BY WINTER'S LIGHT

It was his eyes that held her, that trapped Claire's gaze and her awareness in warmth and something more.

She fell in—into the hazel, into the mind and personality behind—and saw.

Clearly.

Daniel employed no shields, no screens, no guile.

What she saw was the truth—his truth.

And seeing that clearly—being afforded that precious insight—the reckless soul that yearned deep within her broke free and stated unequivocally: *I want you.*

Other titles from Stephanie Laurens

STEPHANIE LAURENS

BY WINTER'S LIGHT

mira

▶ mira™

Recycling programs for this product may not exist in your area.

ISBN-13: 978-0-7783-1227-7

By Winter's Light

First published in 2014. This edition published in 2021.

Copyright © 2014 by Savdek Management Proprietary Limited

The names Stephanie Laurens and The Cynsters are registered trademarks of Savdek Management Proprietary Limited.

This edition published by arrangement with Harlequin Books S.A.

For questions and comments about the quality of this book, please contact us at CustomerService@Harlequin.com.

Mira
22 Adelaide St. West, 41st Floor
Toronto, Ontario M5H 4E3, Canada
www.Harlequin.com

Printed in Lithuania

MIX
Paper from responsible sources
FSC® C021394

This book is dedicated to those who made it possible:

Nancy Yost, agent extraordinaire,
who listened and talked and studied along with me
for the past three and more years as the
publishing industry has morphed about us

and

Tara Parsons, editorial director, MIRA,
who listened and responded with the attitude of:
How can we make this work for all of us?

and

All those at MIRA and Harlequin globally who have
come together to get this book in printed form out
and available to my readers worldwide.
My readers wouldn't be reading this without you!

CAST OF CHARACTERS

Richard and Catriona Cynster's household at Casphairn
Manor, December 1837

Lord Richard Cynster, aka Scandal	married to Catriona, half-brother to Devil, Guardian of the Lady
Catriona, Lady Cynster, Lady of the Vale	married to Richard, mother of their five children
Lucilla Cynster	eldest child of Richard and Catriona, twin to Marcus, future Lady of the Vale, seventeen years old
Marcus Cynster	eldest son, twin to Lucilla, future Guardian of the Vale, seventeen years old
Annabelle Cynster	second daughter of Richard and Catriona, fourteen years old
Calvin Cynster	second son of Richard and Catriona, eleven years old
Carter Cynster	third son and youngest child of Richard and Catriona, ten years old
Oswald Raven	tutor to Richard Cynster's sons, confirmed bachelor
Melinda Spotswood, Miss	governess to Richard and Catriona's daughters, confirmed spinster
Algaria	Catriona's aging mentor
McArdle	ancient retired butler of the manor
Polby	current butler of the manor
Broom, Mrs.	housekeeper at the manor
Cook	just that

Cynster families visiting for the holidays

Lady Helena Cynster, Dowager Duchess of St. Ives, Her Grace	matriarch of the clan, Devil's mother
Lord Sylvester Cynster, aka Devil, Duke of St. Ives, His Grace	married to Honoria
Lady Honoria Cynster, Duchess of St. Ives, Her Grace	married to Devil, mother of their three children
Lord Sebastian Cynster, Marquess of Earith	eldest son of Devil and Honoria, eighteen years old
Lord Michael Cynster	second son of Devil and Honoria, seventeen years old
Lady Louisa Cynster	only daughter, third and youngest child of Devil and Honoria, fourteen years old
Spencer Cynster, aka Vane	cousin of Devil, brother of Demon, married to Patience
Patience Cynster	married to Vane, mother of their four children, sister to Gerrard Debbington
Christopher Cynster	eldest son and eldest child of Vane and Patience, seventeen years old
Gregory Cynster	second son of Vane and Patience, sixteen years old
Therese Cynster	third child and only daughter of Vane and Patience, fourteen years old
Martin Cynster	third son and youngest child of Vane and Patience, eleven years old
Samuel Morris	tutor to Vane and Patience Cynster's sons, confirmed bachelor

Harry Cynster, aka Demon	brother of Vane, cousin of Devil, married to Felicity
Felicity Cynster, aka Flick	married to Demon, mother of their four children
Prudence Cynster	eldest daughter, eldest child of Demon and Flick, sixteen years old
Nicholas Cynster	eldest son of Demon and Flick, fifteen years old
Tobias Cynster, aka Toby	second son of Demon and Flick, eleven years old
Margaret Cynster	second daughter and youngest child of Demon and Flick, ten years old
Rupert Cynster, aka Gabriel	brother of Lucifer, cousin of Devil, married to Alathea
Alathea Cynster	married to Rupert, mother of their three children
Justin Cynster	eldest son, eldest child of Rupert and Alathea, sixteen years old
Juliet Cynster	eldest daughter and second child of Rupert and Alathea, fourteen years old
Henry Cynster	second son and youngest child of Rupert and Alathea, thirteen years old
Claire Meadows, Mrs., aka Medy	widow, governess to Gabriel and Alathea's daughter, has turned her back on marriage
Alasdair Cynster, aka Lucifer	brother of Gabriel, cousin of Devil, married to Phyllida
Phyllida Cynster	married to Alasdair, mother of their five children
Aidan Cynster	eldest son and eldest child of Alasdair and Phyllida, sixteen years old
Evan Cynster	second son of Alasdair and Phyllida, fifteen years old

Jason Cynster	third son of Alasdair and Phyllida, eleven years old
Lydia Cynster	eldest daughter and fourth child of Alasdair and Phyllida, ten years old
Amarantha Cynster	second daughter and youngest child of Alasdair and Phyllida, eight years old
Daniel Crosbie	tutor to Lucifer and Phyllida Cynster's sons, intent on wooing and winning Claire Meadows

Others in the locality

Carrick, Thomas	nephew of the neighboring laird, Mad Manachan Carrick, nearly twenty years old
Hesta	Thomas's very large and impressive deerhound, gray, shaggy, with a lot of teeth
Fields, Jeb	a crofter on Carrick lands, married to Lottie
Fields, Lottie	crofter-wife of Jeb
Fields, Lucy	newborn daughter and first child of Lottie and Jeb
Artemis	deerhound puppy gifted to Lucilla by Thomas Carrick, Hesta's daughter
Apollo	deerhound puppy gifted to Marcus by Thomas Carrick, Hesta's son

Others mentioned but not present

Manachan Carrick, aka Mad Manachan	Laird of the Carricks, a neighboring clan
Nigel Carrick	son and heir of Manachan, cousin of Thomas

Lady Antonia Chillingworth	daughter of Gyles and Francesca, best friend to Lucilla and Prudence
Lady Francesca Chillingworth	wife of Gyles and mother of Antonia, referred to by Cynster children as aunt
Lady Celia Cynster	married to Martin, mother of Rupert and Alasdair
Lord Martin Cynster	married to Celia, father of Rupert and Alasdair
Debbingtons, the	family of Gerrard, artist, brother of Patience Cynster, and his wife, Jacqueline
Randall Meadows	deceased, Claire's late husband
Lady Mott	Claire's chaperone when she was presented to the ton
Therese, Lady Osbaldestone	grande dame, close friend of Helena and well known to all Cynsters

Titles and their meaning:

Lady, the	ancient Scottish deity worshipped in the Vale of Casphairn
Lady of the Vale, the	Catriona's title as principal representative of the Lady in that region
Guardian of the Lady	title held by husband or male protector of the Lady of the Vale, currently held by Richard
Lady	honorific bestowed by locals on those they consider to be the Lady's representative
Lady-in-waiting	refers to Lucilla as her mother's ultimate successor
Lady-touched	denotes Her chosen who have heightened intuition and awareness of the land, and a degree of foresight

BY
WINTER'S
LIGHT

One

December 23, 1837
Casphairn Manor, the Vale of Casphairn,
Scotland

Daniel Crosbie felt as if all his Christmases had come at once. Letting his gaze travel the Great Hall of Casphairn Manor, filled to overflowing with six Cynster families and various associated household members, he allowed himself a moment to savor both his unexpected good fortune and his consequent hope.

About him, the combined households were enjoying the hearty dinner provided to welcome them to the celebration planned for the next ten days—as Daniel understood it, a combination of Christmas, the more ancient Yuletide, and Hogmanay. Seated about the long refectory-like tables on benches rather than chairs, with eyes alight and smiles on their faces, the assembled throng was in ebullient mood. Conversation and laughter abounded; delight and expectation shone in most faces, illuminated by the warm glow of the candlelight cast from massive circular chandeliers depending from thick chains from the high-domed ceiling.

The central room about which the manor was built, the Great Hall lived up to its name; the space within its thick walls of pale gray stone was large enough to accommodate the Cynster contingent, all told about sixty strong, as well as the families of the various retainers who worked in and around the manor, which functioned like a small village.

With no family of his own still alive, Daniel had spent his last ten Christmases with the Cynster family for whom he acted as tutor—the family of Mr. Alasdair Cynster and his wife, Phyllida—but this was the first time in that decade that the Cynsters had come north for Christmas. The six Cynster families present—the six families closest to the dukedom of St. Ives, those of Devil, Duke of St. Ives, his brother Richard, and his cousins Vane, Harry, Rupert, and Alasdair—invariably came together at Christmastime. They were often joined by other connected families not present on this occasion; the long journey to the Vale, in the western Lowlands of Scotland, to the home of Richard Cynster and his wife Catriona in a season that had turned icy and cold with snow on the ground much earlier than expected had discouraged all but the most determined.

Out of long-established habit, Daniel glanced at his charges—soon to be erstwhile charges—seated at the next table with their cousins and second cousins. Aidan, now sixteen years old, and Evan, fifteen, had passed out of Daniel's immediate care when they'd gone up to Eton, yet Daniel still kept an eye on the pair when they were home—an action their parents appreciated and which the boys, at ease with him after all the years, bore with good grace. At that moment, both were talking animatedly with their male cousins in a fashion that instantly, at least in Daniel's mind, raised the question of what the group was planning. He made a mental note to inquire later. Jason, the youngest son of the family and the last of Daniel's true charges, was similarly occupied with the group of Cynster offspring nearer his age. Now eleven, later in the coming year, Jason, too, would start his formal schooling—a circumstance which had, for Daniel, raised the uncomfortable question of what he would do then.

Once Jason left for Eton and there were no more boys in Alasdair Cynster's household in Colyton, in Devon, for Daniel to tutor, what would he do for a living?

The question had plagued him for several months, not least because if he was ever to have a chance at the sort of life he now knew he wanted, and, if at all possible, was determined to claim, he needed to have secure employment — a place, a position, with a steady salary or stipend.

He'd been wracking his brains, trying to think of his options, of what might be possible, when Mr. Cynster—Alasdair —had called him into the library and laid before him a proposal that, in a nutshell, was the answer to all his prayers.

On several occasions over the years, Daniel had assisted Alasdair with his interests in ancient and antique jewelry, with documenting finds and establishing provenances, and also with cataloguing and adding to the collection of rare books Alasdair had inherited from the previous owner of the manor. Alasdair, supported by Phyllida, had suggested that, once Jason had departed with his brothers for Eton, if Daniel was happy to remain in Colyton as a member of their household, they would be delighted to engage him as Alasdair's personal secretary, an amanuensis to assist with Alasdair's ever-expanding interests.

The suggested stipend was generous, the conditions all Daniel could have hoped for. Not only would the new position suit him, it would solve all his difficulties.

Most importantly, it cleared the way for him to offer for Claire Meadows's hand.

He glanced along the board to his right. Clad in a soft woolen gown in a muted shade of blue, Claire—Mrs. Meadows—was sitting on the opposite side of the table, two places down. She was the governess in Rupert Cynster's household; as Rupert and Alasdair were brothers, Claire and Daniel were often thrown together when the families gathered. It was customary in such circumstances that the attending tutors and governesses banded together, sharing responsibilities and each other's company, as they were at present. The manor's governess, Miss Melinda Spotswood, a comfortable matronly sort with a backbone of forged iron, was chatting to Claire. On Melinda's other side, opposite Daniel, sat Oswald Raven, tutor at the manor; a few years older than Daniel, Raven projected a debonair façade, but he was hardworking and devoted to his charges. Raven was chatting to Mr. Samuel Morris, who was seated alongside Daniel and hailed from Vane Cynster's household in Kent; the oldest of the group, Morris was slightly rotund and had an unfailingly genial air, yet he was a sound scholar and very capable of exerting a firm hand on his charges' reins.

All five had met and shared duties on several occasions before; the rapport between them was comfortable and relaxed. Over the coming days, they would, between them, keep an eye on the combined flock of Cynster children—the younger ones, at least. The oldest group, the seventeen-year-olds led by eighteen-year-old Sebastian Cynster, Marquess of Earith and future head of the house, could be relied on to take care of themselves, along with the large group of sixteen- and fifteen-year-old males. But there were six boys thirteen years and under, and seven girls ranging from eight to fourteen years old, and over them the tutors and governesses would need to exert control sufficient to ensure they remained suitably occupied.

There was no telling what the engaging devils would get up to if left unsupervised.

Being governess or tutor to Cynster children was never dull or boring.

Daniel had managed to keep his gaze from Claire for all of ten minutes. Despite the color and vibrancy, the noise and distraction—despite the many handsome and outright stunningly beautiful faces around about—hers was the shining star in his firmament; regardless of where they were, regardless of competing sights and sounds, she effortlessly drew his gaze and transfixed his attention.

She'd done so from the moment he'd first seen her at one of the family's Summer Celebrations in Cambridgeshire several years ago. They'd subsequently met on and off at various family functions, at weddings in London, at major family birthdays, and at seasonal celebrations like the current one.

With each exposure, his attraction to Claire, his focus on her, had only grown more definite, more acute, until the obvious conclusion had stared him in the face, impossible to resist, much less deny.

Utterly impossible to ignore.

"If the weather holds," Raven said, commanding Daniel's attention with his gaze, "and the older crew go riding as they're planning, then we'll need to invent some suitable pastimes to keep our charges amused."

Seated with his back to the table at which the Cynster

children were gathered, Raven had turned and asked what the animated talk had been about. Riding out to assess the position and state of the deer herds had been the answer.

Daniel nodded. "If at all possible, let's get those left to our care out of doors."

"Indeed," Melinda said, turning from Claire to join the conversation. "We need to take advantage of any clear days. If it is fine enough tomorrow, I was saying to Claire that the fourteen-year-olds—the girls—might like to gather greenery to decorate the hall." Melinda gestured to the stone walls hosting various fireplaces and archways, all presently devoid of any seasonal touches. "It's customary to decorate them on the twenty-fourth, which is tomorrow."

"I'd heard," Morris said, "that there's some tradition about the Yule log that's followed hereabouts." He looked to Raven for confirmation.

Raven, his hair as dark as his name would suggest, nodded. "Yes, that's an inspired idea. Not only is it necessary to collect the right-sized logs, but the logs have to be carved. That should keep the boys amused for hours. I'll speak to the staff about organizing whatever's needed."

Daniel nodded again, and his gaze drifted once more to Claire; she'd been following the conversation, her calm expression indicating her agreement with the suggestions. With her glossy mid-brown hair burnished by the candlelight, with her delicate features and milky-white skin, her lips of pale rose, lush and full, and her large hazel eyes set under finely arched brown brows, she was, to his eyes, the epitome of womanhood.

That she was a widow—had been widowed at a young age—was neither here nor there, yet the experience had, it seemed, imbued her with a certain gravitas, leaving her more reserved, more cautious, and with a more sober and serious demeanor than might be expected of a well-bred lady of twenty-seven summers.

Her station—gentry-born but fallen on hard times— was similar to, or perhaps a touch higher than, Daniel's; he didn't really know. Nor did he truly care. They were both as they were here and now, and what happened next... that was up to them.

He'd come to Scotland, to the Vale, determined to put his luck to the test—to seize the opportunity to speak with Claire and plead his case, to learn if she shared his hopes and if she could come to share his dreams.

A gust of laughter and conversation drew his gaze to the high table.

The six Cynster couples were seated about the table on the raised dais along one side of the room, a traditional positioning most likely dating from medieval times. In addition to those twelve—middle-aged, perhaps, yet still vibrantly handsome, articulate, active, and engaged— there were three of the older generation at one end of the board. Helena, Dowager Duchess of St. Ives, mother of Devil and Richard and elder matriarch of the clan, was seated at the end of the table closest to the hearth, and had chosen to summon Algaria, Catriona's aging mentor, and McArdle, the ancient butler of the manor, now retired, to join her there. The three were much of an age and, judging by their glances and gestures, were busy sharing pithy observations on all others in the hall. Having met the dowager and been the object of her scrutiny on several occasions, Daniel didn't like to think of how much she, let alone black-eyed Algaria, was seeing.

A comment in a deep voice, followed by laughter, drew Daniel's gaze back to the twelve Cynsters of the generation that currently ruled. Their children might have been growing apace, might already have been showing signs of the forceful, powerful individuals they had the potential to become, yet the twelve seated about the high table still dominated their world.

Daniel had observed them—those six couples in particular—for the past ten years. All the males had been born to wealth, but what they'd made of it—the lives each had successfully wrought—hadn't been based solely on inherited advantage. Each of the six possessed a certain strength—a nuanced blend of power, ability, and insight—that Daniel appreciated, admired, and aspired to. It had taken him some time to realize from where that particular strength derived—namely, from the ladies. From their marriages. From the connection—the link that was so deep, so strong, so anchoring—that each of the six males shared with his wife.

Once he'd seen and understood, Daniel had wanted the same for himself.

His gaze shifted again to Claire. Once he'd met her, he'd known whom he wanted to share just such a link with.

Now he stood on the cusp of reaching for it—of chancing his hand and hoping he could persuade her to form such a connection with him.

Whatever gaining her assent required, he would do.

Now Fate in the form of Alasdair Cynster had cleared his path, it was time to screw his courage to the sticking point and act.

Hope, anticipation, and trepidation churned in his gut.

But he was there and so was she, and he was determined to move forward. He knew how he felt about her, and he thought she felt similarly toward him. His first step, plainly, was to determine whether he was correct in believing that—and whether with encouragement, "like" could grow into something more.

Claire was very—not to say excruciatingly—aware of Daniel Crosbie's gaze. Of his regard. Of the steady, focused way in which he looked at her.

She wished he wouldn't—or, at least, her mind told her that was what she should wish. Her emotions—stupid giddy things—were more inclined to be flattered and interested…as she'd said, stupid and giddy. And reckless, too.

Yes, Daniel was a handsome, personable, honest, and honorable man; she wasn't silly enough to imagine she was in any danger of receiving any indecent or illicit proposal from him.

Which was the point. With his dark brown hair, thick and straight, his lean face that so fitted his long, lean, athlete's body, and his gentle, intelligent, brownish-hazel eyes, he was too nice, too gentlemanly, too kind—she didn't want to hurt him by peremptorily depressing any pretensions he might harbor. That she greatly feared he was, indeed, intending to voice.

She liked him and valued the quiet friendship that had sprung up between them too much to want to see it damaged, as it would be, quite definitely, if she was forced to say him nay. If she was forced to dismiss the offer she had a dreadful premonition he was intending to make.

There was no future for her with him—or, more accurately, for him with her. For either of them together. But convincing a gentleman like him of that…

Just the thought made her head and chest hurt.

Avoiding him seemed her only real option, but they were fixed at the manor for the next ten days; she would need every bit of ingenuity and quick thinking she could command to successfully keep him at a distance for such a long time.

She didn't like her chances, but what else could she do?

Live through one day at a time. That had been her motto during the days immediately following her husband's death; it was all she could think of that might serve her now.

Turning to Melinda, she said, "Alathea asked me especially to keep an eye on Mrs. Phyllida's two girls—Lydia and Amarantha—given they're the youngest here. If I'm to take the older girls out to gather greenery, do you have anything planned for the younger lot, or should we combine the two groups?"

Melinda shook her head. "The four fourteen-year-olds are too close-knit a clique—and there's Louisa in the lead, too. No need to give her more troops to command."

All the tutors and governesses knew that Devil Cynster's daughter was a handful—too clever, too persuasive, and far too adept at getting her own way.

"I was going to suggest," Melinda continued, "that I take the three younger ones—Margaret, Lydia, and Amarantha—into the kitchen. Cook said she would be making mince pies, and they'll enjoy helping."

Claire nodded. "That they will. All right—I'll take the older four." Surrounding herself with four fourteen-year-old girls should at least keep her safe through the next day. "What sort of greenery is customarily used for the decorations here, where do we get it, and how much are we likely to need?"

Lucilla Cynster, eldest daughter of the house and future Lady of the Vale, listened while her twin brother, Marcus, seated beside her, explained the ins and outs of the local deer hunting season to her cousins Sebastian, Michael, and Christopher. The three were sitting on the other side of the table, forming a wall of broad shoulders and masculine chests that effectively blocked the rest of the room from Lucilla's sight. Glancing down the long board beyond Marcus and Christopher, she saw her five fifteen- and sixteen-year-old male cousins—Aidan, Gregory, Justin, Nicholas, and Evan, all of whom intended to join the exploratory ride tomorrow—leaning forward, hanging on Marcus's every word.

Sebastian, Michael, and Christopher were much more nonchalant, but as Lucilla could feel their eagerness radiating from them, she viewed their expressions of aloofness with skepticism.

Together with Louisa, they— the older six, including Prudence, who was sitting on Lucilla's other side—had been principally responsible for convincing their elders to hold the family Christmas celebrations in the Vale. The girls had wanted to experience the magic of an assured white Christmas in the deep, undisturbed silence of the Vale, something they hadn't known since the last family Christmas held there, when they'd been small children. All of them remembered that time with nostalgic pleasure. The boys, of course, had wanted to hunt, but although the season for does was open, the early snows had sent the deer deep into the narrow valleys in the nearby hills; it had been decided that the group should ride out tomorrow to scout around before mounting a proper hunt on the day after the Feast of St. Stephen.

Beside Lucilla, Prudence—Demon and Felicity Cynster's oldest child and Lucilla's closest cousin, friend, and sometimes confidante—leaned nearer and, as Marcus paused to answer a question from Aidan, said, "I'm for the ride—are you going to come?"

That Prudence would ride was the opposite of a surprise; she lived for horses and always had. Given her parents' obsession with the animals, her fervor was perhaps understandable.

Lucilla thought about the ride, about joining the company. Her gaze drifted further down the table to Louisa— she of the lustrous black hair, pale green eyes, and infallibly engaging manners. If Lucilla remained at the house, Louisa would attach herself to Lucilla, which wasn't a situation to be encouraged. Not because they didn't get on—despite Lucilla's flaming red mane, in temperament they were two peas in a pod—but because, courtesy of the Lady's gifts, Lucilla saw in Louisa a woman who would one day wield great power.

Whenever they were together, Lucilla felt a strong urge to steer or guide Louisa—yet at the very same time, she knew she…shouldn't. Louisa was supposed to find her own way without any help from Lucilla; the trials and tribulations Louisa would face were important, presumably in shaping her for whatever role lay in her future.

Explaining that to anyone who wasn't Lady-touched was impossible. So…

The proposed ride would keep her away from the manor for most of the day. Lucilla nodded. "Yes, I'll come, too." As she always did, she consulted her connection to the Lady—her inner compass—and felt her eyes widen slightly in surprise.

She was *supposed* to ride out with her cousins. As to why… As usual, that wasn't forthcoming.

Up on the dais, at the end of the long table closest to the warmth thrown out by the blaze in the fireplace nearby,

Helena, Dowager Duchess of St. Ives, looked out on those gathered with an indulgent eye. She smiled, more to herself than anyone else, at the sight of her grandchildren, grandnieces, and grandnephews. "They are growing up."

There was immense satisfaction in her tone.

Beside her, Algaria twitched her shawl over her shoulders. "Up, certainly. Older, indubitably. But wiser? I believe I'll reserve judgment."

The third of their number, old McArdle, quietly laughed. "They're like youngsters anywhere—they'll learn."

Algaria stilled, then she murmured, "You're right—there will be hurdles and challenges for each of them, but as to what those might be... We can only guess."

Helena refused to let Algaria's mysterious allusions derail her pleasure. "In truth, it is what amuses me most these days, watching them stumble and fall, then pick themselves up—watching their lives evolve."

Algaria and McArdle looked out at the children. Although neither made any reply, eventually, both inclined their heads.

Helena allowed her smile to deepen, content that, at least on the philosophical side, she had had the last word.

"So!" Prudence thumped her curly blonde head down on the pillow she'd arranged at the foot of Lucilla's bed. She and Lucilla were sharing the bed, top to toe, while the three youngest girls—Prudence's sister, Margaret, and their cousins Lydia and Amarantha—had settled on pallets before the fire. "We'll spend most of tomorrow riding with the others, and then Christmas Day will be full of all the usual eating, drinking, and being merry." Wriggling into a more comfortable position, Prudence went on, "I can't remember—do you do St. Stephen's Day up here? The boxes and all?"

"We most certainly do." Already settled beneath the covers, Lucilla angled her head to look down the bed. "But here it's called the Feast of St. Stephen, and for good reason, so be warned. Mama will almost certainly want our help either tomorrow evening or, more likely, on the morning of Christmas Day for making up the boxes. It's more or less the same as Uncle Sylvester and Aunt Honoria do at Somersham—gifts to all the workers and their families. Here, of course, it's even easier, as even our shepherds live at the manor, and so everyone will be here—in the Great Hall, anyway."

Prudence nodded. "So we have all that filling up the day after Christmas, plus the hunt on the day after that. Then what?"

"We have three days to recover and prepare, and then it's Hogmanay—the end of this year and the beginning of the next."

Prudence was silent for several minutes, then she squinted up the bed and caught Lucilla's eye. "I'm looking forward to next year precisely because it's *not* our coming-out year."

Lucilla nodded in understanding. "In a way, the coming year will be our last year—the last year of our girlhoods, so to speak."

"We should make it count," Prudence said. Warming to her theme, she continued, "We should make sure we do everything we've ever wanted to do, and make sure we leave nothing undone that as girls we can do, but that as young ladies we might find more difficult."

Lucilla chuckled. "Like driving down St. James in an open carriage?"

"Exactly! And riding hell-for-leather in the Park. Isn't it absurd that I'll be able to do that next year—every morning we're in London, if I wish—but the year after, me doing the same thing will be considered indecorous and unbecoming?"

"Society does love its rules, no matter how silly." Lucilla paused. "In fact, now I think about it, next year is going to be the *perfect* year for doing all those slightly risqué things. The better part of society will be so focused on the Coronation and all the events surrounding it that no one will have any attention or disapprobation left over to direct at us."

"Very true," Prudence said. After a moment, she went on, "I have to say I feel for those girls who will be making their come outs next year. I heard Mama say that it's going to be bedlam with all the events planned in the lead-up to the Coronation, and that getting noticed is going to be next to impossible unless you're foreign royalty."

"Hmm." Although she'd never said so aloud, Lucilla was not looking forward to the year beyond the next, the year in which she, alongside Prudence and Antonia Rawlings, would make her formal curtsy to the fashionable world. It was going to be a dreadful bore—and entirely to no purpose. A point she suspected that her mother appreciated, but she doubted her father did, or would, no matter that he usually accepted her mother's Lady-inspired decrees on most subjects. It would be for him that Lucilla would go to London and be presented, and promenade around the ballrooms and in the Park…all to no avail. Her future, she knew, lay here, in the Vale, just as her mother's had before her.

She didn't know who, or how, or when, but she did know where he—whoever he was—would find her.

Here—somewhere in the lands the Lady ruled.

Prudence turned on her side and snuggled down. "It's a pity Antonia and her family couldn't join us."

Lucilla settled, too, tugging the covers over her shoulder. "Aunt Francesca wrote. Mama said that they had wanted to come, but Antonia's grandmama is poorly and they didn't want to leave her at this time."

Prudence mumbled in grudging approval, "Christmas is for families." A moment ticked past. "Perhaps they can come and visit when you come south to stay in the new year." She yawned.

Lucilla yawned, too. "P'rhaps." A second later, she murmured, "Good night."

She heard the smile in Prudence's voice as she replied, "Sweet dreams."

Two

The following morning, along with the other tutors and Melinda and Claire, Daniel shepherded their combined charges—all those still in the schoolroom, plus the fifteen- and sixteen-year-old boys—down the stairs and into the Great Hall for breakfast.

He was sharing a room with Raven and Morris, and they all knew better than to leave their young charges to their own devices. They also knew that the promise of food was the most potent lure to get the lads out of bed, dressed, and ready to behave in a civilized fashion.

On ushering the noisy mob to the tables, Daniel was somewhat surprised to note that the three older members of the company—the dowager, Algaria, and McArdle— had beaten everyone down and were already partaking of rolls warm from the oven and the rich golden honey from the Vale's beehives.

Seeing Daniel's surprise, McArdle grinned wryly. "At our age, laddie, we don't need much sleep."

"And"—the dowager transfixed Daniel with her pale green gaze—"we take great pleasure in the small delights life yet affords us." With that, she took a dainty bite of a pastry.

Finding her penetrating gaze unsettling, Daniel smiled, inclined his head politely, and turned back to his far less unnerving charges.

The girls, who were quartered in a separate wing of the manor, were led in by Melinda, with Claire bringing up the rear. She was surrounded by a trio—fourteen-year-old Juliet, Claire's actual charge, along with ten-year-old Lydia and eight-year-old Amarantha. All four appeared to be deeply engrossed in some discussion.

When handling any such gathering of the families, the tutors and governesses habitually grouped the children by age and arranged activities for each group. Along with Raven and Morris, Daniel walked along the benches, ensuring that the various groups sat together—all six of the younger boys in one group, leaving the five boys aged fifteen and sixteen congregated toward one end of the long table.

Footmen, maids, and undercooks ferried out bowls of porridge and placed jars of golden honey in the middles of the tables. Jugs of milk and mugs appeared, along with racks of toast and marmalade. The boys dove on the food. Sharing a smile with Raven and Morris, Daniel retreated to the center of the long table and sat at the end of the row of boys. Raven and Morris sat opposite, and then Claire arrived. She'd been settling the girls along the bench; she paused when she reached the space beside Daniel, and he turned with a warm smile to give her his hand to help her step over the bench.

She hesitated, her gaze on his hand. Her expression, as usual serious but calm, gave him no hint as to her thoughts, but just as his smile was about to wane, she gave a tiny, infinitesimal sigh and placed her fingers on his palm.

Closing his hand, holding hers, he felt something in him shift, which seemed odd, as he'd taken her hand before... Perhaps it was an outcome of his having made the decision to actively pursue her that gave the moment an extra edge, a deeper significance.

Hiding his reaction, he steadied her as she raised her dark blue skirts and decorously stepped over the bench. Slipping her fingers from his grasp, she murmured, "Thank you," then smoothed her skirts and sat beside him.

She immediately gave her attention to the girls on her other side, making sure they were supplied with what they wished to eat and that all were satisfied with their lot.

Melinda climbed over the opposite bench and sat beside Morris, across the table from Claire.

Claire looked at Melinda, and under cover of asking "Are we proceeding as planned?" continued to lecture her unruly senses. Giddily dizzy didn't begin to describe the whirl they were presently in, all because she'd taken Daniel's hand, offered in the vein of an entirely polite, conventional courtesy. Yes, his long fingers had felt warm and strong when they'd closed so firmly around hers, but he'd just been helping her over the bench, for heaven's sake. As far as her rational mind could see, there was no reason whatever for the silly bubbling warmth that had coursed through her.

And as for the sensitivity that, out of nowhere, had afflicted her nerves, leaving her intensely aware of his nearness as he sat on the bench alongside her—perfectly correctly, several inches away—she found it intensely irritating and could only hope that it would rapidly fade.

At twenty-seven and a widow to boot, her senses had

no business behaving as if she was some giddy miss just out of the schoolroom.

In response to her query, Melinda confirmed their plans to Claire and the three tutors, who in turn fleshed out their ideas for the boys.

"The tradition of the Yule log differs somewhat in different locales," Raven said. "Here, they've combined at least two different ceremonies into one. They cut and bring in the Yule logs on Christmas Eve, and the logs burn in all the main fireplaces from sunset on Christmas Eve to New Year's Day. Because the logs are fresh and treated somehow, they burn slowly, but we still need plenty of logs. In addition, each log is carved with the face of an old woman—Cailleach, the spirit of winter." Raven looked at Morris. "Two of the handymen will come out with us to cut down and help trim the logs, and the carpenter has volunteered his two apprentices to come with us and show the boys how to carve the faces."

Morris looked resigned. "I'll bring the bandages. We're sure to need some."

Raven chuckled, then he leaned forward and looked down the table at the older boys. "Aidan." Raven waited until the eldest lad present looked his way. "Are you going riding, and if so, who else is going with you?"

Aidan looked around the group. "We're all going—me, Evan, Gregory, Justin, and Nicholas."

Morris fixed his charge, Gregory, with a firm look. "Just remember—don't get out of range of your elders. You are released on that undertaking."

They all grinned, but Gregory nodded, and when Morris directed his gaze around the others in the group, they nodded, too. By and large, they were a reliable bunch; all of them rode well, and with the older ones in charge, none of the tutors harbored any real qualms.

Daniel turned back to Melinda as she said, "Good. That takes care of the rapscallions. As for our ladies..."

Melinda met Claire's gaze, then both governesses looked up the table to where Louisa sat, with Therese opposite and Annabelle and Juliet alongside. "Girls," Melinda said, "we're in dire need of some decorations for the hall. Are you four willing to see to it?"

Louisa glanced at Therese, then looked back at Melinda. "What do we need to do?"

"You need to collect evergreens," Melinda said. "That's the tradition here. I asked the gardeners and also McArdle. Apparently, evergreens means holly and fir—you need both. The gardeners said they would leave a sled for the boughs by the side door, along with the right size shears and saws. They recommended boughs about a half inch in diameter or less, and look for longish, well-leafed specimens. For the holly, of course, you want the berries."

"Where do we go to get the boughs?" Louisa asked.

"I know," Annabelle, the younger daughter of the house and one of the fourteen-year-olds, said. "It's not far—just across the bridge over the burn and into the wood on the other side."

"So we get to explore the woods?" Therese grinned. She glanced at Louisa. "We can try out our new boots."

Louisa considered Therese for a moment, then smiled and nodded. "Yes." Raising her gaze, Louisa looked at the hall's largely bare walls. "And it'll be good to make this place look more festive."

"Excellent!" Melinda said. "So we're handing that task to the four of you."

Claire smiled at the four girls. "We'll be relying on you to make this place look wonderful for tomorrow."

As Claire sat back, Melinda caught her gaze and, lowering her voice, said, "It's not far, and there's no chance of you and the girls getting caught even by a freak storm. You'll be able to get back easily."

Claire arched her brows. "Good. I have to admit that, coming from the south, I don't tend to think in terms of freak storms."

Melinda chuckled. "Live up here for a year, and you never forget to allow for Mother Nature." She turned and regarded the three youngest girls, who were sitting closest to her and Claire. Raising her voice, Melinda said, "And that leaves us with you three. I checked with Cook, and she has sunburst shortbread on her list of things to make today, as well as mince pies."

"What's sunburst shortbread?" Margaret promptly asked.

"It's the modern version of an old tradition called Sun Cakes," Melinda explained. "The original cakes were shaped like a ring—round with a hole in the middle. And the cakes had lines drawn on their tops to represent the sun's rays. They were eaten at this time of year to call the sun back into people's lives."

"But nowadays we do it with shortbread," Annabelle explained. "The shortbread is made in rounds like plates, with a circle in the middle representing the sun, and the rays are drawn outward from that."

"Exactly." Melinda glanced at the younger girls. "So are you interested in making sunburst shortbread? And Cook said you can help with the mince pies, too."

"Yes!" came from the three young throats.

Daniel found himself smiling.

"Right, then," Raven said. He clapped his hands together. "I'll supervise the Yule log expedition."

"And I'll assist," Morris said, "armed with bandages."

"I'll need to supervise in the kitchen." Melinda looked at Claire. "Cook's run off her feet at the moment, what with all the preparations for the coming days."

Claire lightly shrugged. "I'm sure the girls and I can find our way to the wood and back, especially as Annabelle knows the way."

Raven, Morris, and Melinda all looked at Daniel.

He opened his mouth to offer his services, but before he could speak, Louisa fixed her large, limpid eyes on Claire and said, "Shouldn't one of the gentlemen come with us? Some of the boughs we want might be out of our reach, or heavy, and the sled certainly will be after we've loaded it up with boughs."

Daniel leapt to fill the perfect opening. "Raven and Morris won't need me as well—I'll come and assist the bough-gathering party."

"That's an excellent idea." Melinda nodded approvingly.

"Much safer," Raven added.

"And Raven and I will also have the two carpenters with us," Morris pointed out. "That's more than enough adults to supervise six boys, Cynsters though they may be." The last was said with a wry look directed at the boys in question, all of whom grinned back.

Daniel turned to Claire and smiled encouragingly. "You lead—I'll bring up the rear."

Claire looked into his eyes and wondered what had become of her grand plan to avoid him. Stifling a sigh and ensuring that no hint of her rising anxiety showed in her face, she inclined her head and, glancing at the girls, rose.

"Come along, girls. Off to get your boots and coats—and don't forget your hats and gloves—and let's get started. Not only do we need to fetch the boughs, we have to get them on the walls before dinner this evening."

She waved the girls up and shooed them along the bench—so she could follow and not have to place her hand in Daniel's again.

If she was to survive the next nine days, she was going to have to do all she could to limit further physical contact.

Richard had arranged for three comfortable armchairs to be set on the dais before the fireplace built into one corner of the hall. Having removed to the comfort of those armchairs, enveloped in the warmth thrown out by the flames leaping in the hearth, Helena, Algaria, and McArdle watched the four groups of youngsters depart the hall, three of the groups under the close guidance of tutors, governess, or—in the case of the four fourteen-year-old girls—both.

"And that," Algaria said, indicating the last group with a tip of her head, "is undoubtedly wise."

Alerted by her granddaughter's comment, Helena watched Daniel Crosbie as he ushered the evergreen-gatherers out—saw his gaze lift to rest on the lady who led the way. Helena's lips curved. "Louisa is very quick, is she not?"

Algaria snorted. "I'm tempted to say she sees too much for her age, but I suspect she gets that from you."

Helena's smile took on a proud edge. "From me, via my son, to her. It goes with the eyes." She, Devil, Sebastian, and Louisa shared the same large, peridot-pale green eyes. "But for my money, Louisa is right—there is a romance blossoming there. All the better to brighten our days."

McArdle, who'd been struggling to follow their oblique

exchange, frowned. "Romance?" He glanced at the last boys filing out of the hall. "What romance?"

Helena and Algaria exchanged a look, then Helena waved. "Never mind. We will just settle back here in comfort and watch events unfold—and then we will see whatever it is that we will see, and whatever we see will be right."

It took McArdle several minutes to sort through that tortuous statement, then he snorted and cast Helena a reproving glance.

Helena laughed.

Claire saw her four charges start up the turret stairs to Annabelle's room, then turned and quickly detoured into the corridor that led to the side door.

Daniel, of course, followed her.

When she tugged at the heavy wooden door, he reached around her, closed his hand about the upper latch that she'd already released, and opened the door for her.

Letting go of the door handle, ruthlessly quelling her utterly ridiculous fluster, she inclined her head. "Thank you." Stepping onto the stoop, she felt compelled to add, "I wanted to check the conditions."

His gaze touched her face, but after an instant's pause, he, too, looked out. "Always a point to remember when up here. I think that in the south, we fall into the habit of taking the weather for granted."

Acknowledging the comment with a nod—it was, indeed, true—she looked out on a world of glistening white and forced her mind to focus not on her senses' obsession but on what lay before her.

Snow covered all the open ground, and the low temperatures of the night had frozen and crisped everything, but the cover wasn't thick, and bare patches showed beneath the trees and larger bushes. In addition, the manor staff had already been out with brooms and shovels, and the paths had been cleared.

"Once we get into the wood, we should be free of the snow," Daniel said.

She nodded. "Their boots should be enough—it doesn't look slushy enough for pattens."

The air was so clear, so pure, it felt crystalline—bright, sharp, and invigorating. She drew a breath deep into her lungs, held it, then slowly exhaled. "But scarves and mittens obligatory, I should think."

She'd seen enough—and the temptation to stand there, with Daniel's warmth at her back, and enjoy the strange, isolated beauty of the manor's surrounds, somehow made more interesting through knowing that he was doing the same, was not one she should indulge. Turning, she had to wait for him to step back, then she led the way back to the stairs.

Of course, the girls hadn't yet come down. "They'll be chattering in their room," she said to Daniel as she started up the steps.

Gaining the next floor, she paused, then glanced at him. He halted on the top step of the flight and she met his eyes—hazel with overtones of rich toffee... Eventually, she recalled what she'd been about to say. "That's where they are." She pointed to a door just along the corridor. "I'll go and get my coat and meet you here—they'll natter for as long as we let them."

Daniel nodded. When Claire headed toward the stairs leading to the floor above, he stepped up and turned the other way. On this level, the manor was a maze of corridors, connecting turrets and towers and the stairs that serviced them, as well as a plethora of major bedchambers and suites. "I'll get my coat." He glanced at her departing back. "Don't forget your scarf and gloves."

She threw him a look—one he caught. He grinned and heard a small huff as she turned and vanished up the stairwell.

The grin lingering on his lips and in his eyes, he strode for Raven's room in the next turret along.

Raven and Morris had already departed. While shrugging on his heavy brown overcoat, then winding a pale knitted scarf about his throat, Daniel wondered if the fact he'd been the one of the three tutors left free to accompany Claire had been lucky coincidence or deliberate assistance. He hadn't said a word of his hopes, much less revealed his dreams, to the other men, yet both were intelligent and knew him well enough to have realized...

Picking up his gloves, he turned to the door; he wasn't entirely comfortable with the thought that his peers might have guessed his intentions regarding Claire, but if they had and felt moved to ease his path, he wasn't such a coxcomb as to refuse their help.

He was waiting at the head of the first flight of stairs when Claire reappeared. A cherry-red pelisse was buttoned to her throat, and a warm knitted scarf much like his dangled about her neck. Looking down, she pulled on a pair of fine leather gloves as she walked briskly to join him.

Halting beside him, she glanced at the door of the room the girls were occupying. "Still no sign?"

As if the words had conjured them, the door opened, and the four girls spilled out in a rainbow of colors. Louisa's coat was a stylish dark green, Therese's a rich brown, Annabelle's a pale blue, and Juliet's a soft mauve-pink.

Claire held up a hand as the four filled the corridor. "Inspection first."

Annabelle and Therese mock-groaned, but all four lined up happily enough and allowed Claire to check their boots and gloves.

Daniel appreciated the necessity; frostbite wasn't something either of them wished to risk, much less have their charges risk.

"Very well." From the end of the line, Claire waved the girls forward. "If you would lead the way, Mr. Crosbie?"

Lips curving wryly, Daniel turned and did, going down the stairs and on toward the side door. That Claire wished to keep her distance from him hadn't escaped him, but he assumed that had more to do with their audience than any rejection…or, at least, he hoped it did. As he hauled open the heavy side door, the notion that she might not be as interested in him—in pursuing a future with him—as he was with her surfaced in his mind; he considered it for only an instant before pushing it aside.

The connection—the right sort of sensibility, the awareness and consciousness of the other, the inescapable reality of being attuned to the other—was there between them; he knew that.

And having been married before, she must have recognized that, too.

Stepping outside, he descended the single step onto the roughly graveled path. As promised, the manor's staff had left a sled for them to ferry the boughs back to the house. It hadn't been there when he and Claire had stood on the stoop earlier, yet now it sat ready and waiting, a sturdy and strong workman's sled with a canvas sling strung between the handles.

The girls poured through the door and joined him on

the path. While they exclaimed at the day, at the snow and the crunchy hoar frost, and at how their breaths fogged in the air, Daniel took stock of the implements nestling in the canvas sling. A collection of handsaws, light enough for the girls to use, plus three pairs of strong shears and a lightweight hatchet, presumably for trimming the ends of larger branches.

He looked up as Claire arrived on the path alongside him. She subjected the sled to a serious, evaluating survey, then raised her gaze to his face. "Will you be able to manage that on your own?"

He arched his brows in faint hauteur. Positioning himself behind the handles, he gripped them, kicked off the brake and pushed; the sled ran easily on its runners, even over the path. Slowing it, he gave Claire an openly cocky look. "Lead on, Macduff, and I'll follow."

Her lips twitched; she tried to straighten them, but failed. She inclined her head, attempting to hide her grin. "Very well." Looking ahead, she called, "Girls!" She waved them from the snow-covered mounds of the raised beds in the herb garden. "Off to the wood. We only have an hour, two at the most, and we need to get enough greenery to decorate the whole hall."

The girls ran ahead, Annabelle in the lead with Juliet beside her, and Louisa and Therese close behind.

Pushing the sled in their wake, keeping to a steady pace with Claire walking just ahead of the sled's front board, Daniel realized his pride had led him to make a tactical error. The pushing bar between the handles of the sled was wide enough to accommodate two people pushing together; he should have claimed he needed her help.

His gaze on her back, on her sweetly turned hips encased in the rich red wool of her pelisse, he murmured to himself, "There's always the return journey."

Making a mental note not to miss that opportunity, he settled to pushing the sled along and making the most of the moment.

Ahead on the path, Louisa paused at the curve just before the first stand of tall firs enfolded their way in cooler shadow. She took only a second to look back and consider all she could see, then she quickened her pace, catching up with Annabelle, Juliet, and Therese.

When they glanced at her, Louisa said, "Mistletoe. We need some." She looked at Annabelle. "Does it grow in this wood? Do you know where?" Without waiting for an answer, Louisa raised her gaze and started scanning the trees.

Annabelle turned, doing the same. Therese was quick to join in.

"It does grow here, yes," Annabelle said. "There should be quite a few clumps, but we'll need to find some we can reach."

"Or that we can climb to," Therese said.

"I thought we were only supposed to get holly and fir," Juliet said, although she, too, was looking for the telltale clumps of draping greenery; her tone made it clear the comment was an observation—a request for clarification, if anything, rather than a disagreement.

"That's what they said, but…well, what's the point in hanging evergreens at Christmas if you don't have mistletoe as well? Mind you," Louisa continued as, with a gentle push, she started Annabelle and Juliet walking again, "I suspect Mrs. Meadows will try to discourage us from bringing it in, so I suggest we don't mention it and hide it amongst the fir and holly."

Falling into step alongside Louisa, Therese cast her a sidelong look. "Is the mistletoe just for general fun or"— Therese glanced back along the path to where Claire walked just ahead of Daniel and the sled—"do you have someone—two someones—specifically in mind?"

Louisa met Therese's eyes and grinned. "I think Mr. Crosbie is sweet on Mrs. Meadows, and that she would be sweet on him if she gave herself the chance—and I like Mr. Crosbie, so I can't see any reason why we shouldn't just…" She gestured.

"Nudge things along?" Therese chuckled. "You sound just like your grandmama."

"There!" Annabelle kept her voice down and surreptitiously pointed to their left, to where a huge clump of mistletoe was growing in a cleft only a yard off the ground. "There's a clearing just ahead that will be perfect for leaving the sled. Then while we're gathering fir and holly, we can circle around and pick some of that, too."

"There's more on the right and some up ahead." Juliet had very sharp eyes.

"Plenty." Louisa glanced at the others; the girls met each other's eyes. "We've never played Cupid before." Louisa grinned. "Think of it as a challenge. Let's see how we do."

Helena, Algaria, and McArdle were still in their chairs, dozing contentedly in the warmth, when the six oldest children straggled into the Great Hall and sat at the section of table they'd claimed as theirs—just below the dais and the high table at which their parents sat.

Said parents had already come and gone, breakfasting on ham, sausages, eggs, bacon, and crisply toasted crumpets, leaving behind the tantalizing aromas of coffee and the cinnamon rolls all the ladies preferred. They'd shared their plans for the day with Helena, Algaria, and McArdle; subsequently, the men had headed out to inspect the herd of shaggy-coated Highland cattle, before continuing into Casphairn to lunch at the local inn. The ladies, meanwhile, had retired to Catriona's solar, to sit, embroider, and talk of their children.

The children most exercising their parents' thoughts were the six who belatedly sat down to break their fast. Helena, feigning sleep, watched them from beneath her lashes. She saw them all often, yet because she did not meet them day by day, she suspected that she saw the changes in them more clearly than most.

And perhaps the distance of the generations also had something to do with her perspective. They weren't her responsibility in the same way they were their parents'; she felt both detached from them and, curiously, more connected at the same time.

They were a joy and a blessing, one she was too old not to appreciate fully and hold very close to her heart.

She doubted she would be there to see them married—perhaps if she was lucky and lived to be as old as her dear friend Therese Osbaldestone. That was in the lap of the gods; for now, she was content to watch them forge on through what would arguably be the most decisive period of their lives. She wondered if they—these six in particular, given they stood on the very cusp of adulthood—truly comprehended that the decisions each made in the coming days, weeks, and months would shape their future.

Would irreversibly mold it, shutting some doors forever, opening others.

Which doors they chose and how they walked through them would define and determine the rest of their lives.

She knew—better than most—that the decision of a moment could change a life. That pivotal instants occurred, where going this way or that would irrevocably alter one's destiny.

That certain knowledge, that understanding born of experience, was not something readily transmitted or absorbed. She could only hope for this new generation that they, too, found the breadth of happiness, the depth of love, that she and their parents had.

Listening to their voices—the rumbling tones of Sebastian, Michael, Christopher, and Marcus already reaching the deepness of the adult males they almost were, spiced with the lighter notes of Lucilla's and Prudence's voices, already strong and clear—Helena let her lids fall. She felt her lips curve as she listened to them plan.

Sleep beckoned; she followed and left them to grow.

Sweet dreams. Seated on the bench, her elbows on the table and her hands wrapped around a mug of strong tea, Lucilla doubted that Prudence's words of the previous night had been intended to evoke the strange phantasms that had haunted her sleep. Yet as she sat sipping tea, ostensibly watching her brother and male cousins consume positive mountains of eggs, sausages, and the last of the kedgeree, she couldn't seem to bring any of the odd images into proper focus.

Normally, her visions were distinct and identifiable—foretellings of something that would happen, or a prediction of something that might or might not. In this case, however, the visions were hazy, at least visually; what she could sense more strongly were the associated emotions, but even those were...confused.

Yet nothing she'd seen had evoked fear, not of any sort. The best she could make of it was that somewhere in her life ahead lurked some possibility where she would have to make some decision—and that decision would lead her either down one road or down some other entirely. And the choice would be mutually exclusive—the chance to take whichever road she eschewed would not come again.

Quelling a shiver—not of fear but of trepidation of the unknown—she forced herself back to the here and now. To the debate raging between Marcus, Sebastian, and Prudence over which part of the manor's lands they should assess first.

Lucilla knew.

Setting down her empty mug, she waited for a break in the discussion, then calmly stated, "We ride to the southwest, into and through the forests and up onto the open levels of the range. From there, we follow the range north—you'll be able to look down into the forested valleys, and with the snow, if you bring the spyglass, you'll be able to see the tracks if a herd has sought refuge in any spot. We can continue north until we reach the cross-range, then we follow that east and so back here."

That hadn't been a route any of the others had proposed.

Across the table, Marcus met her eyes, searched them.

Lucilla held his gaze and allowed him to see, recognize, and appreciate her knowing.

He blinked once, then nodded. "That's a good plan." He looked at Sebastian, seated alongside him. "That's what we'll do."

Sebastian looked at Marcus, then looked at Lucilla, then threw up his hands in surrender. "All right."

Lucilla turned her head and looked at Prudence.

Prudence shrugged. "Whatever you say, cuz."

Michael and Christopher laughed and started getting

to their feet. "Thank you, Lucilla," Michael said. "These three would have taken until lunchtime to decide."

"So can we go already?" Christopher asked.

A clatter of boots approaching the hall had them all looking toward one of the archways. Aidan and Evan appeared, with Justin, Gregory, and Nicholas crowding behind.

"Are you lot ready yet?" Aidan asked in long-suffering tones.

Sebastian glanced at the others about the table, then rose. He was the tallest of the boys, nearly as tall as his father. Stepping over the bench, he nodded at Aidan and the other four. "We'll meet you at the stable."

"Excellent!" Evan said. The five strode off in another roll of thunder.

After rising from the bench, Lucilla and Prudence followed Marcus, Sebastian, Michael, and Christopher out of the hall. Under the archway, awareness tugging, Lucilla glanced back at the three elders enthroned in their armchairs on the dais, but all appeared to be asleep.

With Prudence, she headed for her turret. They were already wearing their riding clothes, gathered skirts falling to their lower calves with trousers tucked into boots beneath, the outfits in their signature colors of forest green for her and cornflower blue for Prudence.

"Scarf, gloves, quirt." Prudence cocked her head. "Will I need a hat, do you think?"

"I would certainly advise it," Lucilla said, taking the lead up the stairs. Unerringly, she glanced to the northwest. "Even among the trees, it'll be cold up on the range."

Regardless of all intentions, it was a full hour later before they were finally mounted and ready to ride. Lucilla had been partly to blame for the delay, but when she'd suggested that perhaps taking food to fill their stomachs at midday might be wise, all nine males had immediately agreed.

Of course, they'd left it to her to petition the kitchens, but when she and Prudence had emerged bearing two large hampers, the boys had been quick to help; they'd gathered around and, with a reasonable degree of civility, had divided the food into their various saddlebags.

Five minutes later, well accoutered and well provisioned, they trotted out into the snow-covered fields. The light covering was still crisp and crunched beneath their mounts' hooves. Horsey breaths fogging around them, they formed up in a loose group with Sebastian and Marcus in the lead. Lucilla and Prudence rode side by side on Marcus's left. All of them were excellent riders, while Prudence, Nicholas, Aidan, and Sebastian could lay claim to the title of exceptional.

Before them, the land stretched under a blanket of white scattered with sparkling motes courtesy of the weak sunshine. This far north, even though the day was fine, there was little warmth in the sun. Luckily, the breeze was a bare whisper, adding negligible sting to the knife-like chill in the air.

Further ahead, past the limit of the fields—indeed, of civilization—the Galloway Hills rose in heavily forested waves to the bald range known as the Rhinns of Kells.

Setting a southwesterly course as Lucilla had directed, in wordless concert the riders leaned forward and thundered toward the dark smudge of the forests and the open range beyond.

Three

It had taken a little while to maneuver the sled into the clearing Annabelle had declared was the perfect spot from which to gather the holly and fir they'd come to collect. After wedging two rocks beneath the back of the sled to hold it in place, Daniel straightened. Brushing off his hands, he raised his gaze and found five pairs of eyes fixed on him.

Four pairs immediately lowered to the sling carrying the tools; expectation lit the girls' faces.

Grinning, Daniel reached for the canvas flap and threw it back. "We have shears or handsaws, ladies. Which will you have?"

Somewhat to his surprise, the girls exchanged a long glance, then Louisa opted for a pair of shears, as did Therese, while Juliet and Annabelle elected to try the handsaws.

Daniel had no idea what they were up to, but that look… He'd dealt with Cynster boys long enough to know what that meant; they were planning something.

Whatever it was, it included collecting the fir and holly boughs they were there to fetch. The four girls set off, tramping into the surrounding forest, pointing to various boughs and comparing their potential usefulness in draping the archways, mantels, and the hall walls.

Daniel turned to Claire. "What implement would you prefer?"

She considered, then said, "I suppose I'd better take a saw, too. I can see myself having to finish off cuts they start."

Daniel smiled. "No doubt." He searched through the various tools in the bag. As she approached, he drew out a handsaw with a sturdy grip. "This is a good one." He held it out.

Claire reached for the saw. Because of the style of grip, it was impossible to take the tool without their fingers touching. Brushing.

Sensation slithered down her spine, delicious, enticing.

She clamped down on the reaction, determined not to let it show...if she could have, she would have stopped reacting altogether, but she didn't know how. She didn't even know why she was so sensitive when it came to Daniel Crosbie.

"Thank you." Lips tightening, she took the saw and turned away.

She pretended to look into the trees, pretended to follow the girls with her eyes; in reality, her every sense had locked on the man standing silent and still beside her.

He was looking at her, studying her face; she could feel his gaze but she was not—absolutely was not—going to meet it.

Daniel saw her resistance quite clearly, carried in her stance, in the rigidity of her spine, in the stoniness of her expression, in the way she stood with her shoulder toward him—supposedly looking into the forest, but that was a sham.

Resistance, yes—but was it truly rejection?

He forced himself to consider that unwelcome possibility...but no. Drawing in a breath, one tighter than he liked, he decided that this wasn't rejection. If she rejected him, he would know it; she wasn't one to mince words or be coy. So she hadn't rejected him, not yet. As for resistance...resistance could be overcome.

For one instant longer, he gazed at her face, let his eyes linger on her profile. The way he saw it, he owed it to her as well as himself to make a push to overcome whatever hurdle she plainly saw standing between them.

If they were to have the future he wanted them to have, he would need to make a push to secure it.

He shifted his attention back to the canvas sling; he reached in and drew out the hatchet. Hefting it, he turned.

The movement drew Claire's gaze.

Meeting it, he smiled. "We'd better get after them." Raising the hatchet, he added, "According to Raven, I should trim the branches before we haul them back to the house."

They worked in a loose group for the next hour, selecting branches and boughs of fir, cutting them down and trimming them, and selecting and cutting bushy sprigs of holly laden with red berries for contrast. Daniel found a fallen tree a little upslope from the sled to serve as a makeshift bench on which to trim the branches. The girls and Claire spread out into the forest around the spot, ferrying the branches they cut down back to him and the hatchet. The time passed swiftly. Daniel was occasionally called to help with this bough or that, while Claire was summoned hither and yon to deal with holly sprigs just out of the girls' reach, or to examine scratches and pulled threads.

It took Daniel a little time before he realized what the girls' plan was; he'd been right in thinking they had one, but they were really very good at hiding their purpose. He'd thought it strange when Louisa and Therese had brightly offered to cart the first pile of trimmed fir boughs back to the sled. He'd watched them go, their arms piled with greenery, and had wondered... He'd returned to his task but had glanced over at the sled in time to see a swift whispered exchange, which had ended with both girls stuffing something else green and leafy in among the fir they'd stacked.

Intrigued, he continued to surreptitiously watch Louisa and Therese as they spread out beneath the trees. Eventually, Therese spotted something; she turned and caught Louisa's eye and beckoned her over.

Louisa reached Therese and, having seen what her cousin had, nodded. With Therese, Louisa moved forward—

"Mr. Crosbie—can you help me split this branch?"

Daniel turned to see Annabelle dragging a bifurcated branch of holly toward him.

She hauled it around so that he could see and pointed. "Quite aside from it being too big, that part is less pretty. We don't want that bit." Annabelle fixed her dark blue eyes on his face.

The urge to look around and check what Louisa and Therese were doing warred with the instinct to respond to Annabelle, to the clear expectation of his immediate attention shining in her eyes.

Instinct—and Annabelle's eyes—won out. Gripping the hatchet, he went to examine the branch.

By the time he had dealt with that, had helped Annabelle to add the neatly trimmed "pretty branch" to the growing pile of holly, and finally looked up, it was to see Juliet and Claire in animated discussion over a particular fir tree that was slightly different from the rest. Annabelle was now trudging back toward them. Straightening and scanning the surrounding forest, Daniel eventually located Louisa and Therese. Instead of being where they'd been when he'd stopped to deal with Annabelle—been distracted by Annabelle? He had to wonder—the pair were now heading toward him with several boughs of fir in their arms.

He knew he could simply ask what they were about, and if he insisted they would probably tell him, but…he remembered what it was like, as a youth, to have plans one kept secret from the adults. That was part of leaving childhood, of growing up. He eyed both girls as they neared, but as he'd yet to see the slightest sign that whatever they were up to posed any danger, either to themselves or to others, he decided he should wait and observe.

Laying down the fresh boughs for trimming, Therese asked, "Are there any boughs ready to go back to the sled?"

Daniel pointed at the mound to his right. "Those are ready for loading." He glanced at the pair in time to see the brief exchange of an eager glance.

Louisa brightly said, "We'll take them down and stack them."

Daniel watched as the two girls divided the good-sized pile between them, then, balancing the unwieldy branches in their arms, headed back down the slight slope to the sled.

He hesitated, then, after setting down the hatchet, he moved silently away from the fallen tree and set off after them.

When the girls reached the sled and halted, Daniel halted, too. From ten yards away, he watched them dump the boughs they'd carried on the ground before the sled.

Then they reached over the sled and drew up a pile of softer-leafed greenery...mistletoe.

They were gathering mistletoe.

Daniel stared. Had they guessed? Had he been that obvious?

Were they intending the mistletoe for him and Claire—playing matchmaker? He certainly wouldn't put it past them.

Or were they simply doing this by way of making the most of the spirit of the season?

As he watched, Louisa and Therese spread the mistletoe in a layer on the boughs already on the sled, then proceeded to cover and conceal the fincr-leafed greenery with the boughs of fir they'd just carried down.

They were probably right in thinking that Claire, at least, would not encourage them to hang mistletoe, but what should he do? What should his stance be?

Regardless of whether they were trying to specifically help him or not, he could use all the help he could get.

"How much have we collected?" Claire said from behind him. "Do we need any more?"

Daniel turned; from the corner of his eye, he saw Louisa and Therese shoot startled looks at him and Claire. Hands rising to his hips, he stood squarely between Claire and the sled, blocking her view of the sudden flurry of activity there. "We have plenty of fir, but I suspect we need more holly."

Claire glanced toward the sled, but he didn't move.

Instead, he pointed upslope to the pile of holly he'd trimmed and stacked beside the fallen tree. "That's all the holly we have so far—at a guess, I would think you might need twice that much."

Boots crunched on pine needles as Louisa and

Therese—both rather breathless—came up. "We've been gathering fir up to now," Louisa said, pale green eyes innocently wide. "If we switch to gathering just holly, it shouldn't take long to finish collecting what we need."

"I can't wait to get back to the hall and hang everything up." Therese's anticipation was very real.

It didn't escape Daniel that nothing but the truth had passed their lips. Looking at Claire, he arched his brows. "That sounds like a viable plan."

Claire tipped her head in agreement. Louisa and Therese went ahead, moving swiftly up the slight slope to join Annabelle and Juliet, who had trailed behind Claire when she'd headed down to the sled. Claire turned and followed the girls, acutely aware of Daniel when he fell to pacing beside her.

But neither felt moved to speak; after reclaiming their tools, they separated, following the girls under the trees. As Juliet was her true charge, Claire tended to gravitate instinctively to watching over her. Luckily, in this section of the wood, the bushes with the best holly—with the greenest of dark leaves and most amply supplied with the reddest of red berries—grew in a single large clump; even though she was watching Juliet, Claire could hear the other girls and could see them as they moved around the bushes.

Somewhat less helpfully, Daniel took up station opposite her, keeping an eye on Louisa and Therese, and also Annabelle when she hove into his sight. Although his gaze wasn't constantly on her, Claire knew he was there; it was disconcerting and somewhat irritating to discover just how much of a lodestone for her unruly senses he had become.

But as they gathered in the holly, paying due attention to the thorny prickles, and nothing occurred to exacerbate her awareness, she gradually relaxed and found herself sharing genuine smiles with Juliet and, all in all, enjoying the moment.

While listening and occasionally responding to Juliet's artless chatter, Claire found her attention repeatedly caught by comments Daniel and the other girls exchanged. She found herself smiling at several; he was really very good with them.

"Watch out!" he called.

Claire shifted; boots scuffed, and she saw Daniel shoot out an arm—a bent-back holly branch, released, slapped against the thick sleeve of his overcoat.

"Oh!" Louisa had been the one in line to get slapped—thorns and all. She looked up at Daniel and smiled, sincerely grateful. "Thank you—I forgot I'd hooked it back."

Disentangling the spiky leaves from his sleeve, Daniel asked, "Do you really need to burrow so far into the bush?"

"That's where the best berries are," Therese pointed out.

"Might I remind you that we will not be *eating* holly berries?" Daniel's tone and the look he bent on the girls were resigned.

When Therese and Louisa just blinked at him, then returned to ferreting past the outer branches to get to the branches with the best berries, Daniel sighed. "You do realize," he said, to no one in particular, "that that would have worked if you'd been boys?"

Several rude sounds were swallowed by girlish laughter.

Softly laughing herself, Claire returned to helping Juliet gather the holly they'd collected.

Juliet considered the pile. "More," she said. She surveyed the bush they'd been plundering, eyes narrowing. "We have plenty of smaller pieces to weave into the fir. Perhaps we should take a larger branch—a signature piece for the main fireplace, perhaps." She walked about the bush, peering this way and that, then she stopped and pointed. "How about that branch?"

Claire looked. It was certainly a larger branch than they'd thus far attempted. "We can try."

Between them, using their coated backs, they managed to press back the outer branches sufficiently to get access to the longer, arching branch Juliet had identified. It was, indeed, a handsome specimen of its kind and would do very well stretched along the mantelpiece over the hall's main fireplace. Claire nodded at Juliet. "I'll hold it—you saw."

Juliet's face lit with eagerness. She set her handsaw in position and started sawing.

The branch was several inches thick. Less than half-way through, Juliet's saw blade stuck.

Frowning in concentration, she tried to push it, then tried to pull it free, but it didn't shift. Juliet released the saw handle along with a sound of frustration.

Claire opened her mouth to suggest they trade places.

Before she could speak, Juliet whirled around. "I'll get Mr. Crosbie."

No! Claire stifled her instinctive response—and Juliet darted out and the branches held back by her body sprang forward.

Trapping Claire where she stood.

She couldn't even move her arms from the branch she was supporting without risking tangling herself even more inextricably…she was trapped in the thicket of holly.

She didn't have time to even start to panic; Daniel,

summoned by Juliet and followed by all the girls, arrived on the scene.

He looked at her, assessing her situation—and she saw his lips firm as he struggled to hold in his laughter.

His gaze collided with hers, and she narrowed her eyes in warning.

Lips twisting, he looked down, then he handed his hatchet to Louisa. "Hold that—I'll probably need it once I get in there."

Luckily, they were all wearing thick gloves. But Daniel had to pick aside each thorny branch barricading his way into the area in which she stood, insinuating his body into place as he did, so that the branches slid and snagged along his back.

He was a great deal larger than Juliet; by the time he was standing where Juliet had been, Claire felt as if she daren't take a breath. Not a deep one, anyway.

After meeting her eyes, humor still very evident in his, he examined the jammed saw. He gripped the handle and tried to shift it, but it moved less than an inch before jamming again. He humphed, then glanced at Claire. "I'll cut the branch using the hatchet, but first I'll need to free the saw." He looked at her gloved hands, still loosely gripping the branch. "When I say, can you bend the branch down?"

When he glanced at her face, she nodded.

He nodded back. "Use all your weight if you have to."

He turned back to the saw, examined it again, then twisted his head and called, "Hand me the hatchet."

Annabelle was the smallest; she wriggled as close as she could and threaded the hatchet, handle first, through the branches. Daniel reached back, grasped the handle, then, after glancing at Claire as if to reassure himself that she was all right, he focused on the jammed saw blade;

he lined up the edge of the hatchet blade and eased it into the same groove. "All right. Pull down now."

Gripping more tightly, Claire dragged the branch down.

Daniel forced the hatchet blade deeper and at the same time wrenched the saw blade free. "Good! Ease up."

Claire did as he bid and watched him twist and hand the saw out to Juliet.

Turning back to the branch, he met her eyes. "Turn your head away. I'm going to hack through the branch, and I don't want any flying splinters cutting you."

It was good advice. The only problem she had in following it was that to turn her head away from him, she had to shift her body, her shoulders... She ended with her shoulder lightly brushing his back.

"Ready?" he asked.

She swallowed. "Yes." Really, this unlooked-for sensitivity was beyond ridiculous, yet her lungs had still seized, and her senses still waltzed.

The sound of the hatchet biting into wood reached her; the branch jarred in her hands, and she tightened her grip, bracing the limb.

"Thank you," he murmured between *thwacks*.

She could feel steely muscles shift fluidly in his back and upper arm as he hacked at the branch; the sensation riveted her senses.

The branch cracked, then, on one last stroke of the hatchet, it came free in her hands. She had to shift to balance the weight, then she glanced at him—they were now standing shoulder to shoulder, their backs to the way out of the thicket, dozens of thorny branches blocking the route to freedom.

She met his eyes; he looked into hers. "How are we going to get out?" she asked.

The laughter in his eyes, just curling his mobile lips, invited her to laugh at their predicament with him.

Somewhat to her amazement, she felt her lips lift in a reluctant smile.

He glanced back, then to either side. "Girls—I want you to stand to either side of the spot Mrs. Meadows and I used to get in here, and then pull back all the branches you can reach and hold, but I don't want you to step into the thicket, all right?"

"Yes, Mr. Crosbie," chorused four voices.

Behind her, Claire heard the girls murmuring to each other; as usual, Louisa was directing. Claire couldn't even turn around far enough to glance back at them. She looked at Daniel. Although his shoulder was still pressed to hers, he'd craned his neck to check on the girls. "Now what?" she asked.

Her question drew his gaze back to her face—and, quite suddenly, it was as if they were alone, private…and if she hadn't been sure, earlier, what he was thinking, what he intended regarding her, she knew now. It was there in his face, in his hazel eyes, in his direct and open gaze.

Instead of the resistance—the refusal, the denial—she expected to rise up…her lungs constricted and her heart beat more heavily, and for one instant, she wondered…

He glanced at the branch. "Is that heavy or can you hold it?"

She blinked and had to think for a second before replying, "No—meaning yes, I can hold it. It's not that heavy."

"Good. In that case"—he glanced again over his shoulder—"we'll need to move slowly and together, or we'll both end up stuck." He met her gaze briefly, then leaned back a trifle to look along her back and past her, then he nodded. "All right. You're going to have to turn toward me. We'll have to juggle the branch—probably lifting it as high as you can and pushing it past me will be the best way. Then just keep turning slowly until you're facing the way out, and I'll keep the branches back and follow close behind you."

Claire nodded. She wasn't going to think about this; if she did, her thoughts would end in a horrendous knot and paralyze her. Instead, she focused on doing as he said, on following his murmured directions as he and she adjusted and shifted, moving in slow motion together.

The maneuver was a lot easier described than accomplished, and performing it inevitably and unavoidably led to their bodies touching, brushing, almost as if they were engaged in a dance, one that placed the partners as close as if not closer than a waltz.

By the time she stepped free of the thicket into the space the girls had created, the prize branch of holly gripped like a staff in her hands, a blush had taken up permanent residence in her cheeks, and a wholly unexpected sense of triumph and exhilaration coursed through her veins.

Smiling, unable to stop herself, she stepped forward so that Daniel could follow, untangling the last of the incommoding branches from the thick weave of his overcoat. At last, he, too, stepped free—and crowing with success, the girls could release the branches they'd been holding back.

That done, the girls literally danced, their spirits high and effervescently infectious.

Claire steeled herself and met Daniel's eyes.

His gaze was warm, reassuring, and conspiratorial. "It looks like we've made their day."

Looking at the girls, she laughed. "Indeed." She glanced

at the branch, then called, "Juliet. Annabelle. Come bear away this bough we've wrested from the holly thicket."

"Yes!" All four girls raced up. The branch was long enough for all four to spread themselves along it and carry it off.

Releasing it, Claire felt a sharp sting on the inside of her wrist and sucked in a breath.

"What is it?"

She glanced up and found Daniel at her shoulder, frowning down at her.

He met her gaze, concern in his eyes. "Are you hurt?"

She blinked, then shook her head. She glanced at the girls, but they were already on their way back to the sled, triumphantly bearing away their prize. Raising her left hand, Claire peeled back the edge of her glove. "A thorn." One long sliver had angled beneath the fine skin on her wrist and broken off. She tried to pull it free, but the instant she released the edge of her glove, it flipped down and covered the spot.

"Here—let me." Daniel was already tugging off his gloves.

Before she could stop him—before she could think— he took her gloved hand, almost reverently cradling it in one large palm, the back of her hand resting securely within his larger one.

She was wearing gloves, but they were fine leather gloves and didn't mute the warmth of his palm.

"Hold back the flap."

She obeyed, and he bent his head. Slowly, he closed his neatly trimmed nails on the protruding sliver. He had the hands of a pianist, his touch strong and firm. She watched his fingers move, felt the caress of his fingertips on the sensitive skin of her inner wrist—and the touch seared her to her bones.

She sucked in a breath, held it—and prayed he thought the reaction was on account of the hurt. A hurt she couldn't even feel—her senses were distracted, awash with him.

Then she felt the slide of the thorn, and the sliver left her flesh.

She exhaled quietly and waited. She couldn't dash away, couldn't run away—and to her surprise, she didn't want to.

He'd been inspecting the damage; she felt his fingers soothe the skin—a caress that tightened her nerves again and sent sensation streaking through her. Then he released her hand and straightened.

He looked into her eyes, and she met his gaze.

The moment—filled with a nascent emotion she couldn't name—hovered between them.

Impulses, urges, flashed through her mind, but the girls were just down the slope, in sight, and...

She dragged in a breath, smiled and inclined her head, and managed a creditable "Thank you."

Head tilting, he held her gaze, then his lips eased into a wholly masculine smile. "It was my pleasure."

Keeping her own smile within bounds required effort; looking away, she waved toward the sled and started in that direction. "I believe we've done our share—our helpers can fetch the rest of the holly."

Bending to retrieve the hatchet and two saws the girls had left behind, Daniel glanced at the piles of smaller branches. "As you say." As it appeared that persuading Claire to accept him was going to be a case of one step at a time, he was already planning his next advance.

Straightening, he set off after her, lengthening his stride

to catch up with her. They were halfway back to the sled when the girls passed them, of their own volition returning to pick up the rest of the holly.

Upon reaching the sled, Daniel busied himself with checking and stowing the tools. After a second of indecision, Claire went to the front of the sled. She leaned down and poked and prodded under the branches; Daniel hoped Louisa and Therese had hidden their secret foliage deeper in the sled. "What are you looking for?"

Claire glanced up at him, then she straightened, drawing a long loop of rope free. "This is a workman's sled, so I thought there should be a rope for pulling as well—and there is."

The girls returned, their arms full of holly. They dumped the branches on top. Daniel loosened the side ropes and looped them over the piled load; with a few quick knots, he secured it. "Girls," he said, still busy with the last knot, "why don't you take the lead position with the rope, and Mrs. Meadows and I will push?"

"Yes!" Juliet rushed to Claire and reached for the rope.

Knot tightened, Daniel straightened and saw that Claire was reluctant to give up the rope, but the girls swarmed, and she had no real choice.

Designed to allow the sled to be dragged, the rope at the front was a loop secured at the junctions of the front axle with the two runners. The girls busily lined up inside the loop, holding it at their waists and shuffling forward to tension it.

A frown in her eyes, Claire walked to join him as he moved to the bar that ran between the rear handles. "You don't really need my help pushing this along—not with the four of them pulling, as well."

"We might not need your help pushing," he said, taking

up position to one side of the bar and grasping one handle, then inviting her with a wave to take her place alongside him, "but we will almost certainly need your assistance to ensure this doesn't run them down, and also stays on the path." Facing forward, he nodded at the four girls, all eager to be off. "There's enough of a gradient that if they pull too hard, the sled might start sliding on its own. And if two of them pull harder than the other two, the sled will slide sideways and might well end up off the path."

"Oh." Her frown deepened a fraction, but then she nodded and, taking a slightly deeper breath, stepped into position alongside him; mimicking his stance, she gripped the back bar with one gloved hand and the handle with her other.

Their shoulders just touched.

He was waiting to catch her gaze when she glanced up. He smiled as reassuringly as he could. "Ready?"

For an instant, she searched his eyes, then she looked forward and nodded. "Indeed."

Quelling a smile, he looked at the girls and found them all staring expectantly at him. "All right, girls—off we go!"

To a chorus of cheers that quickly devolved into soft laughter, punctuated by the occasional feminine shriek, the sled started sliding over the woodland path in the direction of the house.

Daniel kept the pace at a gentle walk, reproving the girls if they tried to go too fast. Claire walked beside him and found herself mesmerized by her awareness of him—of the warmth of his large body pacing so fluidly beside her, of the muscular strength he deployed in correcting the sled's trajectory, of the way her shoulder brushed his steely bicep with every second step.

She told herself she was being unforgivably silly, that such indulgence of her senses was something she would come to regret—the exercise had no purpose and, at best, would only leave her yearning for something she knew she could never have.

Pointless.

She should cease enjoying the moment immediately.

Instead, some reckless piece of her soul she'd thought long dead kept a firm grip on her reins, and she walked on by Daniel's side and, regardless of what she knew should be, found herself smiling.

By their standards, the riding party hadn't ridden hard, but they'd made good time into the hills, through the forests mantling the lower slopes, and had climbed to a bridle path that snaked along above the forests below the bald spine of the Rhinns of Kells.

Turning their horses' heads north, they'd ridden a little way, then had halted at a spot where a collection of larger rocks provided a flattish space sufficiently large to accommodate them all. Leaving the horses grazing in the rough stubble between the rocks and the upper edge of the forest, the boys lugged the saddlebags to the rock, and their company spread out for what was a rather early lunch.

"More like late elevenses," Prudence said, then bit into the chicken leg she held in one hand.

"Pointless to try to keep them from food," Lucilla dryly observed.

"Hmm" was all Prudence offered in reply.

Sebastian had settled on Lucilla's other side, with Marcus, Michael, and Christopher beyond him. With a wave, Sebastian indicated the land spread before them. "If the manor lands end where the forests begin, who owns the land we're riding through?"

"The Crown," Marcus replied around a mouthful of ham. "We have logging rights in the forest, and hunting rights, too, but the land itself is the Crown's—which hereabouts means it's no-man's-land."

"So by our English standards, it's common land." Michael glanced at the crest towering above them. "How far does it extend?"

"To the west"—Marcus gestured to the rounded peaks—"it goes for four or five miles."

"What about to the north?" Christopher asked, squinting in that direction. "Those forests to the north of the manor—are they common land, too?"

Glancing at Marcus and noting that his mouth was full, Lucilla answered, "Only a narrow strip—the highest and densest part of the forests. On that boundary, our lands go into the forests some way, almost to the ridge line, and our neighbor's lands lie further to the north, beyond the strip of common land, which follows the ridge line."

"So where in all these forests are we most likely to find red deer?" Michael asked.

"If I had to guess," Marcus said, "I would say further to the north, closer to the Carrick property—they're our northern neighbors. As with the manor's lands, the Carricks' western boundary lies at the lower edge of the forests, so we can ride and hunt along the ridge as far as we like."

"Right, then." Sebastian gathered his long legs under him and rose. He met Marcus's eyes, then Lucilla's as they, too, got to their feet. "I suggest we ride north along the edge of the forests"—he inclined his head to Lucilla—"as you suggested, and keep a sharp eye out for tracks."

Marcus nodded. "We can ride into the afternoon and see what we find, but we'll need to turn back in good time to return to the manor before full dark."

Sebastian glanced at the others, including the five younger boys. "We're all good enough riders that we shouldn't have a problem riding across open land in moonlight."

Marcus glanced at Lucilla; when she said nothing, he shrugged. "We'll see."

As they gathered the saddlebags and the others started climbing off the rocks and heading for the horses, Lucilla looked up at the crests to the west. This close, they blocked her view of the western sky, yet…

She grimaced and, echoing her twin, muttered to herself, "We'll see."

After picking up her saddlebag, she followed the others off the rocks.

"A little to the left," Helena directed.

Claire exchanged a glance with Daniel, then obediently shifted the long branch of holly a fraction further left on the mantel of the main fireplace in the Great Hall. The cavernous room had a total of four hearths of varying sizes built into the walls. They'd already decorated two mantelpieces to the girls'—and the three older observers'—satisfaction.

Louisa, standing back with the other three girls to observe the critical placement, nodded decisively. "That's perfect."

Glancing at the others and seeing approval in all their faces, Claire resisted the urge to raise her eyes to the skies and instead settled the holly on the bed of fir boughs the girls had laid over the stone mantel.

"We just need a few more sprigs to finish it off." Annabelle went to the huge log-basket they'd filled with their holly sprigs. Juliet followed and the pair began to sort and select branchlets to augment the longer branch.

"We'll get the candles and the pinecones," Louisa said. She and Therese headed to where those items had been stacked on one of the tables.

With Claire, Daniel glanced around the hall at the four footmen co-opted to hang branches of fir over the four archways leading into the hall. Balancing on stepladders and stools, the men were lacing string between nails that had clearly been inserted long ago for just that purpose, creating a web to hold the branches in place. Louisa and the girls had been very clear in their instructions. The green branches were to be secured above and on both sides of the archways, and then later the girls planned to insert sprigs of holly in amongst the fir.

Daniel assumed that, at some point, they also intended to hang their mistletoe under the arches. He had no idea what they'd done with the leafy stuff, but he suspected it currently resided at the bottom of the log-basket, concealed beneath the holly. Upon finishing his survey of the hall, he glanced at Claire. "I think that leaves us to arrange the fir on the last mantelpiece."

Eyes dancing, she arched her brows. "And I suspect we should get started before Louisa or Helena think of something else for us to do."

Daniel grinned and moved with her to the last unadorned fireplace, pausing along the way to fill his arms with a load of the feathery fir they'd left stacked in one corner of the room.

Standing at one of the long tables, helping Louisa prepare and insert candles into a set of beaten silver candleholders, Therese glanced at Daniel and Claire, then, dropping her gaze to her busy hands, leaned closer to Louisa and whispered, "What about the mistletoe?"

Louisa glanced up as Annabelle and Juliet, satisfied with their creation in holly, joined them. Once the other girls had started sorting the pinecones by size, Louisa quietly said, "I think we should hang the mistletoe later." She flicked a glance over her shoulder at her grandmother and the two others in the armchairs on the dais. "I've always thought it's something that works best as a surprise. We could slip down while everyone is getting ready for dinner. That'll be the perfect time. There's really no point in putting it up earlier—I've always heard that the magic of mistletoe starts at sundown on Christmas Eve."

Annabelle nodded. "And hereabouts at least, it's said to remain effective only until sunrise on St. Stephen's Day." After a moment, she added, "There'll be about half an hour when no one will be here—not any of the staff, either."

"Can we leave the mistletoe where it is, do you think?" Therese eyed the log-basket.

"As long as we leave a nice layer of holly on top, no one will notice," Louisa said. "We can make it look like the basket's a part of our decorations."

"I'll mention that to the footmen," Annabelle said.

Juliet glanced at the pair of footmen working at the nearest archway. "We should take note of where they store those stepladders."

"They'll be left somewhere nearby," Annabelle murmured. "They're normally kept in the storerooms near the stable, but no one will want to go out there to fetch them if something falls down, so they'll leave them in some nook. I'll find some reason to ask exactly where."

"Good—so we have the when and how decided, although

we'll need to be organized and quick when we come down." Louisa met the other girls' eyes and smiled. "So for now, we can simply enjoy ourselves finishing these decorations."

The others smiled back.

They fell to with a will, and the next half hour sped by.

Daniel halted beside Claire and surveyed the results of the girls'—and theirs and the footmen's—labors. "I will own to being astounded at just how much four school-girls can achieve."

"*If* they set their minds to it," Claire returned. "In this instance, they've seemed well-nigh driven, and I have to admit that the result is quite amazing."

Previously rather bare, the Great Hall now stood ready for the festivities, garlanded with holly and festooned with fir, with pinecones and candles arranged on all the mantelpieces and down the center of the long tables. The fires had been built up in all four fireplaces; warmth pervaded the room, and the dancing flames bathed the scene with a cheery glow.

Watching the four girls pirouetting in the center of the huge room, their faces alight with unabashed delight at the transformation they had wrought, Daniel murmured, "They've been inspired."

He was feeling inspired, too, but by sudden, unsettling uncertainty. He looked at Claire and found her consulting the small watch pinned to her collar.

"Heavens! It's just after midday. Where has the morning gone?" She raised her gaze and looked at the girls, not at him. "Girls! Come along—it's time to wash and get ready for luncheon."

Daniel hovered as, in true governessly fashion, Claire gathered the girls, had them collect their coats, hats, gloves, and scarfs, and herded them out of the Great Hall…all without looking at him.

Not once.

He'd thought they were getting along well, that her resistance, whatever it sprang from, was waning, fading, yet as soon as they'd entered the Great Hall, something had changed.

She'd pulled back, retreated, and suddenly there was a certain distance between them, one he wasn't sure he should attempt to reach across…perhaps her sudden buttoning-up was because of the three observers on the dais.

Regardless, concern over her unexpected retreat had collided with another realization—that although their respective families were supposed to remain at the manor until the second day of the new year, he couldn't count on either her family or his not being called away earlier. Although the dowager had made the journey north, none of the others of her generation had felt strong enough to risk it. What if one of those others—Celia or Martin Cynster, for example—were taken ill? Or what if there was some investment crisis and Rupert Cynster took his family back to London? Or if Alasdair was called to assist with some antiquity and removed his family either back to Devon or somewhere else?

Such incidents had been known to occur. Which meant Daniel could only count on him and Claire being there, together at the manor, until the day after St. Stephen's Day. It was unlikely they would move before then, but more to the point, it was unlikely that any news from the outside world would reach their employers to summon them elsewhere before then.

So in the matter of his campaign to convince Claire to throw her lot in with his, he could count on having the rest of Christmas Eve, and Christmas Day and St. Stephen's Day, but no longer.

Two days and an evening.

The driving need to ensure that she'd instituted the sudden distance between them purely for social appearances, that it was a smokescreen and nothing more, drove him to dog Claire's heels and follow her into the manor's front hall.

Chattering and laughing, the girls started up the curving stairs. In their wake, Claire was about to set foot on the first tread when Daniel caught her hand.

"Come out to the front porch for a moment." Without further explanation, he drew her toward the front door. "I want to speak with you."

Claire's feet seemed to move of their own volition. Speak with her? Her heart started to thud. She should resist—make some glib excuse...before she had time to think of any words, Daniel had opened the door and checked outside, then he stepped back, ushered her through onto the porch—and there was no easy way to hang back as he followed and drew the door almost shut behind him.

Facing him, she clung to the mask she'd assumed as soon as they'd reached the house and she'd realized that her easiness with him—her relaxing in and enjoying his company, appreciating the dry wit of the comments with which he'd enlivened the return journey to the house— was not in keeping with the distance she was determined to maintain between them.

She could be an acquaintance and not much more, and she hadn't been honest in adhering to that line.

For his sake, she was determined to do better from now on. Searching his eyes, she tried to read his expression; it seemed sober and rather serious. Her chest tightened; she raised her chin fractionally. "What did you wish to speak about?" Best they get this dealt with now—best she nip any aspirations he might harbor in the bud before they developed any further.

He held her gaze; he'd said he wanted to speak with her, yet he hesitated...then he cleared his throat and looked out at the landscape, brown blotches showing through the light dusting of snow. "I..."

Then his jaw firmed, and he looked back and met her eyes. "I have recently had some good news. News I wanted to tell you about, in which I hope you might have some interest." He drew breath, then went on, "As you've most likely noticed, Jason is nearly twelve, and will go off to Eton next year. He's the last of my charges, and so I was facing the possibility of having to move on, to find another post and leave Alasdair Cynster's household, but instead, Mr. Cynster has offered me the position of amanuensis, assisting him with his collection, his library, and his interests in those spheres."

He paused, then continued, his gaze still holding hers; she found it impossible to look away. "The position comes with an increased stipend, one sufficient to support a wife and family."

She couldn't suppress her reaction—the instinctive stiffening—even though she retained the presence of mind not to act on the impulse to take a definite step back. The impulse to shake her head.

This was precisely what she had feared, that he would read too much into her liking for his company, into the easy rapport that from the first they'd shared.

Into the connection that had always seemed to be there

between them—gentle, understated, nascent perhaps, yet a link of sorts nonetheless.

That link made it impossible for her to pretend she didn't comprehend his direction, that she didn't understand the question in the depths of his eyes. That she didn't hear the emotion underlying his words when, voice low, he said, "I wanted to ask if there was any hope. For me...for us?"

Inwardly gathering herself, holding his gaze even though that cost her dearly—she owed him that much—she opened her mouth to say what she must...only to discover that the words she'd been so sure would be there, ready to trip off her tongue, had vanished. Gone.

She stared, confounded, surprised, and suddenly lost. She knew she had to say no, that she had to let him down gently yet make it clear that such a hope on his part could never become a reality, not with her...

Seeing her confusion, he hesitated, then said, "I'm not pushing for a firm answer—I just wanted to know if...the *possibility* was there." When she still didn't respond, his face tightened. "If you would consider—just consider—spending the rest of your life with me."

Her heart was suddenly in her throat, strangling her vocal cords. Again, she tried to speak. Again, the words wouldn't come.

Epiphany struck.

And left her reeling.

She couldn't say the words, couldn't give voice to them...because they weren't the words she wanted to say.

The realization rocked her. When had this happened? Surely not... How could this be?

Was she—that restless, reckless her she'd successfully suppressed for so many years—actually considering...

No.

Yes.

He'd started to frown. She had to say something. She moistened her lips—saw his gaze deflect to them.

Felt something inside her hitch. "I…"

"Mrs. Meadows! *Medy?*"

Juliet, calling from the front hall. Claire hauled in a breath. Suddenly desperate—and she didn't know why—she searched Daniel's eyes, then she gripped his arm.

"Later." She felt the steel of his forearm beneath her fingers and gripped tighter for emphasis. "I promise I'll give you an answer later."

Once she'd formulated the right answer and put it into words.

Before he could reply, she released him, whirled to the door, pushed it open, and went through.

As she closed the door behind her—leaving him alone on the chilly front porch—Daniel heard her say, "Here I am—what's the matter?"

Feeling…utterly discombobulated—was her response a yes or a no? How could she have managed to leave him with neither?—he looked out, unseeing, at the snow-draped landscape.

He replayed the exchange, searched every word and nuance, every glance, for some clue to her intention, and found none.

She'd understood him—and she hadn't answered.

Was he supposed to interpret her non-answer as a no? Or was she sincere in saying she would answer him properly later?

Even if she did, would her answer still be no? Had she simply grasped the chance offered by Juliet to take more time to find better words in which to say him nay?

He snorted. "I couldn't have surprised her. She knew—knows—that I feel for her in that way."

But what did she feel? That was the point on which he'd sought elucidation.

All he'd received thus far was an even greater degree of complexity and confusion.

The chill air started to penetrate his suit coat; he'd left his overcoat inside.

He finally focused on the landscape and realized that its empty bleakness was a perfect analogy for what his life would be—would feel like to him—without Claire in it.

Straightening, stiffening his spine, he drew in a breath, then turned back to the house.

Regardless of what her answer proved to be, he wouldn't be giving up—on her, on them, on their future— so easily.

To reach the tower in which Raven's room—the one Daniel was sharing—lay, he had to cross the Great Hall.

Head down, wrestling with the hideous tangle of his thoughts, he was halfway across the large room when an imperious "Mr. Crosbie" fell on his ears.

Looking at the dais, he saw the dowager beckoning.

Stifling incipient wariness, he diverted toward that end of the room; Her Grace, the Dowager Duchess of St. Ives, was not a personage it was possible to refuse.

Halting before the dais, he met Helena's pale eyes and essayed a polite smile. "Yes, Your Grace?"

Folding her hands, she studied him, her penetrating gaze as always unsettling.

To his relief, she didn't study him for long. A small, commiserating—to Daniel, rather worrying—smile curved her lips. "From your demeanor when you came into the hall just now, I take it your embassy didn't meet with instant success."

How had she—they—known? A swift glance showed Algaria nodding in sober agreement; McArdle, at least, was decently asleep.

"That being so," Helena continued, for all the world as if his embassy and his lack of success were entries in an open book, "I wished to advise you to stay your course."

Daniel opened his mouth, then closed it; he wasn't sure what to say. Eventually, forcing himself to meet Helena's uncanny gaze, he steeled himself and asked, "Are you sure?"

In the present situation, he'd take help and encouragement from any quarter that offered.

Algaria snorted, yet the sound conveyed approval of his question—which, of course, implied acceptance of Helena's pronouncement. "We're as sure as anyone can be when people and emotions are involved."

Helena's smile deepened. "But yes, I am sure." She paused, then added, "In such affairs, one should remember that anything worthwhile is indubitably—self-evidently—worth fighting for."

He considered both her words and her expression, and—insensibly, perhaps—felt heartened.

Politely—with all due grace—he inclined his head. "Thank you."

He took a step back, then turned and continued on his way—inwardly shaking his head when he looked within and discovered that he did, indeed, feel more confident, certainly more sure and determined on his path, than he had when he'd entered the hall moments before.

From their chairs on the dais, Helena and Algaria watched Daniel leave the hall.

When he disappeared from sight, Helena sighed. "Such a nice young man." After a moment, she cocked a brow at Algaria. "May we trust in your Lady to see to it that he receives his just reward?"

Helena wasn't surprised when Algaria tilted her head, her gaze growing distant as if she was listening to something Helena couldn't hear.

After a moment, Algaria blinked, then shook herself. "Him—and her, too. I believe we can count on it, regardless of what's to come."

Helena arched her brows. "I don't suppose you would be willing to share what's to come?"

Algaria pulled a face. "I would if I could, but that's the sum of all I know."

Helena grimaced lightly. "Ah, well." She looked toward the archway through which Daniel had gone. "In that case, we will simply have to have faith in those powers that are greater than us all."

Four

Claire had never dithered in her life. Even when the worst had befallen her, she'd been shocked, aghast, horrified, but she'd always known her own mind. Yet now, faced with Daniel and his plans for a future with her as his wife, she…had no idea what she thought. What she felt? That was a different story, but she'd long ago learned that giving in to her impulses led to heartbreak, that her feelings were unreliable indicators as to sensible, much less safe, behavior. She'd learned the hard way not to trust her instincts.

At least, not when it came to men and marriage.

The gong finally rang for luncheon. Having presided over a brief sewing session to repair the hem on Juliet's overcoat—Alathea Cynster was a firm believer in her children knowing the basics of survival, and sewing was one such necessary skill—Claire walked into the Great Hall in Juliet, Louisa, Therese, and Annabelle's wake. A quick glance around revealed that, with the older children still out riding, the three tutors and Melinda had elected to join the remaining children at their table, filling the spaces normally taken by the fifteen- and sixteen-year-old boys.

Whether by design or simply luck, the space awaiting her was alongside Daniel.

Claire hesitated for only a heartbeat, then, with wholly spurious calm, went forward to claim her seat; she couldn't create a fuss over such a minor thing...and she wasn't such a coward. She had to give Daniel some form of answer. She'd told him "later," but hadn't specified when "later" would be.

Sadly, despite her thoughts having churned furiously ever since she'd come in from the porch, she was still no nearer formulating the right response—one that accurately conveyed her reaction to his suggestion.

He'd been so heartbreakingly direct and honest. She simply couldn't allow herself not to be the same.

Which meant she had to grapple with the totality of the unexpected, unprecedented, and entirely unanticipated emotions his words, their implication, and even more him—just him—evoked in her. Not even over her late husband could she recall experiencing this depth of emotional wrenching, as if something buried deep inside her was struggling to break through. To break free.

She was dimly aware of the others in the hall—of the Cynster couples filling the high table, the three older members at one end like three wise men, and the many other members of the manor household gathered about the tables. In a bustling stream, footmen and maids were ferrying covered dishes from the kitchen, delicious aromas wafting through the air as they passed.

Then, noticing that the four girls had arrived, Richard Cynster, their host, rose and raised his goblet. "To the gatherers of the evergreens—well done, girls!"

"The hall looks lovely!"

"So pretty with all the holly."

"Perfect for the season."

With those and similar comments coming from all quarters, the girls beamed, accepting the accolades with becoming pleasure.

Claire smiled appreciatively at the foursome, too. They had worked diligently, and the hall did, indeed, look wonderfully festive.

Daniel rose as she neared. "Mrs. Meadows." His gaze found hers as he offered his hand to help her step over the bench.

Meeting his gaze only briefly, Claire inclined her head. "Mr. Crosbie." Maintaining her mask of unimpaired serenity took effort; she steeled herself against the contact, put her hand in his, and allowed him to assist her over the bench. Strangely, this time, the sensation of his fingers closing, warm and firm, over hers steadied rather than unnerved her. Reluctantly slipping her fingers free, she sat and settled her skirts.

Juliet joined Louisa, Therese, and Annabelle in the places to Claire's right, while beyond Daniel, the six boys who, supervised by Raven and Morris, had gathered and prepared the Yule logs were in full flight, describing their activities of the morning and eagerly discussing the ceremony that was to follow that afternoon.

From his place at the far end, Raven leaned forward to speak down the table. "It'll take at least an hour to bring all the logs in and get the fires set and blazing. The whole household usually gathers to watch. In this house, the ceremony involves the four fireplaces here, plus the one in the entry hall and the one in the drawing room. The burning of Cailleach, the spirit of winter, is a very important ritual to all those who live here—to the locals, it's a critical part of marking the turn of the year."

Morris, seated opposite Raven, humphed. "With the snow freezing on the ground and icicles hanging off the eaves, it isn't hard to see why."

Raven grinned. "It'll get a lot worse before spring comes, and I believe that's part of the meaning behind the Yule log ceremony—that it acknowledges the hope and expectation that, in time, the weather will once again improve."

The children, predictably, were more interested in the details of the ceremony; as soup was dispensed and consumed, they peppered Raven, as well as Annabelle, Calvin, and Carter—the three of Richard and Catriona's children present—with questions that the four did their best to answer. Then pots of stew replaced the soup tureens, and the heartier fare claimed the children's attention; gradually, the rowdiness faded.

Sampling her helping of the rich savory stew, Claire wrestled with her dilemma—with her difficulty facing the unexpected, disconcerting truth Daniel's speaking of his wishes had revealed, and of how to be honest with him while simultaneously guarding them both against hurt.

She didn't want to risk being hurt again, but she didn't want to hurt him, either. She knew all about that particular type of hurt. It wasn't one she wished to court again, yet neither did she wish to visit it on him.

"I..." She hadn't made a conscious decision to speak, but some part of her awareness—the part that any good tutor or governess developed—had noted that all the others around them were presently engaged in and distracted by conversations of their own. Seizing the moment, she swallowed and, keeping her voice low, continued speaking for Daniel's ears alone. "I need to explain...well, several things."

She wasn't sure how to go on and took a sip of the wine

the Cynsters had sent to their table. Conscious of Daniel's gaze resting on her face, of being the cynosure of his attention, she cleared her throat, set down the glass and went on, "Your...vision of your future. Perhaps it shouldn't have been a surprise, yet it was. It wasn't something I'd considered—"

"Mrs. Meadows—can we help the boys bring in the logs?" Therese fixed her blue eyes on Claire's face.

Claire blinked. She glanced up the table at Raven, then briefly met Daniel's gaze before turning back to Therese and her three cronies. "Perhaps not the hauling in, but you can certainly supervise the setting of the fires—that would be more appropriate, don't you think?"

Louisa was quick to agree, and the girls fell to dividing up the fireplaces, with each claiming responsibility for one of those in the hall.

"Supervising?" Cynical amusement rang in Daniel's tone. "Very adroit."

"One has to be, dealing with those four," Claire replied.

After an instant's pause, his gaze on her profile, he prompted, "You were saying?"

Without looking his way, she drew in a breath and forged on. "As I was saying, I hadn't thought—hadn't envisioned the prospect at all...or, at least, not in the sense of it being a real prospect. Not in the sense of having to answer your question—the one you asked me on the porch." She felt breathless, rattled, ridiculously nervous; drawing in another quick breath, she hurried on. "*However*, that doesn't mean that I don't *wish* to give you an answer. I just..."

She shifted on the bench. Turning her head toward him, but unable, still, to meet his eyes, with her voice lower still and some emotion akin to desperation seeping into her tone, she forced herself to say, "I *thought* I knew the answer. I was sure I did—that in any such situation, the answer was—would be—obvious and straightforward, because after being married once, why would I wish to marry again? But instead..."

The vise about her lungs cinched tight and she stopped.

Then on a spurt of strength, she met Daniel's eyes. "I'm babbling. I owe you an answer—I *want* to give you an answer. But—"

"Medy." Juliet waited until Claire looked at her to ask, "Even if we're not helping with the pulling, we can go out with the boys and all the others to cheer them on as they bring in the logs, can't we?"

What? Claire was momentarily at a loss, but she was too experienced to agree to something without understanding what she was agreeing to.

Daniel saw her confusion. He'd already heard the details of the ceremony; quietly, he said, "The whole household usually goes out to line the way as those bringing in the Yule logs haul them to the front door. The logs are already beside the stable, so it's no great distance."

"Ah, thank you." Claire looked at Juliet and the other three girls. "Yes, of course—just make sure you put your coats back on, and proper boots, hats, and gloves."

On a chorus of cheery assurances, the four girls returned to their planning.

Claire turned back to Daniel, one hand rising to rub her temple. A frown formed between her brows. After a moment, she sighed. "I'm sorry—I've lost my train of thought."

Her thoughts hadn't been coherent enough to have a train. That beneath her outward calm she was agitated hadn't escaped Daniel; that she was agitated disturbed him. Clearly, what he'd thought a simple question wasn't so simple for her. *After being married once, why would I wish to marry again?* Although he'd known she was a widow, that question hadn't occurred to him. And what did it mean? Was he competing with the memory of her late husband? Was there some comparison, some standard he had to meet?

"Mr. Crosbie." Jason, seated opposite and two places along, was waiting to catch Daniel's gaze. Jason grinned, all but bobbing with anticipation. "You have to come and see my carving of Cailleach—before it burns."

Daniel summoned a smile and directed it over all the boys' eager faces. "Of course—we'll all want to see the carvings before they go up in flames."

The boys smiled delightedly and went back to organizing the order of their Yule log procession.

Turning back to Claire, Daniel shifted, then murmured, "Perhaps it might be better to postpone this discussion until later." He met her eyes as they rose to his. "By which I mean later in the day, perhaps after dinner, when our respective distractions have gone to bed."

If there was something about her previous marriage that was going to stand in his way, he would, he felt sure, require a certain degree of privacy to persuade her to tell him—he couldn't overcome a hurdle if he didn't know what it was—and, quite obviously, here and now was not the time.

Claire held his gaze for an instant, then looked across the table, unseeing. She was conscious of rising frustration; she'd made the effort and spoken—and all the exercise had proved was that she didn't yet know her own mind well enough to explain. When she'd walked into the hall, she hadn't wanted to talk to Daniel—not about what lay between them—but now she'd screwed up her courage and broached the subject, she wanted to press on... not least because, despite her rambling, hearing herself stumble through her own assumptions and feelings—and into the clash between said feelings and the lessons of her past—had helped.

Perhaps if he and she talked further, it would help still more, until she saw her way forward clearly.

"Yes." Lips thinning, she glanced at Daniel, met his eyes. "You're right. This evening. Somewhere where we can speak with some degree of privacy."

He nodded, his gaze serious and direct. "Yes. Exactly."

On the words, the boys called to him, and Annabelle spoke to Claire, and their duties reclaimed them.

Yet even as, over the dessert of sticky date pudding, Claire listened to Raven announce the finalized details of the Yule log ceremony to be played out immediately after the company rose from lunch, she was very aware that, while one half of her wanted to push forward and see if some golden future with Daniel could ever be, her older, wiser, more experienced and cynical half remained immovably convinced that such a shining future was nothing more than fool's gold.

Everyone at the manor—from the blacksmith's little daughter, her tiny hand engulfed in her father's giant fist, to the dowager, leaning heavily on her cane and supported by both her sons—participated in the ritual of bringing in the Yule logs.

The day remained fine, but the wind had picked up, and dark clouds were massing to the north and west. Yet the sun still shone weakly and the air was crisp and clear as the assembled company formed up on either side of the path leading from the rear yard around the side of the house to the front door.

Raven, Morris, the carpenter and his men, plus all the stable hands were assisting the boys to pile their logs onto various sleds. There were logs enough for each boy, apprentice, and stable lad to haul; they needed multiple logs per fireplace to last through the days to Hogmanay and into the new year.

Relieved of further duty on that score, Daniel walked back up the path to where Claire and Melinda stood with their charges spread out to either side. After circling to stand between the governesses, Daniel clapped his hands and stamped his feet; the temperature was falling. "After all this activity, the boys will sleep well tonight."

"For which," Melinda said, slipping her gloved hands into her coat sleeves, "we should all, no doubt, give thanks."

Daniel saw a slow smile curve Claire's lips, then she glanced at him. "One might be forgiven for wondering if, while the Yule log tradition might be widely observed, the precise details as practiced here might have been designed to achieve just that. Having all the excitable boys exhausted and ready to fall into their beds and sleep tonight is a boon any parent would give thanks for." She tipped her head to the many couples, girls, and younger children lining the path. "There are many families here, after all."

"Hmm," Melinda said. "I hadn't thought of that. And it wouldn't surprise me one little bit if you were right. I must ask Algaria—she would know."

A cacophony of cheers and calls from farther down the path announced that the first boy pulling his logs had left the rear yard.

Claire looked down the avenue formed by the onlookers. Beside her, Juliet and the other girls leaned forward and peered, too, then Juliet crowed and clapped. "It's Henry!"

Confirming that Henry, Juliet's brother, was leading the procession alongside one of the brawnier stable lads, both boys hauling a sled loaded with logs, Claire glanced at Daniel. "Was it drawn straws or...?"

Daniel grinned. "Somewhat to our surprise, the boys reached agreement entirely on their own. It's oldest first, which is Henry, then youngest, then second oldest followed by second youngest—each of them paired with one of the manor families' boys—then our middle two, Toby and Martin, together, and the last of the six sleds will be hauled in by the two carpenter's apprentices."

"Six sleds—one for each of the fireplaces?" Claire asked.

Daniel nodded. "It was that or a much longer procession." He tipped his head toward the darkening horizon. "Raven and the manor folk say there's a major storm coming, so while we have to have the procession, it needs to be kept short."

Looking down the path, Claire saw several small children dart out from the lines to look more closely at the logs, then turn and, pointing and chattering, race back to their parents.

"According to local custom," Daniel said, "whoever carves the best depiction of Cailleach is assured good luck in the coming year."

Claire smiled and glanced at him. "Boys can always do with more good luck."

Daniel grinned back. The differences between their

charges was a frequent topic of conversation—and good-humored contention—between the governesses and tutors.

Claire faced forward. Seconds later, Henry drew level with their position. He grinned at Juliet. She, Louisa, Therese, and Annabelle all stepped out to join the younger children in examining the faces carved into the upper surfaces of each of the ten logs loaded on the sled.

The four girls looked, then laughed and nodded to Henry and the stable lad. As the girls stepped back, Claire, Melinda, and Daniel stepped forward to look, too.

Claire saw that the two boys had carved five logs each, with the same design of face repeated on all five. Her lips twitched when she saw the likeness Henry had created. "The archetypal witch-hag-crone." The stable lad's design was similar, but with a different aspect.

With a smile for both boys, Claire stepped back in line. As Daniel joined her and the two boys hauled the sled on, she murmured, "I can see there's going to be stiff competition for that dose of assured good luck."

The other boys came toiling along with their respective sleds; Carter, Richard and Catriona's youngest child, a cheeky character who was a favorite with the manor staff, was on the second sled and created quite a stir.

"As is his way," Melinda dryly said.

When, invited by a flourishing bow to examine Carter's carvings, Claire laughed and joined the girls in doing so, she discovered that, in addition to his theatrical flair, Carter had the soul of an artist. He'd envisioned Cailleach as a beautiful Norse-like wind goddess, with streams of hair swirling about a hauntingly beautiful face rendered with remarkable precision.

Claire arched her brows in surprise and added her sincere compliments to the girls' rather more effusive declarations.

Rejoining the line, after Daniel, too, had looked and stepped back, she murmured, "It's going to be hard to beat that."

"Indeed." Daniel glanced at Melinda. "Has anything been said of getting Carter art lessons?"

Melinda nodded. "They're going to send him to Mrs. Patience's brother—the one who's the famous portrait artist—over this coming summer. He'll still have to go on to Eton, of course, but if the arrangement suits, he might be spending his holidays—or at least some of them—in London, learning more about art." She paused, then went on, "Mind you, I'm not sure how well Carter will take to that arrangement."

Daniel frowned. "I've met the Debbingtons—they're a nice family. We occasionally see them when they travel down to their house in Cornwall. It's a fabulous place, too, with incredible gardens and views over the Channel. I would think Carter would enjoy it immensely."

Melinda shrugged. "Perhaps. But if you get a chance, ask to see his portfolio." When Daniel arched a brow, clearly asking why, Melinda said, "It's full of landscapes of hills and mountains and"—she waved her arm in an all-encompassing sweep—"the wide skies hereabouts. I suspect he'll miss this—and for someone who has spent most of his life here, it's the sort of place that leaves a mark on your soul."

Daniel inclined his head. "I imagine that's true."

They all turned to view the next sled in the procession. Henry's sled had reached the front porch and was being unloaded by several footmen and older men under Polby's direction.

The cheers and calls of encouragement were getting

louder as all six sleds were now somewhere along the path. The carpenter, his crew, and the other men who had been helping in the rear yard were following the last sled, collecting those watching on the sidelines as they came, the extended household swelling into a crowd, all laughing and talking. The noise welled in a pleasant cacophony and washed over the scene.

Just then, Calvin, pulling the fourth sled, drew level with their position; he grinned at the girls and paused while they duly examined his handiwork and that of the stable lad grinning alongside him. Then both boys leaned into the ropes they had drawn over their shoulders—

Calvin's boot slipped on a patch of re-freezing ice. The stable boy slipped, too, and started to topple.

Claire blinked, and Daniel—who had been standing alongside her—was at Calvin's side. He caught Calvin's elbow and held him upright, and all but simultaneously reached across and anchored the rope the stable lad was clinging to—and hauled the stable lad back to his feet, too.

Both boys were embarrassed and also a little shaken. They stammered their thanks.

"Just ice," Daniel said. "No harm done."

Melinda waved to one of the older men standing on the other side of the path, closer to the house. "We need some extra gravel here—there's ice on the path."

The man nodded, stepped back, and hefted a bucket left ready, then ambled over. "Get along now, boys, and let me tend to this patch."

Daniel released both boys and put a hand on the top logs on the loaded sled. "Go on—we'll give you a push to get you started."

Several men joined in and helped ease the sled back into motion; with gradually returning confidence—

gradually returning smiles as people on both sides called encouragement—the boys continued up the path.

When Daniel came back to stand by Claire's side, she was tempted to compliment him—only, between governesses and tutors, it wasn't customary to compliment each other on doing their jobs. Yet he'd been amazingly quick, and he'd rescued both boys without making them feel foolish or childish—and boys of that age were prone to being sensitive.

Indeed, she doubted either Raven or Morris, kind and caring souls though they were, would have acted so swiftly, or so tactfully.

The festive atmosphere increased as the fifth sled went by, and then the last sled, hauled steadily along by the carpenter's apprentices, both grinning fit to burst, was before them.

The four girls and the other children swarmed the sled; Claire, Daniel, and Melinda also looked and smiled appreciatively at the two very strong portraits of Cailleach-as-the-crone carved into the logs.

As the boys leaned into the ropes and the sled moved on, Claire joined the following crowd. Smiling, swept up in the welling gaiety, she fell in along the edge of the small army, keeping pace with the four girls over whom she was still keeping a watchful eye.

Melinda was walking just ahead, like a mother hen ushering the three youngest Cynster girls ahead of her.

Every sense Claire possessed was ridiculously aware that Daniel had elected to pace alongside her, on her other side.

Deeper in the crowd, Louisa stumbled, knocking Juliet into Claire.

Instinctively, Claire caught Juliet and prevented her from

falling, but in righting her charge, Claire lost her own balance. She stifled a cry as her boot soles slid on the icy ground.

Daniel caught her. Easily held her.

She'd fallen back against him, her senses jarred by the sudden contact. Against the back of her shoulders, he felt like an oak, solid and immovable.

The crowd parted about them, streaming toward the front porch; the girls looked back at them and giggled, then were swept on.

Despite the crowd, for an instant it was as if they stood alone on some island, just the two of them.

A man strong enough to catch you and hold you up when you stumble.

Still supported by Daniel, Claire looked up—into his face. Into his hazel eyes. Some part of her mind noted—again, avidly—his clean-cut features, the chiseled planes, the perfectly squared jaw below lips created by some celestial artist.

But it was his eyes that held her, that trapped her gaze and her awareness in warmth and something more.

She fell in—into the hazel, into the mind and personality behind—and saw.

Clearly.

He employed no shields, no screens, no guile.

What she saw was the truth—his truth.

And seeing that clearly—being afforded that precious insight—the reckless soul that yearned deep within her broke free and stated unequivocally: *I want you.*

The afternoon was waning, and the air beneath the trees in the forests had turned cold. Bone-chillingly cold. A portent Lucilla and Marcus had read with ease.

They'd promptly insisted that a storm was closing in

and that the riding party had to head back to the manor immediately.

To give the others their due, after taking a long look at her and her twin's expressions, Sebastian, Michael, and Christopher had agreed without argument, even though they'd yet to sight any deer.

That had been fifteen minutes ago. They'd turned on the bridle path they'd been following northward—they'd been riding to the west of Carrick lands by then—and backtracked to the junction with the path running eastward through the forest that lay along the manor's northern boundary; that path was their fastest, most direct route back to the manor.

Lucilla kept her mount close behind Prudence's; her cousin was riding behind Michael and Sebastian, while Marcus brought up the rear, riding behind Lucilla. Falling as he always did into the role of leader, Sebastian had set Christopher, arguably their best rider in terms of picking out the safest route, in the lead, with the younger boys strung out behind him and ahead of Michael.

The storm was going to be a tempestuous one; even without being able to see the sky, Lucilla knew that—and she was certain Marcus did, too. She might be the Lady's future representative in these lands and therefore afforded greater insight, but Marcus was Lady-touched, too; he, like Lucilla, was attuned to the forces that ruled this land.

They were perhaps a third of the way home, following the bridle path that ran more or less along the northern ridgeline, when a thrashing in the bushes downslope on the side away from the manor lands brought Lucilla's head up—and had Sebastian swerving his heavy hunter to a stamping halt, facing the unknown threat.

Both Lucilla and Marcus likewise veered to come around, flanking Sebastian.

Prudence, having sunk into being one with her mount as she usually did when riding, yelped, swore, and diverted around Sebastian, then expertly wheeled to come back and take station beside Lucilla, with Michael—who had called a warning to the others before swinging his mount around—at her heels.

The five cousins reined their skittish horses in. They were sitting their stamping, shifting mounts, eyes trained on the source of the noise, when a man in rough home-spun came crashing through the bushes beneath the trees.

The man looked up and saw them. He halted, his wide eyes skating over their line, but then his gaze landed on Lucilla and his fraught expression dissolved into one of abject relief. "Oh, thank God, and the Lady, too."

Whether from relief or exertion, the man—a crofter, by his clothing—swayed. Abruptly, he crouched, head down, breathing hard.

For an instant, no one moved, then Lucilla nudged her horse forward.

Sebastian's hand rose as if to hold her back, but then he let his hand fall and instead set his horse to pace beside hers.

Without looking, Lucilla knew Marcus was following at her back.

Reining in when she was closer, but not too close to the affected man—his chest was working like a bellows—she gave him a moment more, then said, "You were seeking me." No question about that. "Why?"

The man was exhausted, but he got to his feet even though he weaved. He raised his head, met Lucilla's gaze and gasped, "Lady—I—my Lottie—we need your help."

Now they were closer, Lucilla could see how deathly

pale the man was, could see in his eyes the fear and near-blind panic that still gripped him.

"What ails your wife?" She kept her tone even, letting compassion flow beneath it.

The man's gaze turned pleading; he looked at her with his heart in his eyes. "She's not ill, Lady—she's having a baby."

Lucilla blinked. Scanning the man again, estimating his age as in the early twenties, she asked, "Is it her first?"

The man nodded. "Aye—and she's having a time of it." He wiped a shaking hand across his lips. "She says the babe's coming early. We'd planned to go to the laird's after Hogmanay—it would have been all right with the midwife there. But now..."

Abruptly, the man went down on one knee, pressed his palms together and raised them to Lucilla in supplication. "Please, Lady—please help."

"Yes, of course." Lucilla couldn't imagine doing anything else. "How far is your cottage?"

The man rose to his feet, hope washing some of the stark panic from his face. He pointed down the slope, north and a little west. "It's a little ways along that way. I heard your party on the main track and prayed... I ran as fast as I could."

"Lucilla?" Sebastian caught her eye. "The storm."

She nodded. "Yes. You and the others should get back, but I have to help..." She glanced at the man. "What's your name?"

"Jeb, m'lady—Jeb Fields."

Jeb was tall, thin, and gangly; his very long legs could have covered a fair distance in the ten minutes or more he must have run.

Sebastian glanced around as all the younger boys and

Christopher came back along the track. Sebastian briefly met Michael's eyes, then exchanged a glance with Marcus, then Sebastian sighed and nudged his mount forward. "We all stay together until we see what the situation is." Freeing one boot from his stirrup, Sebastian halted his mount alongside Jeb; leaning from the saddle, he held out his hand. "We'll get there faster if we ride. Come up, and you can show me the way."

To Lucilla's mind, it spoke volumes of Jeb's panic, of how completely his worry for his wife dominated his mind, that he didn't even blink, just grasped the hand of the Marquess of Earith and swung up behind Sebastian.

Gathering his reins, the instant Jeb had settled, Sebastian asked, "Which way?"

Jeb pointed over Sebastian's shoulder back along the bridle path. "There's a little track leading off just around that curve. On horseback, that's the fastest way."

Without further ado, Sebastian set his horse trotting.

Lucilla wheeled her mount and followed. The others fell in behind.

One didn't argue with Lucilla when she was on her Lady's business. Sebastian had learned that truth a long time ago; in such circumstances, arguing was always wasted effort, and, worse, he would lose.

He never liked to lose, so he'd learned not to argue.

He didn't have to like it. And he liked this particular situation even less when he caught his first glimpse of their destination through the thinning trees.

The crofter's cottage was little more than a rude hut built of split logs and roofed with shingles. The cottage stood in a clearing at the top of a narrow valley opening to the north; the front of the cottage faced west, into the clearing, while the rear was protected by the thick forest that bordered the clearing on three sides. A thin trail of smoke rose from the single chimney.

Jeb had directed them onto the track, then had proceeded to fill Sebastian's ears with a litany of panicked gibberish; the man was so clearly unhinged by worry over his wife and imminent child that despite the irritation, Sebastian felt sorry for the poor sod. Sorry enough to push the pace. Even so, it was a good ten minutes after they'd left the ridge when he drew rein before the cottage door.

Jeb tumbled off Sebastian's horse and ran to hold Lucilla's mount.

Unnecessary, but Lucilla thanked Jeb with a nod; she slipped her boots free of the stirrups and slid to the ground before Sebastian or any of her other male kin could help her.

Prudence was on the ground a second later. Grabbing her saddlebags, Lucilla shot her cousin a summoning glance. Reaching for her own saddlebags, Prudence waved her on. "I'm right behind you."

Leaving Sebastian doing what he did best and organizing everyone else—admittedly, in this instance, with Marcus's input—juggling her saddlebags, Lucilla swept up the skirts of her riding habit and marched through the snow to the cottage door. With the clearing being on the north face of the ridge and at higher elevation than the manor, the covering was already a solid six inches deep.

There'd be more after the storm hit.

Having handed her mount's reins to Marcus, Jeb came racing up to open the door.

When he lifted the latch, thrust the simple wooden door wide, and awkwardly half bowed, Lucilla waved at him to precede her. "Tell Lottie I'm here." She had no idea what she would find in the cottage, what state Lottie would be in, much less what she might need to do, but barging in unannounced on a pregnant woman in extremis was not a good move on any number of counts.

Jeb bobbed his head and stepped inside.

Lucilla paused on the threshold; eyes adjusting to the low level of light—indeed, gloom—inside the cottage, she saw a rectangular deal table, and beyond it a crude but solid stone fireplace built into the wall directly opposite the main door. Although the fire in the grate was presently feeble, the hearth was swept, and split logs were neatly stacked to either side. A quick scan of the implements in the hearth and the pots, pans, and bowls arrayed on the surrounding shelves confirmed that she would have all she might need in that regard; Jeb and Lottie Fields might be poor crofters, but they possessed at least the necessities of life.

Hearing low voices from the shadows to her left, Lucilla could tell from the female tones that Lottie was still very much aware—and that she, too, was eaten with fear for her babe and herself. Lucilla stepped into the cottage and turned to face the young couple.

Lottie proved to be as pale as Jeb, but not quite as thin. She lay on a bed comprised of a rough timber frame supporting a decently plump, straw-filled pallet placed with its head against the cottage's front wall. Panting, her hugely distended belly covered by several thin blankets, Lottie lay propped up by two pillows. Her wide, shadowed eyes locked on Lucilla's face, then Lottie let out a sigh of relief—that hitched into a whimper as her eyes closed and her face contorted with pain.

"Let me see." Setting her saddlebags on the table, Lucilla went quickly to the nearer side of the pallet. Aware that Prudence had followed her inside, Lucilla said, "I need better light." She glanced at Jeb, and caught his still wide eyes. "Do you have any lamps? Or even candles?"

They had one good lamp and a handful of tallow candles. Prudence helped Jeb to clean and fill the lamp, then trim the wick and light it.

Meanwhile, Lucilla knelt beside the pallet and took one of Lottie's limp hands in hers. "How long have the pains been coming?"

Lottie glanced briefly at Jeb; reassured he was occupied, she lowered her voice to a whisper. "Since yesterday. I didn't want to say and worry him—I thought maybe they'd pass. But they haven't."

Lucilla smiled and poured comfort into her expression. "I'll know more in a moment, but have the pains been steadily building since then?" When, biting her lip, Lottie nodded, Lucilla calmly continued, "Then I suspect that there's nothing actually wrong—it's just that your baby is ready to make his or her appearance and isn't about to wait."

Lottie's fine brown lashes swept down, then rose; her pale blue eyes searched Lucilla's face, then some of the tension tightening her features eased. Her fingers curled and gripped Lucilla's hand. "I do so hope it's just that, and praise be Jeb found you and you came."

Light suddenly bloomed and came nearer; Lucilla glanced around as Jeb carried the lamp toward them.

At the same time, faint shadows slanted in through the open door.

Leaving the table, Prudence made for the door. Catching hold of the panel, she spoke to whoever stood outside.

"We don't need you at the moment—stay outside." With that, she shut the door.

Stifling a grin, Lucilla turned back to her patient. Jeb had halted at the foot of the pallet. Lucilla waved him to the spot opposite where she knelt. "Stand there and hold the lamp directly over Lottie."

While Jeb moved to obey, Lucilla smiled at Lottie and reached to free the rough blankets. "I'll be able to tell what's happening if I look. Is that all right?"

Lips compressed, Lottie nodded. She held still, tense and nervous, as Lucilla swiftly examined her, but she responded readily to Lucilla's directions and instructions.

Several minutes later, having seen enough to confirm her suspicions, Lucilla resettled the blankets, then sat back on her heels and met Jeb's anxious gaze, then Lottie's. Lucilla smiled as confidently as she could. "It's as I thought—the baby's coming." She glanced at Jeb. "Quite aside from the storm that's blowing in, it's too late to even think about moving Lottie down to your laird's house. This baby is going to be born here."

Lottie reached out and gripped Lucilla's hand. "Will you stay?"

Lucilla met Lottie's eyes and returned the pressure of her fingers. "Yes, of course. That's why I'm here."

The latter words had spilled from her lips without conscious thought, but, hearing them, she knew they were true. The Lady had sent Jeb to find her and lead her here—here was where she was supposed to be, bringing this child into the world.

"I've assisted at many births—it's part of my training." Lucilla squeezed Lottie's hand and set it back on the blanket-covered mound. "So yes, I'll be staying, and although the baby's appearance is some way off, we'll use the time to get ready." Rising, she looked down at Lottie. "Rest. Doze if you can, in between pangs. Meanwhile, Jeb and I and my cousin will sort things out."

Lottie's smile was wan but real. "Thank you, Lady." Her eyes drifted shut.

Satisfied, Lucilla turned away.

Across the cottage, she met Prudence's gaze. Lucilla raised her brows. "You'll stay?"

"Of course. I've assisted at any number of foalings, and although humans and horses aren't entirely the same, the basics aren't that different."

"Indeed." Lucilla hesitated, then looked at Jeb as, leaving Lottie's side, he brought the lamp to the table. "My cousin and I"   Lucilla glanced at Prudence—"will need to talk to the others. While we're doing that, Jeb, can you find a length of rope we can use to stretch across the cottage so we can hang up some blankets and give Lottie a bit of privacy?"

Jeb blinked at the notion, but nodded. "I've got some rope in the stable-barn." With his head, he indicated a narrow door set into the cottage's rear wall.

Lucilla realized she'd been hearing the shuffling of hooves and the occasional soft bleat from beyond the rear wall; until now, she hadn't paid attention to the sounds. Crofters in these parts were usually shepherds to flocks of sheep belonging to their lairds; presumably Jeb's stable-barn was home to his flock through the harsh winter. "Good. You sort out the rope and find us some blankets or sheets. Meanwhile, we'll sort out the rest."

Specifically their male relatives, who, if she knew anything of them, were even now contemplating hammering on the door and demanding to be told what was going on; she reached the door and opened it before they could.

Sure enough, Marcus, Sebastian, Michael, and Christopher stood in a group mere feet from the door. Stepping outside, Lucilla waited until Prudence joined her and shut the door firmly before looking first at Marcus, then Sebastian. "I need to stay until the baby's born."

"And I need to stay with Lucilla," Prudence said. Her tone, even more than Lucilla's, somewhat belligerently stated that argument was futile.

His hands in his breeches pockets, Sebastian met Lucilla's steady gaze, then Prudence's blue eyes, then he glanced at Marcus. Finding no comfort there, lips compressing, jaw setting, Sebastian half turned and looked at the trees. The strong features he'd inherited from his father were relatively easy to read; he wanted to simply say no, but he knew very well that there was no point.

With patience born of unshakeable confidence, Lucilla waited for his capitulation, but she, along with Prudence, was too wise to prod him.

At eighteen the eldest by a full year, Sebastian was invariably—inevitably—viewed by their parents as principally responsible for any decisions they made. He was their leader, and that was, in fact, never in doubt. Yet in situations such as this…leadership came in many guises.

After half a minute of communing with the trees, his pale green eyes narrow, Sebastian looked back at Lucilla and, his features set, nodded. "In that case, I'll be staying, too." He barely spared a glance for Prudence before looking at Marcus and arching a brow.

Marcus nodded. "I'll remain, too, of course."

"And me," Michael said. When Sebastian directed a questioning look his way, Michael said, "If this storm settles in and you need to send for help, you'll need to send two of us." He nodded at Marcus. "Me and Marcus—it'd be madness to send either one of us alone."

Marcus grunted in agreement. "That's a possibility that might turn into a reality, so yes, there should be at least three of us males all told."

"Very well." Sebastian turned to the last member of their group.

Christopher grinned. "And that leaves me to lead the younger crew"—with a jerk of his thumb, he indicated the five younger boys still sitting their horses—"back to the manor and explain where you are and why."

Sebastian read Christopher's expression and raised his brows. "You don't mind?"

"Actually, no." Christopher tipped his head toward the cottage. "If there's a baby going to be born in there in the next few hours, I really would rather be elsewhere."

Lucilla watched as that point sank home with Sebastian, Marcus, and Michael. All three unquestionably shared Christopher's aversion, yet although they shifted and frowned, none were, she judged, remotely likely to change their minds about staying.

"Very well. Now that's settled"—Lucilla looked at Christopher—"you need to get moving. Ride as hard as you can." Both she and Marcus glanced to the northwest, to where a brooding gray-white mass was roiling and spilling over the peaks.

"If you leave now," Marcus said, his narrowed gaze on the clouds, "you should make it back to the manor without difficulty, but that storm will be on your heels."

"In that case, we'll get going." With a general nod and a breezy salute, Christopher walked off to where his brother Gregory held Christopher's mount's reins.

The five cousins left before the cottage door watched

as Christopher mounted, then gathered the group and led them back up the track to the ridge.

Lucilla stirred and caught Michael's eye. "Jeb has what he calls a stable-barn at the rear—the horses need to be taken in, tended, and secured. The winds coming with the storm are going to be ferocious, I think."

Marcus nodded. "I think so, too. And we won't have that much time before they hit."

Prudence shifted from foot to foot, then gave up and headed for her mount. "I'll take care of Gypsy."

Knowing Prudence's attachment to horses—all horses—Lucilla merely nodded. "Jeb and I can handle putting up a screen." With the others collecting their horses and hers, too, she turned to the cottage door. "I'll unlatch the door between the cottage and the stable-barn so you won't have to come outside to get in."

Opening the door, she went into the cottage, leaving the other four leading the five horses to the barn.

Five

Louisa, Therese, Annabelle, and Juliet crept silently down the main stairs and, valiantly suppressing the urge to giggle, tiptoed through the front foyer and slipped into the Great Hall.

It was early evening; outside, the sky had darkened. Thick gray-white clouds were closing in, shrouding the surrounding hills and sending the temperature plummeting from icy to freezing.

And as the girls had hoped, in the half hour before dinner, the huge hall was deserted.

They were already dressed for the evening, had rushed and hurried and helped each other neaten their hair and hunt out their evening slippers.

"We'll need to be quick." Louisa led the way to their festive log-basket.

The other three followed. Donning the leather gloves they'd stuffed into their pockets, they fell to, lifting out the upper layer of holly and piling it to one side.

As soon as they uncovered the mistletoe beneath, Therese stopped and looked at Annabelle. "Let's go and get those stepladders."

Annabelle nodded. She and Therese left Louisa and Juliet carefully lifting out the more delicate mistletoe, separating the individual branchlets, with their drooping leaves and clusters of white berries.

Hurrying through one of the archways into the corridor that ultimately led to the kitchen, Annabelle and Therese turned into the cluttered alcove where the footmen who had earlier helped deck the hall with evergreens had left the pair of stepladders. "I hope we're tall enough to reach with these." Annabelle hefted one of the ladders.

"We will be." Therese grabbed the second ladder. "We're nearly as tall as the footmen, and they were only using the second step of the three—I watched."

"That's true." Annabelle huffed as she carried the heavy ladder back to the hall. "And anyway, we're only going to be hanging the mistletoe under the archways, not above them."

Louisa and Juliet, both all but jigging with impatience, met Annabelle and Therese as they re-entered the hall. Juliet went with Annabelle to the archway leading to the library.

Louisa halted Therese under the archway through which the girls had returned. "Let's do this one first."

Therese obligingly set the stepladder beneath the archway. Lifting her skirts with one hand and carrying a bunch of mistletoe branchlets in the other, Louisa climbed the ladder. Using the strings she'd left hanging when she'd tied up the bunch, she quickly tied the mistletoe to the evergreens on either side of the archway's apex.

Carefully, she released the mistletoe—as they'd hoped, it hung in the center of the archway.

"Yes!" Therese crowed. She took a step back, eyed the archway measuringly, then nodded. "It's still high enough that not even Uncle Sylvester will have it drag over his head."

"Excellent!" Eyes bright, Louisa quickly backed down the ladder. She glanced to where Juliet was still fiddling with the bunch she was attaching to the library archway. "Let's do the archway into the front foyer—we saved the biggest bunch for there."

She and Therese carried the stepladder across the hall, then with Louisa directing, Therese—who was the taller of the pair—secured the large bunch of trailing greenery and berries in place.

Louisa grinned. "Perfect!"

Juliet and Annabelle had already crossed to the last archway, the one that connected the stairs from three of the upper towers to the dais. Leaving them to finish there, Therese picked up the stepladder and carried it back to the alcove while Louisa quickly placed the holly back into the log-basket, piling it up so that the loss of the mistletoe beneath didn't appear too obvious.

Annabelle came to help while Juliet took the other stepladder back, and then it was done.

The four girls gathered in the center of the hall, in between the tables, and turned in a slow circle, examining the totality of their decorations.

Then they turned to each other and grinned.

"Yes, indeed—and you have every right to be delighted with yourselves."

The words—in a voice they all knew well—had them spinning around to look at the archway giving onto the dais.

Helena stood beneath it, looking up at the dangling mistletoe, then she lowered her gaze and beamed upon them.

"Very timely, my dears. For, after all, what is Christmas without mistletoe?"

Helena used a cane; she was holding it in her hand. None of the girls could understand why they hadn't heard her coming down the stairs…then Helena moved forward and Algaria joined her, and they realized Algaria had helped Helena down.

Looking up at the mistletoe, Algaria audibly sniffed. "It never did anything for me, but for others, I suppose, it's much as that other saying. *Is blianach Nollaid gun sneachd.*" Lowering her gaze, she looked pointedly at Annabelle.

Annabelle screwed up her face in thought, then offered, "Christmas without snow is poor fare…or what is Christmas without snow?"

Algaria nodded approvingly. "Good enough."

Helena tipped her head as if listening to noises above, then she looked at the four girls. "If you wish to play the role of secret mistletoe fairies, then you might not want to be the only ones here when others arrive."

Louisa blinked. "Good point."

With her cane, Helena waved toward the far archway. "The library should be a useful place to retreat to for now, so that you can emerge later and be as amazed as everyone else."

Louisa grinned. "Thank you, Grandmama!"

Annabelle echoed the sentiment, while the other two chorused, "Thank you, Grand-aunt Helena!"

Helena shooed them off, and they went, giggling as they hurried out of the hall toward the library.

Slowly making her way to her place at the far end of the high table, Algaria said, "I find it comforting that they are still at the giggling girl stage, and so still find delight in such minor events. Heaven help us all when that lot grows up."

Looking after the four, Helena thought it very likely she would be in Heaven by that time. But instead of acknowledging the inevitable turning of time's wheel, she tilted her head and, focusing on the ball of mistletoe hanging beneath the arch through which the four had gone, murmured, "Still, I feel it is a very good thing—a very necessary thing—that they have done."

By the time Prudence, Marcus, Sebastian, and Michael came in through the door from Jeb's stable-barn, Lucilla, with Jeb's help, had strung the rope he'd found across the width of the cottage between nails sunk into the log walls, then draped old blankets over the rope and placed logs on the ends trailing on the floor to create a wall screening Lottie and the pallet from the rest of the cottage.

Sadly, that was only the beginning of their making do. The others came in, stamping their feet and rubbing warmth back into their hands. They crowded around the deal table, setting the saddlebags they'd carried in on the empty board.

Coming out from behind the curtain of blankets, Lucilla saw them—saw them all turn to look at the front of the cottage just as she, alerted by some visceral sense, did the same.

Abruptly, the wind shrieked and struck the cottage's exposed front face. The force of the blow was an elemental slap that rattled the structure and left it moaning and groaning.

All five cousins looked up and around at the timbers surrounding them, the creaking beams holding up the roof, the walls with their gaps too numerous to count, and the rickety shutters covering the glassless windows.

"Sounds like the storm's arrived," Michael said.

Lucilla looked at Marcus and met her twin's eyes. It was Marcus who, somewhat diffidently, said, "Actually, no. That was just the precursor—a harbinger, if you like. The winds come first. The storm itself is still an hour or more away."

Turning from studying the less-than-sturdy shutter over the window to the left of the front door, Sebastian bent a richly unimpressed look on Marcus. "So it's going to get a lot worse."

Marcus nodded.

Sebastian looked back at the shutter and sighed. "In that case, we'd better use that hour to see what we can do to shore this place up."

"I saw timber and sheeting at the back of the barn, and there must be tools somewhere." Michael looked at Marcus and Lucilla; Jeb was behind the curtain with Lottie. "Is it all right if we use whatever we can find to make this place more sound?"

Marcus glanced at Lucilla.

"I'll ask," she said.

When applied to, Jeb blinked at her in incomprehension. With Lottie clinging to his hand, gritting her teeth as she waited out another painful pang, Jeb couldn't seem to gather his wits enough to focus on anything else.

It was Lottie who, as the pang eased, drew in a deeper breath and gasped, "There's all sorts o' bits and bobs left over from when they built the stable-barn last summer. Jeb was hoping to use the stuff here and there for repairs."

"Good." Lucilla patted Lottie's hand and squeezed Jeb's shoulder. Rising, she said, "You stay here with Lottie, Jeb, and we'll get busy and do some of those repairs for you." To Lottie, she said, "If you need me, just call."

Lucilla went out past the curtain to discover that Sebastian, Michael, and Marcus, having heard the exchange, had already gone back into the stable-barn to see what they could find.

In the end, Prudence went, too; she was more comfortable doing things in barns than in kitchens.

While the others found and ferried timbers, boards, and bits of shingle, as well as a plethora of tools, into the cottage, Lucilla built the insipid fire into a respectable blaze. Satisfied, she turned her attention to searching the cupboards.

And found next to nothing.

A meagre hoard of flour, not enough to make even one decent-sized loaf. Some turnips. A few chestnuts. And a cooking pot containing a small portion of leftover rabbit stew.

Looking into the pot, Lucilla pulled a face.

Setting down the tools she'd ferried in, Prudence saw and came to peer into the pot. She considered the evidence, then met Lucilla's gaze and whispered, "Is that all there is?"

Lucilla nodded and whispered back, "And that will have to go to Lottie." Setting the lid back on the pot, she returned it to the side of the hearth. "I'll add water and make it into a broth. Whether she eats it now or later, she'll need the sustenance."

Prudence shrugged. "It's not as if going hungry for one night is going to hurt us."

"No." Lucilla shut her lips on the question of what might occur if they were snowed in; both she and Prudence knew how their menfolk ate, but they would deal with that if it happened.

The ferocity of the wind had increased; it howled about

the cottage like some savage animal hell-bent on tearing and rending. Every now and then, a more severe buffet sent snow and sleet peppering the exposed front of the cottage; the fury of the storm seemed a live thing intent on forcing its way inside through every crack and crevice.

"Water." Lucilla found the water jug half full. She grimaced. "We'll need a lot more than this, especially when the baby arrives." Raising her head, she listened to the wind. "Better we get it in now."

Going back around the curtain, she found Jeb talking quietly to Lottie, who had closed her eyes and might have been dozing. "Jeb," Lucilla whispered. When he looked at her, she held up the water jug. "Where's the well?"

The answer proved to be in the trees a little way beyond the back of the barn. Lucilla gathered all the receptacles that would hold a decent amount, and piled them into her cousins' and brother's arms. "Bring back as much as you can, but please don't get frostbite."

Jeb had offered to get the water, but the difference in size and build between him and the Cynster males was too marked to allow any of them to even consider that.

Having tactfully insisted that Jeb remain with Lottie, Lucilla watched her four relatives troop out into the barn. Securing the narrow door behind them, she returned to the hearth, added water to the remnants of the stew, stirred the mixture, then set it hanging over the blaze to simmer.

In the barn, Sebastian squinted out of the main door into the trees. "I can just see the well. It's not that far."

"Draw straws to see who goes," Michael said.

Sebastian glanced at his brother, then shook his head. "No. I'm the heaviest." He shrugged. "And the strongest. I'll go."

Neither Michael nor Marcus thought that a sound idea and said so; an argument looked set to ensue.

They were all in hunting clothes; none of them had overcoats, or even thicker gloves. Hugging a bowl to her chest, Prudence said, "If I might make a suggestion?"

Three pairs of male eyes swung her way.

"What?" Michael asked.

Inwardly sighing, Prudence outlined her idea and, of course, it made the best sense.

Without actually admitting that, the boys accepted her suggestion of forming a short line and passing the bowls and pails back and forth. As she had pointed out, it would be the fastest way to get what they had to do done, and would also involve the least expenditure of energy for each of them.

Sebastian—as he had stated, the heaviest and strongest—went first. It was he who reached the well, lifted the simple lid, and dropped the bucket down. He who turned the wheel to pull the filled bucket back up and tipped the water into the containers.

Michael was next in line, receiving each filled receptacle and passing it back to Marcus before giving Sebastian the next empty vessel. Marcus carried each filled receptacle back to Prudence—forbidden by all three boys from venturing out of the barn; taking it, she set it carefully aside while Marcus picked up the next empty pot and trudged it out to Michael.

Marcus didn't have to trudge far, and Sebastian didn't need to shift from the well. They worked quickly and efficiently, and in the shortest possible time, all the cousins were back in the barn and had hauled the doors shut and dropped the bar across.

Eying the rattling doors in the light of the old storm

lantern they'd earlier found and lit, Sebastian humphed. "Just as well this side of the cottage is protected by the ridge and the trees."

They ferried the filled containers back into the cottage. Lucilla had them place the pots and bowls in one corner, out of the way. Marcus and Prudence returned to the stable-barn to check their horses and Jeb's sheep.

Sebastian and Michael came to warm themselves by the fire.

Holding his hands to the blaze, Michael murmured, "We should block the gaps in the walls where the wind is pushing in."

"Hmm." Sebastian turned his back to the fire and critically surveyed the cottage. "I think the main structure is sound enough—and regardless, we haven't got the materials to do anything about that—but those shutters, the left one especially, look far from secure. If one of them goes, the storm will be inside the cottage."

Straightening, Michael nodded. "You do the shutter. I'll work on the walls."

Marcus and Prudence returned. After a brief discussion—to which Lucilla listened but didn't contribute— Sebastian and Marcus went to work trying to stabilize the rickety shutter, working solely from the inside and without opening it, not a straightforward task. Michael started working his way around the walls, plugging whatever gaps he found with straw or by hammering in slivers of wood.

Prudence turned to Lucilla and tipped her head at the blanket-screened alcove. "Is there anything that needs doing there?"

Lucilla shook her head. "We'll need you later, almost certainly, but as yet…"

Prudence lowered her voice. "How's she going?"

Lucilla met her gaze, then whispered, "I'm not sure. Matters are progressing as they should, and yet…something's not quite right. The baby's position is still not as it should be." She paused, then added, "I tried to shift it around, but that didn't work—it's already too late. I think it's going to be a breech birth."

Prudence shrugged. "That happens with foals sometimes. As long as there's help, it usually works." She studied Lucilla's face. "Have you delivered a breech before?"

Lucilla grimaced. "I've seen it done twice. But seeing is different from doing." She met Prudence's eyes. "You?"

Prudence pulled a face. "Same as you—seen, but not actually done."

Lucilla shrugged lightly. "We'll just have to manage."

"Well, until you need me, I'll help Michael."

"Actually," Lucilla said, "it would help if you did the walls behind the screen. They're just as much in need of patching as the rest."

Prudence saluted and turned away. "Will do."

After checking her stew-cum-broth, Lucilla checked on Lottie, but with Jeb beside her, the young woman was holding her own; as far as Lucilla could tell, they were still at the slow, steady, and repetitive stage.

Prudence, a small mallet in one hand, was shifting around the walls in the narrow space, tapping softened wood plugs into gaps.

But Lottie was a Scotswoman; the rules of hospitality were bred in her bones. Rallying in the aftermath of a birth pang, she looked at Lucilla, her expression aghast. "I just realized… Jeb didn't get a chance to check his traps. And I haven't baked, and there's no flour because we didn't expect the storm, and Jeb would have gone today—"

"Don't. Worry." Lucilla's tone brooked no argument.

"While you're bringing this child into the world, you are absolved of all other duties." When Lottie blinked at her, Lucilla calmly continued, "None of those here are in danger of starving. We have plenty of water, and at present, that's our only essential need."

Lottie didn't look convinced. "But it's Christmas Eve. You and"—she glanced at Prudence, then tipped her head at the screen—"the others should be sitting down to a great feast."

Lucilla shrugged. "But we're not. We're here. We chose to come here, we chose to stay, and I'm quite sure that here is where we're supposed to be. If we miss a meal, then that, too, is part of what should be."

When Lottie frowned, unsure how to answer, Lucilla smiled and patted her hand. "You concentrate on what you have to do and don't worry about the rest of us—not even Jeb. I'm going to brew you a tisane—I'll bring it in a few minutes."

Lucilla went back around the screen, drew up a stool, sat at the table, and pulled her saddlebag from under the pile. She sorted through the herbs she habitually carried. Several would be useful after the birth, to help Lottie recover, and Lucilla had the makings of a tisane that would support Lottie through the next few hours by taking the sharp edge from the pangs, but there was precious little that would aid during the crucial stage of delivery.

Inwardly shrugging, Lucilla brewed the calming and supportive tisane. She poured the concoction into a plain tin mug and set it aside to cool, then, straightening, she glanced at the others—at Michael wedging a piece of wood into a crack above the shuttered window to the right of the door, and at Sebastian and Marcus working on the shutter covering the other window.

As Lucilla watched, Sebastian and Marcus stepped back and surveyed their handiwork. The shutter still rattled, but only with the worst of the gusts, and it certainly wasn't shuddering as it had been.

Marcus said, "That's the best we can do."

Sebastian nodded and, a hammer dangling from his hand, turned away. He saw Lucilla watching and caught her eye. Sebastian glanced at the screen, then mouthed, "Food?"

Lucilla shook her head and mouthed back, "None."

Sebastian grimaced, then shrugged resignedly. Both he and Marcus joined Michael in hunting out and blocking the worst of the gaps in the walls.

Registering that, despite the drop in temperature due to the oncoming storm and the chilling effect of the icy winds, the temperature inside the cottage had actually started to rise—or, at least, was no longer precipitously falling—Lucilla returned to the fire and piled on three more logs.

When the flames caught and flared, she straightened.

Staring into the flames, her own words replayed in her head. *We chose to come here, we chose to stay, and I'm quite sure that here is where we're supposed to be.* She knew truth when it fell from her lips, but in fact, the road that had brought them there stretched back much further than the decisions made that day.

They'd *planned* to be in Scotland for Christmas, a plan they'd hatched while at Somersham Place, principal residence of the Duke of St. Ives and the family's ancestral home, for their Summer Celebration, which lauded and revolved about one thing—family. On that August day, while strolling around the lake, they'd talked about hunting after Christmas, and the boys had, even then, spoken of the need to go riding on Christmas Eve.

They'd started down the path that had landed them in the cottage, with a storm about to hit in full force outside and a woman about to give birth inside, a long time before.

Feeling the increased warmth the fire was throwing into the room, Lucilla turned—just as a long, mournful, whistling howl swirled about the cottage.

Lucilla met Marcus's eyes. *Soon.*

Marcus nodded.

Lucilla swung back to the fireplace, picked up the mug with her tisane, blew lightly on it, then carried it to Lottie.

What would come would come. They would deal with it when it did.

I want you.

Of course, Claire hadn't let the words past her lips; she'd grown so accustomed over the last years to suppressing that part of her that preventing her tongue from blurting out the telltale words had been instinctive, yet those words nevertheless, and the welling compulsion behind them, continued to resonate within her.

Filling her mind. Feeding her reckless, wanton soul.

Drawing that other self closer to her surface.

She'd almost forgotten what it felt like, that yearning and reaching fueled by passionate naivety, by unsullied belief in the goodness and rightness of all she felt.

Of all she yearned for.

Experience had taught her a bitter lesson, had opened her eyes and forced her to see, yet…when it came to Daniel Crosbie…

It wasn't so much that he'd turned back her clock as that he'd somehow reached deep and opened the locks she'd set inside, and he'd freed, resurrected, brought back to life that younger her—the one who believed in the shining wonder of love.

She felt the change within her, recognized the re-emergence of that more youthful self...and still could not quite make her older-and-wiser self believe, accept, and stand aside.

She still didn't know if setting aside the wisdom of her years and re-embracing the reckless wonder of youth was the course she should take.

Didn't know whether she should encourage Daniel or, as gently as she could, refuse him.

Summoned by the dinner gong, she stopped by Annabelle's room but found it empty; her four charges of the day had, it appeared, already gone downstairs. She continued down the turret stairs and walked on toward the Great Hall. Noise and gaiety spilled out through the archways and drew her on; the warmth from all the blazes, spiced with the curious tang of the smoke rising from the slowly burning effigies of Cailleach, wrapped around her, and the evocative scent of evergreens perfumed the air. Outwardly, she remained focused on her governessly duties, but inside her mind revolved—as it had since her reckless self had served up those three little words—on the conundrum of what she should do next.

Of what answer she should give Daniel when they finally talked.

Walking into the Great Hall, Claire saw that the riding party had still not returned. Regardless, the tutors and Melinda were once more sitting at their normal table. Refusing to back away from the challenge before her, Claire checked that her four charges were, indeed, in their accustomed places, then calmly walked to the empty place beside Daniel.

He, Raven, and Morris all rose as she neared. Daniel smiled and offered his hand to help her step over the bench.

Taking his hand, registering—reveling in—the sensations, yet refusing to let her reactions rattle her, she smiled at the others, stepped into the space, then, slipping her fingers free of Daniel's warm clasp, she sat, and the gentlemen subsided again.

The group had been in the middle of a discussion; as they returned to contrasting the various depictions of Cailleach the boys had produced, Claire exchanged a smile with Melinda and settled to listen.

Following the procession—and those three little words—for her the rest of the afternoon had passed in a blur of festivity, excitement, and heightened nerves. The logs delivered to the front porch had been arranged around the entry hall for all to admire and, ultimately, to decide which "Cailleach" would burn in which fireplace. Each of the six major fireplaces was to have two depictions of the spirit of winter burning through the days until Hogmanay. Along with Daniel and the four girls, Claire had circled the room with the rest of the crowd, examining anew and exclaiming over the carvings, now displayed in warm lamplight.

In the end, pride of place in the main and largest fireplace in the Great Hall went to Carter—whose Norse-goddess Cailleach was unanimously declared the most outstanding—along with one of the carpenter's apprentices, the runner-up in the competition. The other carved logs were divided between the remaining fireplaces, with one Cynster boy's work and one manor household boy's work set to burn in each hearth.

Then the lighting of the Cailleachs had begun. That had proved hilarious because the carved logs had been treated to slow their burning, which in turn made them difficult to set afire, but luckily there were enough old hands in the household who knew the knack of setting the carved logs atop logs already crackling; soon enough, Cailleachs were burning in all the appointed fireplaces, and mulled cider and the sunburst shortbread the younger girls had made was ceremonially passed around, much to those girls' and everyone's delight.

The fun-filled afternoon and the relaxed ambiance of the ceremonial gathering of the household and guests had made the sudden spiking of anxiety over the riding party's continued absence all the more jarring.

By the time all the logs had been lit, the sky outside had darkened. Shortly after, the wind had whipped up, and the Cynster parents had started wondering where their older children were. The ladies had started glancing toward the side door, as if doing so might make it open sooner.

Now dinner was about to be served, and there was still no sign of the bevy of males who would normally never miss a meal.

Even though they'd been discussing something else, the male tutors were tense, as was Melinda; Claire, too, was conscious of welling concern. If something had happened...

Raven glanced at the high table. "The duke and the others went out to the rear yard earlier, but they couldn't see anything through the snow."

"It's set in, by the looks of it," Morris said. "I went up

to the highest tower, but even from there the view is obscured."

"They're all old enough to keep their heads," Melinda said. "Whatever's happened, we'll hear about it as soon as they can manage—they're not irresponsible children anymore."

Claire nodded. "That's true." Juliet's older brother, Justin, was one of the riding party. Although he retained the exuberance to be expected of a sixteen-year-old youth, underneath, Justin had his mother's steadiness and his father's courage. "Justin wouldn't unnecessarily cause anxiety for his parents and siblings. I doubt any of the others would knowingly worry their families, either."

Raven pulled a face and was about to add something when the sound of a door banging open was followed by youthful male voices and the clatter of boots.

All talk ceased; everyone looked toward the archway from the front hall.

Christopher Cynster appeared first. With one sweep of his gaze, he took in the heightened tension, the concern... He looked at the high table. "Sorry—nothing bad's happened. No accident or anything of that nature. All of us had to divert for Lucilla to tend a pregnant woman, a crofter's wife, and then the storm came in hard—we've only just ridden in."

Vane Cynster, Christopher's father, and Devil Cynster had risen to their feet; their gazes touched each boy as Christopher walked further into the room and the younger members of the riding party crowded in behind him.

Rising, too, Richard waved the boys to the fireplaces. "Get warm first, then sit down—no need to change."

Christopher led the way forward; the younger boys peeled off to the fireplaces to warm their hands, then hustled to fill the gap at their usual table. Christopher continued to the end of the table below the dais—the space he shared with the other older children, none of whom had appeared.

The duke leveled an interrogatory look at Christopher. "Where are the others?"

Halting at his usual place, Christopher said, "They stayed at the crofter's cottage. Lucilla said she had to remain until the babe is born, and, of course, Marcus stayed with her, and Sebastian and Michael stayed, too, in case of need, and Lucilla asked Prudence to stay and help, which, of course, she did."

Claire noted the several "of courses," stated and implied, in that brief report, but she suspected Christopher had included them deliberately. Familial support was a trademark Cynster trait, one Christopher's elders adhered to without question.

Devil, Vane, and Richard, and all the others about the high table, nodded in reluctant acceptance. As the men sat again, Devil waved Christopher up to the dais. "Come and sit with us, and you can satisfy our curiosity."

Christopher obeyed; staff hurried to set a place for him beside the dowager, who insisted that Christopher be accommodated next to her, the better for her old ears to hear.

Which was nonsense; the dowager's hearing was excellent. But from the look Claire saw Christopher send the dowager's way, he was grateful not to have to sit surrounded by the as-yet-to-be-fully-appeased parents.

The platters were ferried out, the meal commenced, and while the tension had eased significantly from its earlier high, there remained an undercurrent of watchfulness, of unsettled uncertainty.

From the table where the rest of the riding party sat rose

eager questions and answers regarding the cottage and the storm. The deep rumble of the elder Cynster males' voices, punctuated by the lighter tones of their ladies and pauses during which Christopher answered their many questions, drifted from the high table.

Unable to hear any of the comments clearly, Claire didn't bother straining her ears; she would get the full story—embellished with fine detail—from Juliet later. For herself, Claire was thankful that Christopher had led the sixteen-year-olds home without incident; the banshee-like shriek of the wind and the gusting of the storm—the raging of an elemental force outside—could be heard even here in the Great Hall, in the center of the manor, surrounded by so many thick walls and with several floors above them.

Seated alongside Claire, Daniel discovered the true meaning of the word *distraction*. While his uncertainty over Claire—about where she stood vis-à-vis him and what the hurdle she perceived standing between them was—circled in his mind, he was also concerned over the older children's fate. Although none of the five yet to return had ever been his personal charge, he nevertheless knew them—in particular he'd interacted with the three boys, now almost young men, over many years.

From the look in his eyes, Morris, too, shared Daniel's worry, even though Morris's charges, like Daniel's, were now all safely home.

Somewhat strangely, Raven and Melinda, both of whom were most closely associated with Lucilla and Marcus—and to some extent Sebastian, Michael, and Prudence, too—were the most sanguine. Raven waved a general dismissal and fell to attacking his roast beef. "They'll be back safe and sound—no need to worry about that lot."

"No, indeed." Melinda held a platter of roasted vegetables for Claire to serve herself. "No need to fear for them, not even in this storm."

It was Claire who, puzzled, commented, "You seem very confident that no harm will befall them."

Chewing, Raven nodded. He swallowed, then said, "They're Lady-touched. Well, Lucilla and Marcus are, and you may be certain they won't allow the others out of their sight, so Sebastian, Michael, and Prudence will be protected, too."

"Protected?" Morris asked.

Looking at his plate, Raven nodded. "That's one of the things you learn if you live here long enough." He glanced up and gave them all a faintly sheepish, self-deprecatory smile. "The trick of it is that you don't have to believe in the Lady, you just have to accept, and if you live here long enough…" He shrugged and went back to slicing his beef.

"If you live here long enough," Melinda said, "you see too much *not* to accept that there's…a *mystery* that operates hereabouts, one the locals believe in, and regardless of whether you believe in it or not, it works, and you can have faith in it doing so."

Raven nodded. "Well put. We can be perfectly certain those five will return, hale and whole, although exactly when is the point still in doubt."

Across the table, Daniel exchanged a look with Morris, then the older man shrugged and gave his attention to his meal.

Daniel looked down at his plate as Claire said, "That is reassuring…that all one needs to do is accept."

He glanced at her, but she'd looked down, too; he couldn't tell whether her last words had been intended to convey the more personal allusion he thought he'd heard in them.

Regardless, he was intent on engineering the moment they needed—that she'd requested—for them to talk. Later, by his estimation, meant at the end of the meal, after their charges had trooped off upstairs and they were, finally, free of all distractions. There had been so many demands on his attention through the day that he'd made no headway in getting a grip on what, exactly, was troubling Claire and preventing her from agreeing to marry him. Something about her previous marriage, possibly, although from what he could remember of her disjointed revelations, even that was conjecture at this point.

The meal ended. As the platters were being cleared, Catriona—lady of the house and Lady of the Vale—rose to her feet at the high table. Smiling serenely, she looked around the room; as her gaze touched those gathered, they fell silent. An expectant hush spread over the assembly; her voice even and perfectly modulated, Catriona spoke into it. "My family, my friends. There's an old Christmas Eve tradition that we haven't enacted for many years, although I recall it from my childhood. *Oidche Choinnle*— for tonight is the Night of Candles. The tradition calls for the setting of lighted candles in our windows, supposedly to guide strangers to the safety of our doors, the candles symbolizing goodwill and a promise of a fire to be warmed by, and a light to be guided by. But tonight, with five of our number far from home and a storm holding the land at its mercy, I propose that we place our lighted candles in our windows"—Catriona waved and maids and footmen emerged from the kitchen archway with boxes of plain white candles—"to guide our loved ones safely home."

She paused as the candles were passed around, then went on, "There are hundreds of windows in the manor. If you would, I ask that each of you present here tonight take a candle, light it, and set it on the stone sill of one of those windows. One candle per window, to light our children home."

Catriona paused to draw breath. Her gentle smile bathed the room in radiant assurance, then she raised her arms and directed, "Take your candle, light it, and place it in an empty window, and then please return here to share a sip of our Christmas wassail and enjoy one of Cook's famous mince pies."

The children were the first on their feet; they gathered at the fireplaces, each lighting their candle before rushing into the front hall, and from there throughout the house proper.

"At least they can't run," Daniel dryly remarked to Claire and Melinda, "not without risking blowing out their flame."

The tutors and governesses, each with their own lighted candle in hand, spread out through the house in the wake of their collective charges, yet they weren't called upon to rein anyone in; the atmosphere remained good-natured and joyous, and there were many other adults about, plus youths, maids, and younger children from the manor's families, as well as the Cynster parents. Daniel even saw Algaria, Helena, and McArdle assisting each other from the dais; he looked back before he exited the hall and saw them making their slow way toward the library. There were plenty of windows on that side of the house, but most of those in the hall had made for the higher windows in the manor's many turrets and towers.

With the others, Daniel circled the manor on the upper

floors. He found an unadorned window and paused long enough to set his candle in it.

Claire was passing; she halted beside him and peered out into the swirling blackness of the night. "To anyone out there, this place will look utterly magical with candles twinkling in so many windows."

"As our hostess said, shining with the promise of safety," Daniel replied.

Claire glanced at him and smiled, then the girls called from somewhere and she hurried on, her own candle still in her hand.

Daniel was tempted to follow her, but the voices of several of the boys echoing in a nearby stairwell drew him in the opposite direction. He investigated, but all was well; the boys were simply waiting for the last of their number to set his candle firmly in the melted wax he'd dribbled on a stone sill before returning to the Great Hall.

"Don't want to miss the mince pies!" Calvin said. He led the group away, heading for the stairs to the front hall.

Daniel circled back more slowly, checking the various turrets and towers as he went.

When he reached the northwest tower, he heard the low murmur of voices and glanced up. Around the curve of the stairwell, he glimpsed the duke and duchess standing before one window. The duke had already set his candle somewhere and was empty handed; he stood beside the duchess as she melted wax onto the stone sill, then carefully set her candle upright and held it in place while the wax set. Then she raised her head and looked out of the window.

Neither she nor the duke spoke again, but the duke raised his hand and closed it comfortingly on his wife's shoulder, and together they stood silently and looked out into the black night.

Both their sons were out there, in some tiny crofter cottage up in the forest at the mercy of what was, by anyone's yardstick, a ferocious winter storm. No matter how much their intellects knew that their children were old enough, strong enough, sensible enough to keep themselves safe, Daniel understood that the heart still worried.

Parental anxiety wasn't something even the most powerful in the land could avoid.

Slipping silently away and leaving the ducal couple to their vigil, Daniel continued on, only to come upon his host and hostess high in the neighboring northwest turret. Richard Cynster, like his brother the duke having already divested himself of his candle, lounged against the edge of an alcove in which Catriona, like her sister-in-law, was setting her own candle.

Daniel saw Richard, his dark blue gaze on his wife, hesitate, then quietly say, "You do realize that they almost certainly won't be back in time to see any candles still burning."

Catriona turned her head slightly and met Richard's eyes. "It's the thought that counts—quite literally. There's energy in doing and in intention, and it matters. It makes a difference."

His gaze on his wife's face, Richard didn't argue. If Daniel had to guess, he would have said that Richard would have done just about anything to ensure his eldest children returned safe.

Turning away, Daniel continued his sweep.

Ultimately assured that all the Cynster children, girls as well as boys, were at the very least on their way back to the Great Hall, Daniel went down the main stairs and strode back to the hall himself.

Entering via the main archway, he heard piping voices singing the old carol "Here We Go A-Wassailing"—very appropriate, as huge wassailing bowls filled with spiced ale had been brought out and set on several tables. An impromptu choir had gathered before the end of the dais, below the currently empty chairs of the three oldest of the company.

The smiles on everyone's faces told of a moment of shared joy as children from the youngest to the oldest—some from the local families, others from the Cynsters—raised their voices, led by a few robust parental baritones, tenors, sopranos, and altos.

An irrepressible smile spreading across his own face, Daniel looked around and saw Raven and Morris returning from the direction of the library. Each was assisting one of the old ladies, and McArdle was stomping in their wake. The old ladies' eyes had already fixed on the choir with, at least in the dowager's case, unfettered delight.

A swift survey of heads assured Daniel that all their charges had returned, and all were busy either singing like angels, or else sipping the small samples of wassail they'd been allowed and munching enthusiastically on mince pies.

Smiling more broadly—infected by the welling happiness all around—Daniel crossed to where Claire and Melinda stood, also sipping wassail and rather more delicately consuming golden-crusted pies. Before he reached the pair, a maid bobbed up in his path to offer him one of the larger wooden beakers of wassail and a platter of mince pies; accepting the beaker, Daniel chose a pie, thanked the beaming maid with a smile and a half bow, then continued to Claire's side.

The conversation had turned general; the heavily spiced fruit-filled pies were delicious, and the wassail, a golden ale redolent with spices, eradicated the last remaining tensions. Even though the lighting of the candles hadn't miraculously transported the five older children home, there was a sense of the company having done everything necessary to ensure that those absent five would, eventually, return safe and sound.

Raven and Morris came up and joined their group. Along with the others, Daniel kept a weather eye on their charges, but this was Christmas Eve—as soon as they'd consumed their pies and slurped up the small tots of wassail, the children headed for the stairs.

Melinda chuckled. "No need for us to chase them to bed tonight."

"No, indeed." Morris grinned. "This is the one night in the year that governesses and tutors have no need to chivvy our charges to their slumbers."

The departure of the Cynster children acted like a catalyst; soon, the manor families, sleepy children draped over shoulders or cradled in arms, murmured their good-byes and drifted out through the archways.

Surrendering his empty beaker to a still-smiling maid, Raven stifled a yawn. "I'm for bed, too. It's been a long day." He arched his brows at the others. "Coming?"

Morris and Melinda nodded. Daniel glanced at Claire and caught her eye. "We'll follow in a moment."

Meeting his gaze, Claire nodded, then glanced at Melinda. "I'll be up soon."

Turning away, Melinda waved. "Don't rush on my account. Regardless of what night it is, I'll check on the girls

anyway, just to be sure, so you can come straight up—
don't worry about them."

"Thank you," Claire called.

Standing beside her, Daniel watched the others make
their way out into the front hall. As they passed out of
sight, he glanced around. The crowd had thinned dramati-
cally. Other than the Cynster parents, the older three settled once again in their armchairs on the dais, and several
staff clearing the last platters, bowls, and beakers, he and
Claire were the last of the company remaining.

The Cynster ladies were gathering their shawls, and
their men were stretching; clearly, they, too, were about
to leave.

Touching Claire's arm, Daniel nodded toward the inglenook beside the main fireplace. "Let's sit there. It looks
as if everyone else is leaving, so we should be able to talk
freely—privately despite being in public, so to speak." He
suspected she would find the latter reassuring.

She nodded readily, and together they made for the
stone bench built into the alcove beside the fireplace. The
bench was large enough to comfortably seat them both,
and once they'd sat, the shadows of the large overmantel
enveloped them, adding a further element to the privacy
the spot afforded.

A spurt of laughter reached them, then the duke and
duchess led the other Cynster couples past and on toward
the main archway, no doubt making for the drawing room,
where the group usually spent the latter hours of most
evenings.

With the duchess on his arm, the duke reached the
archway—and halted.

Both Daniel and Claire had been watching the small

procession. They saw the duke look up, saw a slow, distinctly devilish smile spread across his harsh features.

He was looking at a dangling bunch of mistletoe.

What with the anxiety over the riding party and the excitement before and after, until then, no one had noticed it.

Abruptly, the duke looked down—at his duchess, who had only just followed his gaze upward.

"Oh!" Her dark eyes widened.

"Indeed." His arm sliding about his wife's trim waist, the duke bent his dark head and kissed her—thoroughly.

The other couples looked on with indulgent smiles.

Eventually, the duke raised his head, and the duchess broke from the kiss on a laughing gasp. "Really, Your Grace!" She tried to frown, but she was smiling too much to manage it.

Devil Cynster, Duke of St. Ives, cast a glance at his brother and cousins, waiting their turn to pass through the archway. Unrepentant, he grinned; looking up again, he reached up, plucked one of the white berries, and tucked it into his pocket. "Plenty more berries left on the bough." Without looking back, he urged the duchess on. "Come, my dear. As ever, it falls to us to lead the way."

There were laughs and hoots at that, but one by one, the other couples did, indeed, follow the lead of the head of their house, sharing long, passionate, yet gentle kisses under the dangling mistletoe before continuing on to the drawing room.

At last, Daniel and Claire were alone in the hall, except for the three oldest of the company, but a quick look their way showed all three dozing in their armchairs by the fire.

They were as alone as they could hope to be.

Daniel turned to Claire, but before he could speak, she laid a hand on his arm. Drawing in a breath, she glanced at him briefly, then, her voice low, said, "I need to explain so you'll understand." She moistened her lips, then went on, "I have believed—*believe*—that…" She drew in a tight breath, let it out on "That I would—*will*—never be able to commit to another marriage. That I would never want to—and this has nothing to do with the gentleman involved. This has to do with me—with what I feel—felt—after my previous marriage, with the vows I made to myself then."

She paused, then cast a quick sidelong look at him and drew back her hand. "I felt—still feel—that were I to receive an offer from any earnest and sincere gentleman, then to accept that offer would be the worst sort of fraud."

Daniel frowned. He opened his lips, but she glanced his way, and before he could speak, she rushed on, "Because I can't give that gentleman what he would deserve." Finally meeting his gaze, searching his eyes as if she could somehow impel understanding, she stated, "It would be wrong of me to accept any gentleman's offer of marriage because I cannot…" She frowned, clearly struggling to find the right words. "Because I cannot be sure—I cannot *trust*—that I will be able to be a true wife to him—to give him the affection, the support, the respect he would be due. I do not know that I *can* marry again, not anyone." She paused. Then, as if her tongue had finally found the right phrase, her gaze growing distant, she softly said, "I do not believe—do not know if—my heart would be up to it."

After a moment, she amended, "If my heart would be in it."

Daniel…didn't know what to make of that. Didn't know what opening it left him. Clearly, her first marriage and her husband's untimely death had marked her; he'd expected that to be the case, but he hadn't dreamed that the impact would be so far-reaching. That her husband's shade could reach out from the grave and prevent her from marrying again.

His mind circled the revelation in a dizzying whirl; before he'd made any conscious decision to speak, words had found their way to his lips. "Would your late husband have wanted that?" Swiveling on the bench, he caught her eyes, trapped her gaze. "Would he have wanted his memory to hold you back for the rest of your life? To prevent you from having any happiness, regardless of what life sends your way?"

Stunned, Claire blinked—and stared. For one long moment, she felt as if the world heaved and swung around her; only Daniel's steady hazel gaze anchored her. For a moment, shock—the shock of realization, of a fundamental epiphany—was so profound it stole her breath. With an effort, she forced air into her lungs. Looking away, still mentally reeling, she murmured, "I never thought of it like that."

She hadn't.

She'd thought that by vowing not to allow herself to even consider marriage again she'd been protecting herself... Could it be that, instead, she'd been harming herself? Restricting herself? Cutting herself off from life and all she might have?

The sudden insight was so blinding she was temporarily struck dumb. Numb. Unable to think.

Much less speak.

When she didn't, Daniel leaned closer. "I can understand that you feel it important to honor his memory, to put all you and he shared on a pedestal and not let a relationship with any other man mar that. That's honorable, but it's an intellectual stance." He took her hand in his, and through his touch, through the intensity of his gaze, she sensed his earnestness, his commitment when he said, "I can understand that you might think that, Claire—but what do you feel?"

I want you.

The words echoed in her mind, trembled on her tongue, but she was still too caught by shock and confusion to let them fall. Meeting his gaze, she swallowed and, in a voice barely above an anguished whisper, said, "I feel...torn." When he would have spoken, she swiftly raised her free hand and placed a finger across his lips. "No, please. It's hard to speak of this, and I'm still not sure I understand myself... For so long I've believed, deep down in my heart and soul believed, that I could never bear to face an altar again. That I simply didn't have it in me—no, don't speak. This is not what you think. It's not you—it's me. I just don't know if I have what it takes to wed a man again. I would have to trust...and I don't know that I have any trust left to give."

She forced herself to sit there, to hold his gaze and not turn away—to not rise and run away.

I want you.

Some part of her clung to that—refused to subside and allow her to deny this, deny herself and him, even though the rest of her was still convinced denial was inevitable.

That there was no chance, no possibility, no future. Not for her, not for them.

His eyes held hers.

She felt something inside her crumble, walls falling, yet still she didn't have the strength—or the courage—to grasp what she most wanted. "I don't *know*."

The words were a breath of confusion, of tortured emotion; instinctively, Daniel closed his hand more firmly about hers. "It's all right."

She's wounded. The knowledge burst on his mind with crystal clarity. He was accustomed to dealing with the turmoils of others; she might not be a pupil, a charge—no, she was even more important. She stood even more firmly in his care.

Even if she didn't yet understand or accept that.

In that moment, he knew his own path with absolute certainty.

"It's all right," he repeated with greater assurance. He searched her face, saw enough in her expression, in the emotions clouding her lovely eyes, to know that this was not the time to push further. Not yet.

He needed to think, to assess—and she was too wrought up with emotion; they both needed time.

He glanced around at the now empty hall, then looked back at her and found a reassuring smile. "It's late. We should go up. Melinda will be wondering where you are."

She swallowed, nodded, and rose; sliding her fingers from his clasp, she turned toward the archway. By the time she took her first step, she'd drawn her shields back into place; she was Mrs. Claire Meadows, widow and governess, once more.

He'd risen as she had. He walked by her side toward the archway.

A flicker of movement at the edge of his vision had him glancing at the dais.

McArdle was snoring, but the other two...he realized they were pointing, gesturing madly. He looked to where—and saw the mistletoe.

Claire reached the archway. He put out a hand, caught her elbow, and stopped her.

She turned, brows rising.

He bent his head and kissed her, there under the mistletoe.

And it seemed as if he'd been waiting all his life to set his lips to hers, to feel hers soften, then—wonder and joy—firm as she kissed him back.

Not ravenously, but definitely.

For an instant, his heart stood still; in the next, it started to beat more heavily.

Almost certainly by instinct rather than design, she raised a hand and her fingertips lightly grazed his cheek while her lips continued to meld with his.

He didn't want to end the caress, yet he didn't want to frighten her. Knew he couldn't push too hard, not yet.

Yet he couldn't resist drawing her closer—just a touch. Just enough to feel the promise of her in his arms.

Couldn't resist letting the simple exchange play out, his lips moving on hers with just enough pressure to evoke a response, perhaps more instinctual than intentional, yet a response nonetheless.

He knew the instant she realized and stopped—and mentally drew back.

Raising his head, he looked into her face. The thud in his bloodstream remained, a needing. Holding her gaze, he quietly stated, "I won't stop pursuing you." The truth and nothing more. "I want you as my wife, and I'm not going to give up—on you, on me, on us. I will keep trying to persuade you."

Sensing the fragile tension that held her, he gently ran the back of one finger down her cheek. "Just so you know."

Claire blinked. "What if I can't? What if I say no?"

His gaze didn't waver; if anything it gained in intentness, in intensity. "I'll keep asking until you say yes." He paused, then caught her hand, raised it, and brushed a kiss across her knuckles, holding her gaze all the while. "I'm not going to go away, Claire—I'm not going to give up on you."

Commitment, devotion, and more shone clearly in his eyes. Claire read the emotions, felt them, recognized and knew them.

There was nothing she could say—there was nothing to be said.

Not now. Not tonight.

Slowly, she stepped back, out of his embrace; he let her go, his arms falling from her. Without a word, she turned and led the way to the stairs.

Daniel followed.

On the dais, Helena sat back in her chair, a smile of smug satisfaction on her lips. "Excellent! I do believe he'll do."

Algaria snorted, but didn't argue.

Six

The wind shrieked and pummeled the cottage. Snow and sleet raked the walls.

Lucilla was distantly aware of the elemental fury outside, of the murmured concerns of her menfolk, and of Jeb, too, as they sat about the table before the fire, but, kneeling by the side of the pallet behind the blanket-screen, she had no time to spare for such minor matters; the baby was definitely on its way into the world, and the manner it had chosen was not going to make its path easy.

She held on to one of Lottie's hands—or rather Lottie's fingers had tightened about hers in a crushing grip as she rode out yet another of the increasingly intense contractions. Prudence, steady as a rock, sat on the other side of the pallet, holding Lottie's other hand. She'd found Lottie a leather strap to bite down on, and in the gaps in between contractions, as Lottie panted and tried to catch her breath, Prudence bathed Lottie's face with a cloth dipped in snowmelt.

As Lottie's labor had continued, Jeb had grown increasingly distraught to the point that he was more hindrance than help. To the point that Lottie had to struggle to find the strength to reassure him, rather than him being of comfort to her. Lucilla had stepped in and sent Jeb to sit with the other men; Lottie had nodded, and he'd gone, leaving the three women to deal with the arriving baby without distraction.

"Gah!" Lottie exclaimed around the leather strap. As the fierce grip of the contraction abruptly eased and, gasping, she fell limp, Lucilla quickly examined her, then let the sheet fall back.

"Everything's progressing as it should." Lucilla lightly squeezed Lottie's hand—and exchanged a meaningful look with Prudence. Progressing, yes, but the baby hadn't turned. It would be a breech birth. The baby hadn't yet entered the birth canal proper, but soon would—and then everything would need to happen quickly for the child to survive. For them to have any chance of helping it into the world alive.

"How are things going in there, ladies?" Marcus spoke from the other side of the blanket-screen. "Do you need anything?"

"Just keep the fire well stoked and the water hot." Lucilla glanced at Lottie's face. "We'll be a few hours yet."

Lottie met Lucilla's eyes; if she hadn't already been wrung out to limpness, Lottie would have slumped.

"Best to think of tomorrow morning." Prudence chafed Lottie's hand. "Of waking up and seeing your new baby in its basket, of holding it in your arms."

Around the leather strap, Lottie managed a wan smile. "If they'd told me it was this much work, I'd've thought twice about the business."

A smile tugged at Lucilla's lips. "You'd still have opted to have a bairn. For all that it's a tortured path to get them here, it's worth every second in the end."

"Aye." Weakly, Lottie nodded. Her eyes drifted closed.

Lucilla looked at Prudence. "I'm going to get some more of the tisane. If Lottie can manage to take a few sips when she rouses again, it'll help."

Prudence nodded. Lucilla rose. She stretched her legs, spine, neck, and shoulders, then she turned and sidled out from behind the makeshift screen.

A heavy thud fell on the outer door.

Everyone looked at the thick planks. A branch flung by the wind?

The thud came again, then the latch started to lift.

Sebastian, seated on a stool on that side of the table, rose and lunged to catch the door before the wind could slam it wide.

A snow-encrusted figure—a man—staggered and all but fell inside. A huge, hairy beast the size of a small pony pushed in beside him.

Marcus had rushed to help Sebastian; fighting against the force of the wind, they wrestled the door shut again and managed to get the iron latch back into place.

The huge beast shook itself, sending gobbets of snow and ice flying, and revealed itself to be a huge deerhound; its curious amber gaze traveled the room, then the massive beast sat, its head as high as a man's elbow, and watched them all.

Lucilla returned her gaze to the stranger. What manner of man came out in a storm like this?

He was tall—as tall as Sebastian—but all else about him was concealed beneath a thick, fur-lined cape. The cowl was up and shaded the man's features; the body of the cape bulged oddly, as if there were more than a man beneath it.

Judging by the movement of the cowl, the man was

scanning the occupants of the cottage from right to left—
Michael, Jeb. The man's gaze reached Lucilla and halted.
Arrested. But then, satisfied that the door was secure,
Sebastian and Marcus moved back into the room and the
man's gaze continued to them.

After a second of assessing silence, the man raised a
mittened hand and put back the cowl.

Jeb reacted instantly. "Mr. Carrick, sir!" Jeb blinked.
"Whatever are you doing out on such a night?"

Thick, wavy hair of dark chestnut was speckled with
snow. Eyes of richly veined amber perfectly set beneath
dark slashes of brows regarded Jeb with a steady gaze. A pa-
trician nose, sharply delineated cheekbones, angular cheeks,
and a chin chiseled square completed a striking face.

Thomas Carrick's gaze shifted to Lucilla. His eyes
held hers for a fleeting instant, then he inclined his head.
"Miss Cynster."

Before she could respond —she knew who he was,
but she hadn't set eyes on him for years—Carrick's gaze
passed on to Marcus. Carrick nodded. "Cynster."

Marcus nodded back. "Carrick."

Carrick's gaze passed on to Sebastian, who now stood
on his left. Carrick's brow arched in polite query.

Marcus obliged. "Thomas Carrick—Sebastian Cynster,
Marquess of Earith, our cousin. And"—Marcus nodded
across the table—"Michael Cynster, Sebastian's brother."

"And," Lucilla said, indicating the screened area with
a wave, "Prudence, another cousin, is sitting with Lottie."

Carrick's eyes again met hers.

Lucilla realized what his principal question must be.
"We were riding along the ridge and Jeb heard us and
rushed out to intercept us. He and Lottie needed help, so
we came."

Carrick half bowed. "Thank you."

He returned his attention to Jeb; lips twisting—whether in a simple grimace or in self-deprecation Lucilla couldn't tell—Carrick answered Jeb's earlier question. "None of the other shepherds had seen you for the last few days, and when you and Lottie didn't come down ahead of the storm... Well, it's Christmas Eve, and knowing Lottie's time was near, I thought perhaps you could do with some extra fare."

Carrick's shoulders fluidly shifted; the cloak parted as he lifted a jumble of oilskin-wrapped bundles onto the table. "I've brought food, and drink, too. I thought you might need it."

Eyes locking on the bundles, the other men converged on the table. Curious, Lucilla approached the table, too. Carrick appeared to have carried half a larder up the ridge.

"However did you manage to carry all this up through the snow?" Jeb asked.

Turning from removing his cloak and setting it on a peg near the door, Carrick tipped his head toward the side of the cottage. "Sled. I left it out there."

"You didn't ride?" Sebastian asked.

Carrick shook his head. "Too dangerous to try to get a horse up that track in weather like this."

He joined the other men in opening the neatly tied, oilskin-wrapped packages. In short order, cheeses, bread, mince pies, shortbread, a small pat of butter, lard, a ham, bacon, a pie, and various already cooked meats tumbled out onto the table's surface.

Reaching for a bottle-shaped package, Michael glanced at Carrick. "Bit of a risk, coming out in such a storm alone."

Carrick didn't look up from the string he was untying. "I wasn't alone." When silence greeted that pronouncement,

Carrick's lips curved and he looked past Michael to the huge hound who, apparently having decided its master was safe enough, had circled to sit to the side of the hearth. "Hesta was with me. She would have pulled me out of any drift."

They all looked at the huge hound; jaws slightly gaping, huge teeth on display, she looked back at them calmly.

"Useful." Sebastian had unwrapped one of the three bottles. He held it up. "Whisky. That makes you doubly welcome."

Carrick's long lips lifted in a fleeting grin.

Michael had unwrapped a smaller bottle. He frowned. "Gin. Not a drop I favor."

Carrick glanced at Lucilla. "The midwife told me it might be useful."

She nodded. "It will be." She reached for the bottle. While the men separated the various foodstuffs, she uncorked the gin and sniffed; the scent of juniper berries was strong. Going to the pot of tisane she'd earlier brewed and left to the side of the hearth, she picked up the beaker Lottie had been using and tipped a small amount of the gin into it. After corking and setting the bottle aside, she ladled tisane on top of the gin, swirled the concoction, then rose and turned back to the table.

Casting her eyes over the food now spread out on the board, as Jeb brought a collection of tin plates to the table, she instructed, "Set aside slices of that pie for Lottie, Prudence, and me, also some bread and cheese, and make sure there's some of that ham left on the bone—Jeb and Lottie can use that in the pot, along with any other meats left over."

Already pulling up stools to the table, the males merely nodded or grunted. Leaving all five to replenish their reserves—sincerely grateful to Thomas Carrick for having thought of Jeb and Lottie's need and having struggled through the storm to reach them—Lucilla slipped behind the screen again.

Lottie was just regaining her breath after battling through another bout of gripping pain. Lucilla handed her the beaker, and she sipped—then her eyes widened, and she looked questioningly at Lucilla.

"I put some of the gin Mr. Carrick brought into it. It'll help." Assuming that Lottie and Prudence had heard everything said beyond the blankets, Lucilla looked at her cousin. "You must be hungry—why don't you slip out and have some of that pie before it vanishes?"

Prudence thought, then shook her head. "I'm settled here, and Lottie and I know where we are at present. Better you eat, then perhaps bring something for Lottie to see if she can manage it, and I'll go out and eat then."

Accepting that Prudence was correct in suggesting that she, Lucilla, would be needed more later rather than immediately, Lucilla nodded and rose again. "All right. I'll get what I want and something for Lottie and come back right away."

There was something about Thomas Carrick that... disturbed her. She saw no reason—felt no inclination—to eat at the table with the men.

Ducking back around the hung blankets, she was immediately conscious of Carrick's gaze—as if he'd been listening and had been determined to look at her the instant she reappeared. He started to rise; suddenly ridiculously flustered, she waved him to sit again. None of the other males had thought of the courtesy.

Ruthlessly suppressing her awareness of Thomas Carrick, holding it to one side in her mind, she scanned the shelves and saw a rough wooden tray. She lifted it down. Next, she found three well-worn trenchers. She set two on the tray and one at that end of the table, then piled each with slices of pie, ham, cheese, and bread. She placed a chicken leg on Prudence's trencher.

Satisfied she'd provided well enough for Lottie, Prudence, and herself, Lucilla was about to heft the tray, leaving Prudence's trencher on the table, when Carrick, who was sitting alongside Marcus at the nearer end of the table opposite the fire and whose amber eyes had watched her throughout, said, "I brought mead, too, if you and your cousin, or Lottie, might prefer it."

With one large palm, he pushed a bottle and several small beakers toward the tray.

Lucilla paused. She and Prudence needed to keep warm, and the mead would certainly help. Releasing her grip on the tray, without meeting Carrick's gaze, she inclined her head. "Thank you."

Before she could reach for the bottle of mead, Carrick picked it up. Unstoppering it, he poured golden liquid into first one beaker, then a second, then he paused. "Two or three?"

"Just two." Lucilla took the first beaker and reached for the second; her fingers brushed Carrick's as he released it. Resisting the urge to suck in a breath— to bite her lip, to react in any way—she calmly set the beakers on the tray. For some unfathomable reason, she felt forced to add, "I doubt Lottie will be able to handle it at the moment, but later the mead will be an excellent tonic, especially in this season."

He'd put thought into what he'd brought; on top of the fact he'd brought anything at all—that he'd battled the storm to reach them—her understanding of the care he'd taken demanded at least that much acknowledgment, however oblique.

"In that case," he murmured, his voice low and deep, deeper than even Sebastian's, "I'm glad I brought it." He caught her gaze. "How is Lottie faring?"

Lucilla looked into his amber eyes. No, he wasn't asking to keep her there, nor was he merely passing the time. He truly wanted to know—and he was the only one of the males to have asked. The stiffness she'd been trying to maintain between them wilted. "She's managing."

She, too, had kept her voice low, their exchange submerged beneath the discussion about local hunting raging between Michael and Marcus further up the table.

Carrick didn't release her gaze; she felt strangely trapped as he looked into her eyes…then he said, his voice even quieter, "There's some problem, isn't there?" One dark brow arched.

In his eyes, his expression, Lucilla read his certainty— he knew. Alerted somehow, as she had been, he, too, had known and had come.

She had been summoned, and so had he.

Slowly, she nodded. "It's a breech birth, but Lottie's strong and, with luck, all will be well."

"How much longer?"

She raised a shoulder. "An hour. Perhaps more."

Carrick inclined his head and lowered his gaze, releasing her. "Thank you."

Lucilla looked down at his dark head for an instant, then she picked up the tray and went to help Lottie deliver her baby.

Seated beside Carrick, Marcus glanced his way—and watched Carrick watch Lucilla retreat behind the blanket again.

This close to the man, Marcus could sense…something similar to the aura he sensed around Lucilla, around his mother and Algaria, and even, at a lower level, around his father, Richard. Marcus had always assumed it was a feature of being, as the locals described it, Lady-touched. As Thomas Carrick was a local, born and bred in these lands, perhaps it wasn't surprising that he might rank among the chosen, too, yet overall there were not that many who were Lady-touched... Marcus wondered if his twin had picked up Carrick's standing; she hadn't as yet been that close to him. At least the width of the table had been between them thus far.

Turning back to the conversation, which Sebastian had not-so-artfully swung from hunting in general to hunting dogs, Marcus hid a grin as Sebastian—who loved dogs, especially big ones—leaned forward to look down the table at Carrick.

"I take it your Hesta is a deerhound?"

Carrick nodded. "We—the family —breed them."

For the next hour, they filled their ears with talk of hounds and deer, and anything else they could think of to keep their minds away from the sounds emanating from the other side of the blanket and, even more, from what those sounds implied.

Apparently deciding that the only thing he could presently do to help Jeb and Lottie was to keep Jeb sufficiently distracted from all that was going on, Carrick focused his attention on the crofter.

Sebastian had left the table to crouch by the huge hound, stroking her head; he cocked a brow at Marcus as he, together with Michael—also drawn by the big dog— joined him. Voice low, Sebastian asked, "Who, exactly, is Thomas Carrick, and the Carricks?"

Marcus had expected the question. He whispered back, "The Carricks are the lairds of the lands on this side of the manor's northern boundary. Their holdings are roughly the same size as the manor's, but the land's rougher and rockier. The family isn't wealthy, but they hang on. They run mostly sheep and so have a lot of scattered crofters and small outlying cottages, but otherwise, although they don't have a Lady of the Vale as we do, the community works similarly to that in the Vale."

"Lots of connections, all answerable ultimately to the principal family?" Sebastian asked.

Marcus nodded. "Exactly." He glanced over his shoulder, but Carrick was still deep in conversation with Jeb. Turning back to Sebastian and Michael—and the dog, who was watching him with an interested expression—Marcus continued, "Thomas Carrick is the nephew of Mad Manachan Carrick, the head of the family. The Carricks as a whole are widely regarded as... Well, to call them eccentric would be kind."

"Mad as insane," Michael murmured.

Marcus nodded. "He's not insane, of course, but Manachan is an unpredictable old despot who actively likes to shock the county. Thomas"—Marcus tipped his head toward the other man—"is widely regarded as the only sane Carrick around. Sadly, he's not Manachan's heir—his cousin Nigel is—and Nigel is truly mad as a hatter, albeit in a distinctly calculated way."

Sebastian was silent for a moment, steadily stroking the hound's head, then he murmured, "So the Carricks are intelligent, but don't play by anyone else's rules."

Marcus blinked but then nodded. "An excellent summation."

He rose, returning to the table just as a horrendous, ill-suppressed scream rent the air.

Jeb jerked, half rose, then fell back on his stool.

Across the table, Marcus met Carrick's gaze, then Marcus slipped onto the stool beside Jeb and tugged the man's sleeve. "I noticed the ewes you have in your stable-barn. Their fleece looks nice and thick—have you been grazing them on the higher pastures?"

Jeb blinked, slowly processed the question, then he answered haltingly.

Between them, Marcus and Thomas Carrick settled to the task of assisting Jeb through his last hour into fatherhood.

High in one of the manor's towers, on a truckle bed in Melinda Spotwood's small room, Claire lay on her back beneath the covers and stared, unseeing, into the darkness.

In the narrow bed on the opposite side of the room, Melinda lay on her side, facing the wall.

Claire had been staring upward since she'd slid between the sheets more than an hour ago.

Suddenly, Melinda sighed. Without turning, she asked, "Why aren't you sleeping? I can almost hear you thinking."

Claire glanced across through the gloom. "I'm sorry."

"Don't be." After a moment, Melinda said, "Is there anything I can do to help—even if all I can do is listen?"

Claire hesitated. There was one thing. "Did you ever think of marrying—of having a family of your own rather than spending your life helping other families?"

"Oh, yes." Unexpectedly, Melinda's tone held the warmth of remembered pleasures. "I was engaged once to my own young man. All I thought about was marrying him and raising a family of our own." Melinda's voice softened. "We had a lovely two years of courting, and were all set to name the date when Napoleon escaped Elba and he—my love—marched off to war..." Melinda paused, then said, "Sadly, he didn't come back. After that... I had other offers, but my love lived on in my heart."

Melinda glanced over her shoulder at Claire. "But you must know how that goes."

Claire was grateful for the darkness.

Resettling, Melinda went on, "The important thing was that, despite mourning what I didn't get to have—a life with my love—I did have that love. I knew what it was like to love and be loved, and to have that hope that some- how shines from within and lifts you up, and to experience the delight of looking forward to a much-desired shared future. I had all that, and not even his death could strip that experience away. So the one thing I learned from that time—and that I teach my girls, every last one —is that when happiness offers, take it. Don't just accept it. Seize it with both hands, because you never know what the future might hold, but you can decide to fill your present—your here and now—with happiness and, if the offer includes it, with love. If you do that and accept what fate sends you, then no matter what happens, you will at least have memories to warm you into your old age, as I do. But if you refuse, and fate later passes you by and you don't get another chance at happiness and love, what will you have to cling to through the lonely days and nights?"

Claire let the words sink in. After a moment, she mur- mured, "Thank you."

Melinda chuckled softly; the covers rustled as she set- tled deeper in her bed.

Claire continued to stare upward as—inevitably—she replayed her discussion with Daniel in her head. She'd managed to convey to him the gist of her problem—that she didn't believe enough, didn't trust enough to marry again. She hoped he'd understood that it wasn't him she distrusted but herself. After her first marriage, she didn't trust herself to love—not properly—ever again.

He'd then thrown all her careful certainty into chaos.

Would your late husband have wanted that? Would he have wanted his memory to hold you back for the rest of your life? To prevent you from having any happiness, regardless of what life sends your way?

It had never occurred to her to see her reaction in that light, but Daniel putting the matter like that—casting her position in those terms—had turned her perceived foundation of both her life and her future on its head.

Only a fool made the same mistake twice. She'd fallen in love and married, and that path had led to disaster. She'd been very certain that she did not need to go that way again.

Yet what she had felt for Randall had been…a girl's dreams, something light and airy—ultimately insubstantial. She hadn't known that at the time, but she could own to it now. In contrast, what she felt for Daniel—the instant focusing of her senses, of her awareness whenever he was near, the intensity and depth of sheer feeling he evoked, the connection between them—that was something she'd never before known.

Only a fool didn't learn from hard experience, but had she learned the right lesson? Had she misconstrued the message, making it into a justification to mask her cowardice—her refusal to risk ever being hurt like that, damaged like that, again?

She would be damned if she allowed Randall, that dissolute deceiver—he who had single-handedly wrecked her life—to reach out from the grave and keep her from… what? Happiness and love with Daniel? Was that what he was offering? If so, was Melinda's sage advice the path Claire should follow?

She'd told Daniel the truth; she felt as if his words had ripped apart the fabric of her understanding of herself and left her adrift.

As if she had to find her compass, her true north, her lodestone again.

As if she hadn't actually been able to sense it and follow it, not over the years since Randall's death.

If Melinda was correct—and the sensible, rational part of Claire's no-nonsense psyche recognized wisdom when she heard it—then if what Daniel was offering was love, it behooved Claire to set aside what she now saw was simple fear—fear of being hurt, nay, devastated again—and chance her hand by taking Daniel's.

By accepting his suit, his proposal, if and when he made it.

But all that hinged on the question of whether he truly loved her. She'd thought a gentleman had loved her once, but that had turned out to be a foolish fiction.

Regardless of Melinda's advice, Claire would be foolish indeed to make *that* mistake twice.

So...did Daniel love her?

How could she tell?

Perhaps if she asked him why he wanted to marry her? Perhaps he could convince her that his regard was love, well enough at least to allow her to believe enough to take the chance and accept him.

But did he love her? How could she truly tell?

She fell asleep with that question revolving, unanswered, in her head.

Seven

The sounds emanating from behind the blanket-screen were enough to make the bravest man blanch.

Thomas, at least, had to be there and, regardless, could not have escaped the ordeal, but the three male Cynsters had ended up being trapped in a small space with a woman giving birth and a storm blocking all routes to relief through no fault of their own.

He had to give Sebastian, Michael, and Marcus Cynster credit for not retreating to the stable-barn. Earlier, Marcus had done his best to distract Jeb by getting him to show off his long-haired ewes, but now Jeb sat across the table from Thomas, his hands clasped tight about a beaker of whisky—the better to stop them from shaking. Jeb's face was as pale as a winter's moon as he stared in mounting horror at the blanket that screened his wife.

Who had progressed from incoherent screams to partially discernible curses—several of which were directed at Jeb. Others were directed at men in general. Several were highly inventive.

Thomas had heard that such things happened in even the most content of marriages. Menfolk were not intended to hear—because they were not intended to be within hearing.

Sadly, that was not the case tonight.

At least they were warm. Reminded by the other girl—Prudence—when she'd brought out the empty trenchers, to keep the fire built up and to ensure there was a good supply of water brought to a boil, then left to cool to use-able warmth, Thomas and the three Cynster males had duly obeyed; despite the storm, the air in the cottage was approaching livable.

Surreptitiously, Thomas checked his watch. An hour, perhaps more, Lucilla had said; by his estimation, they were most of the way through that hour.

Hesta had stretched in silent somnolence to one side of the hearth; suddenly, she raised her head.

Thomas saw, tensed.

The shutters at his back tore free of their latch and whisked open, slamming against the cottage wall.

Icy air carrying snow and sleet swirled inside, whipping around and diving past the blanket.

Three female voices shrieked.

Thomas was already at the door. Pausing only to tell Hesta, "Stay!" he hauled the door open and plunged into the night.

The door swung free behind him, but he didn't stop; he'd glimpsed the Cynsters racing after him—they would hold the door until he returned.

He had to get the shutter closed and secured again, or the baby, when it came, would freeze, or at the very least take a lethal chill.

The fury of the storm was waiting. The wind slapped into him and sent him staggering back a step. But he leaned into it, dug his boots into the snow, and pushed forward. Then he pivoted and bulled his way along the front wall of the cottage.

The drifts reached nearly to his knees. Every step was a battle.

Then he reached the first shutter, grasped the edge, and ignoring the cold stinging his fingers, forced the shutter away from the wall. Fighting the wind every inch of the way, he shifted his grip and, clinging to the edge with near desperation, used his entire weight and shoved the shutter back into place.

He glanced at the second shutter; he couldn't reach it while simultaneously holding the first in place.

"I'll get the other one."

Thomas turned his head to see Sebastian Cynster moving past him, plowing through the drift toward the other shutter.

He watched as Sebastian tried to tug the shutter away from the wall, but the power of the wind defeated him.

Sebastian, Thomas had gathered, was eighteen years old. Thomas was nineteen, nearly twenty. Although they were the same height, the eighteen or so months' difference showed in their weight; Thomas was the more heavily muscled, especially across the chest.

Sebastian was the heaviest and strongest of the other males in the cottage, but Thomas was stronger still.

Moistening his lips, already badly chapped, Thomas yelled over the wind's whine, "Come and hold this one. I'll get that one."

Sebastian hesitated, but thankfully only for a moment. Accepting that Thomas could do what he could not wouldn't have come easily; Thomas could only be grateful that the eldest Cynster had sufficient self-assurance that he didn't need to cling to his dignity.

Sebastian reached Thomas's side and threw his weight against the shutter. Thomas released it; stepping around Sebastian, head down against the strafing wind, he forced his increasingly heavy feet the extra paces to the other shutter.

He gripped it—and could barely feel anything through his fingers. Gritting his teeth, he set himself and pulled.

Tugged. Inwardly swore and threw his weight fully against the wind—which suddenly paused.

Thomas stumbled and nearly fell as the shutter, no longer held back by the force of the gale, slammed over and closed.

Sebastian slapped a palm onto the second shutter, pinning it in place while Thomas regained his balance and his footing.

As soon as Thomas leaned against the second shutter, Sebastian reached for the latch. And swore. "The anchor-point's gone. It's been wrenched off."

Thomas glanced up. The iron circle the latch hooked into had been ripped away. But the arctic gale was blowing again; they had to secure the shutters, and neither of them could stay out much longer. Struggling not to breathe too deeply—to invite the frigid air to sear his lungs—he let his gaze fall…to the thick wooden sill. And the narrow gaps at the base of the shutters.

Lifting his head, Thomas screamed against the wind, "I have an idea. Can you hold them closed by yourself?"

Leaning into the shutters, Sebastian met Thomas's gaze and simply nodded.

Thomas hauled in a shallow breath, pushed away from the cottage wall, and headed around the corner to where he'd left the sled. He gave thanks that that side of the cottage was better protected from the blast and the snow hadn't drifted quite so high; despite his numbed fingers, it took him less than a minute to pull out what he needed from the box in the sled's base.

He shoved the chocks used to stabilize the sled into his pockets and hefted the mallet that went with them. Ducking his head, he rounded the cottage. The wind struck him anew, and he had to battle against the icy blast.

Sebastian was simply holding on, holding the shutters closed. He watched as Thomas fought his way to his side, fleetingly grinned when he saw the chock Thomas pulled from his pocket and wedged beneath the second shutter.

Two minutes later, Thomas had bashed all four chocks into place, two to each shutter.

Sebastian pushed back, removing his hands from the shutters. They both waited, but although the wind ripped and tugged, the chocks held firm.

Sebastian caught Thomas's eyes and tipped his head toward the door. Stuffing the mallet in his pocket, Thomas nodded. Speech was beyond him.

They started off—and Thomas staggered.

Sebastian stopped, then reached back and linked his arm with Thomas's. "Together," Sebastian rasped. "Easier that way."

It was; their combined mass stabilized them both and gave them added momentum when they moved.

They regained the door and fell against it; immediately, it opened, and they were both grabbed and hauled bodily inside.

Thomas found himself manhandled to the table and pushed down to sit on a stool; it was Marcus who did the handling. Beside Thomas, Sebastian was likewise shoved onto a stool by his brother.

"Hands first!" a female voice ordered from behind the blanket-screen.

"Yes, we know," Marcus muttered. Grabbing Thomas's hands by the wrists, he thrust them one after the other into a bowl of barely warm water. Or was it cold water? Thomas couldn't tell.

Before he'd fully absorbed what had happened, Marcus caught his jaw and angled his face upward; standing alongside Thomas, Marcus started smearing some ointment onto Thomas's skin. Thomas tried to pull away but Marcus growled, "Don't. If you want to try arguing with Lucilla, you can attempt it later."

"Indeed." Somewhat grimly, Michael was slathering the same concoction onto Sebastian's face. "Just be thankful we didn't eat the butter. If we had, this would be made with lard."

Thomas was still trying to find his breath, along with his ability to think. As the coldness of his coat registered, he started to shiver.

"The instant they start shivering, get them in front of the fire." Lucilla's voice rang out, loud and clear. "And get their coats off, too. Wrap them in the blankets I threw out there."

Thomas and Sebastian were relieved of the basins in which their hands had been thawing, stripped of their coats, swathed in blankets, and duly bullied to sit on two stools set before the fire. Hesta came to sit by Thomas; she leaned her heavy head against his thigh and looked up at him almost accusingly. If hounds could frown, she frowned. Thomas reached down and ruffled her ears. His hands, while reddened from the cold, showed no sign of frostbite.

Sebastian, too, was examining his long fingers. "Just as well we weren't out there too long."

They'd been outside long enough. Thomas made a mental note to remember the trick with the water and the oily concoction.

Both Michael and Marcus were working to build up the fire.

Prudence erupted from around the screen. "Warm water—quick!" She pointed to a bowl left half full by the hearth. "That one."

Michael leapt to obey. "The baby?" he asked as he placed the bowl in Prudence's hands.

"Nearly here." She whisked herself and the bowl back around the screen.

Behind the curtain, Lucilla crouched by the end of the pallet and prayed harder than she ever had in her life. She had one of the baby's tiny, slippery feet, but she quashed the impulse to pull on it; she needed the hips, or both thighs at least, to pull the babe free.

But she didn't want to dally—the baby didn't have much time. As Prudence set down the bowl, Lottie gritted her teeth over a tortured wail.

"Push now!" Lucilla ordered. "Come on, Lottie—one big push and we'll be done."

Lottie hauled in a huge breath. Supporting Lottie's shoulders, Prudence pushed in behind Lottie's back to give her something solid to push against.

Lottie strained.

Lucilla, eyes on the emerging babe, waited… As she sensed Lottie easing back, Lucilla pushed her fingertips up the baby's tiny legs, reached—and found the hip bones. Gripping as lightly as she could, she started easing the babe free.

Fraction by fraction, as fast as she could, she drew the babe—a tiny girl—free of Lottie's body. Then in a slithering rush, the infant was in her hands.

Working frantically, Lucilla unwound the cord that was wrapped once around the child's neck; the baby's face was puce, but not blue. As fast as she could, she cleared the babe's tiny mouth, then gripped her feet, raised her, and smacked her tiny bottom.

Nothing happened.

Lucilla met Prudence's eyes.

"Harder!" Lottie gasped. She stretched forward and gave her daughter's bottom a resounding slap.

The child jerked, then drew in air and a thin, high wail issued forth.

A cheer came from the other side of the curtain, followed by clapping.

Lucilla slumped with relief. She grinned at Lottie, then looked at Prudence.

Buoyed by welling elation, they grinned at each other.

Then they set to, to clean up the babe, to help Lottie, and generally tidy up.

The next hours flew by, punctuated by vignettes that Lucilla suspected she'd remember all her life. The moment she laid the babe, cleansed and wrapped in warm swaddling, into Lottie's arms. The look of maternal joy on Lottie's face. The corresponding look of awe and wonder in Jeb's.

While they were still working behind the blanket-screen with Lottie and the babe, Lucilla had remembered and looked out at the now much more relaxed gathering before the hearth to ask, "What time was the baby born? Is her birthday Christmas Eve, or Christmas Day?"

Perhaps fittingly, it had been Thomas Carrick who met

her eyes. "She was born at ten minutes past midnight, so her birthday is Christmas Day."

Lucilla's lips had already been curved, but she'd felt her smile deepen. "Thank you." Christmas children were a source of extra special joy, of extra special hope—at least in their communities.

At some point, the storm moved on. Finally, with Lottie absorbed with nursing her tiny daughter in an ancient rocker in the corner by the bed, and with the pallet itself stripped and remade and all else in the area tidy and clean, Lucilla and Prudence stood and watched Lottie for a moment, then they smiled, met each other's eyes, and turned and left mother and infant in peace.

Stepping into the main part of the cottage, Lucilla was all but pounced on by Jeb. "Can I go to them again?"

Lucilla couldn't stop smiling; she nodded. Jeb had come in earlier, but had retreated again to allow Lucilla and Prudence space to tidy up.

On cautious feet, Jeb approached the hung blanket and peered around, then, with a look of reverence stamped on his face, drawn and clearly helpless to resist, he went forward.

Standing beside Lucilla, Prudence sighed. "That's so sweet."

Smiling still—Lucilla wondered when she would stop—she turned to face the others and realized... She looked at the front door. "The wind's died. Has the storm passed?"

Now that she was listening, all she heard was silence.

Her menfolk—and Thomas Carrick—had been standing before the fire, beakers in their hands. Marcus, Sebastian, and Michael all cocked their heads in near-identical fashion, listening, too. Like Lucilla, Thomas looked at the door; she suspected that he was assessing with all his senses, as she had.

Sebastian set down his beaker and walked to the door. He cracked it open, looked out for a moment, then reported, "It's still black as a—black as ever. There's no wind, but snow's still coming down, and the clouds are still thick overhead."

"We're in the aftermath," Thomas offered. No one argued.

Redirecting her attention to the males, Lucilla swiftly took stock—of them, Prudence, and herself. None of them had slept a wink, yet, carried on a wave of triumph and elation, not one of them was showing any sign of tiredness.

Good—they had work to do before they could leave and head for their beds.

Switching her attention to the table, Lucilla surveyed what was left of the provender Thomas had brought. Moving forward, she said, "I want to make what meals I can from what's left, so that Lottie won't have to stir on that account."

Prudence wasn't much help with cooking; instead, she undertook to direct those not assisting Lucilla in setting everything they possibly could in the tiny cottage to rights. Marcus, Sebastian, and Michael opted to work with Prudence, while, somewhat to Lucilla's surprise, Thomas Carrick volunteered as kitchen boy.

Keeping her mind on her task, Lucilla sorted the foodstuffs. "Thanks to you, there's plenty of meat." She frowned. "I wish I had more vegetables for the pots."

Thomas held up a finger. "One moment." He walked to the blanket-screen, but didn't go further. "Jeb?" he quietly called. "Where's your root cellar?"

Not only did Jeb have a root cellar reached via a trapdoor in the stable-barn, when Lucilla followed Thomas Carrick down the ladder—with Marcus keeping watch from above—she discovered a decent variety of roots and tubers. She chose what she thought would work best to flavor and add goodness to the remnants of their Christmas Eve feast; Thomas volunteered the pockets of his coat and, when they were full, carried the extras.

As she climbed back up the ladder, Lucilla again consulted her inner consciousness over Thomas Carrick. She was both curious and uncertain about him, and compounding both, she didn't know what to do with her unexpected and unprecedented reaction to him.

Regardless of all else, now was not their time. That she knew beyond question. They were both too young; even the reactions she found unsettling enough now were mere harbingers of what was to come. That she understood; that she knew in her bones.

So why were they there? Why had the Lady—for it was assuredly by Her edict —brought them together there and then, in such a way?

Reaching the top of the ladder, she grasped Marcus's hand and stepped up into the stable-barn. Marcus and Michael had been delegated to feed and water Jeb's animals; in the far corner, Lucilla glimpsed Michael—unquestionably the most socially debonair of them all—sitting on a stool milking an old cow.

Thomas emerged from the cellar and stepped clear; as he had his hands full of onions, Lucilla bent and helped Marcus close the trapdoor.

With a noncommittal grunt, Marcus went back to spreading feed for the sheep.

Gathering Thomas with a glance, Lucilla led the way toward the cottage. As she reached the door, Thomas, at her heels, spoke softly. "I'll make sure our midwife checks on Lottie and the babe."

As Lucilla glanced back at him, he added, "And I'll do what I can to get Jeb to relocate to Carrick Manor, at least until the worst of the winter is past."

She nodded. "That would be best. While the little one is so very young, both she and Lottie need better protection from the cold. You can tell Jeb I said so."

Thomas inclined his head. "Thank you. That will help."

Lucilla opened the door and led the way inside.

She and Thomas spent the next hour chopping and cooking. He proved to have a hunter's expertise with a knife; she left him to carve the meats and pry the last useful pieces from the bones. The meat she used for stews; the bones she used for soup.

And all the while, with her senses prickling with awareness of him as he stood alongside her at the table, she thought about Thomas.

She'd known who he was, had recognized him instantly; they'd been introduced when they were children, and she'd noticed him any number of times over the years at local fairs and similar events. The last time she'd set eyes on him, he must have been fifteen, tall and gangly. He was taller now, but much less gangly.

Ruthlessly terminating the ensuing train of thought, she refocused on him, on the man he now was—the one who was, without complaint, chopping onions alongside her.

Locally, he was widely spoken of as "the sane Carrick"—the only adult male in his family considered so. His parents were long dead, and since his tenth birthday, he'd been raised within his uncle's household. Manachan Carrick was widely regarded as unstable; to Lucilla, he appeared intelligent, wily, and cunning, as well as eccentric in the extreme and totally unreliable and unpredictable, which was what made all the other landowners nervous. She was of the opinion that Manachan liked everyone else to be nervous about him.

But Thomas was a very different sort of man. For a start, he was Lady-touched, which she found curious. Neither Manachan nor any of his numerous sons were; she was sure of that. While for women—such as herself, her mother, and Algaria—being Lady-touched meant nurturing, caring, and guiding, for men being Lady-touched equated with guardianship, with a selfless protectiveness that went to the bone.

Why Thomas should be Lady-touched she didn't know; there really weren't that many of Her chosen about at any given time. Yet he was, and he was there, and so was she, and she knew beyond question that there was meaning and purpose—the Lady's purpose—in that.

Sebastian and Prudence had been working around them, checking their repairs to the walls and shutters and generally neatening the cottage. Straightening from shifting a heavy trunk so Prudence could sweep behind it, Sebastian paused, then walked to the front door and opened it. He looked out, then grunted. "The wind must have scoured the area in front of the cottage—the cover isn't that deep. At least we won't need to dig ourselves out."

He went outside, leaving the door partly open, but returned seconds later and latched the door again. "It's clearing, but it's not yet clear enough—light enough—to ride." He met Lucilla's gaze. "We should leave as soon as we can."

She nodded. Everyone at the manor would be waiting to see them ride in, and she and the others couldn't rest—not really—until they reached the manor again.

As she worked the dough for dumplings—Thomas had even brought flour as part of his supplies—she thought through her mental list of what the new baby and Lottie most needed.

Her gaze on her hands as she kneaded and rolled, she eventually asked, "Will you be staying here?"

Thomas grimaced, but he, too, kept his eyes on his work. "I'll have to, at least for a few days. The best way out of here and onto Carrick lands is via the valley, and as it faces north, the snow will be piled deep along the upper reaches. I'll go and investigate first. Once I'm sure I can get through, I'll go down, then bring back a few men to help move the family as well as their animals down to the manor."

Lucilla nodded. "That's a sensible plan."

From the corner of her eye, she saw Thomas's lips quirk, but "Indeed" was all he said.

It was an hour later when, after setting aside two pots of stew and a big cauldron of soup to cool, Lucilla looked in on Lottie, Jeb, and their tiny daughter. The babe was sound asleep, but despite their weariness, both Lottie and Jeb were as yet too full of euphoria to rest.

Lucilla smiled. "We'll be leaving shortly." Sebastian and Marcus had agreed that there was light enough to venture forth.

Lottie looked up. "If you please, Lady-miss, we—Jeb and me—was wondering if you and"—Lottie nodded at Thomas, who had come up behind Lucilla—"Master Carrick would agree to stand godparents to our little one."

Lucilla smiled. "I would be delighted." She glanced back at Thomas.

He, too, inclined his head. "It would be an honor, Lottie. Jeb."

Lucilla looked back at the new family and felt something inside swell and burgeon with more than simple satisfaction. "Send word to the manor once you know when you'll be doing the naming, and I'll come." Within six weeks of birth was the usual time, and she would still be at the manor through that period.

"Thank you." Jeb rose. "And thanks be to the Lady and all of you that you were here to help us in our need." He looked both humble and proud as he bowed to them both.

Lucilla smiled, then she walked forward, bent, and placed a kiss on the baby's pink forehead. "Welcome to the world, little one. May your life be long and fruitful, your days filled with laughter and joy, with nary a care to disturb you hereafter." It was an old benediction reserved for the very young.

Still smiling softly, Lucilla met Lottie's eyes, pressed one of her hands, then with a nod to Jeb, she turned and walked toward the end of the blanket-screen.

Thomas Carrick watched her as she approached him; head rising, although she didn't meet his gaze, she was conscious of his regard every step of the way.

But he said nothing, simply inclined his head to her as she passed.

Stepping beyond the screen, she heard him tell Jeb and Lottie that he would remain with them for the present, and heard Jeb's heartfelt thanks on that account, too.

Still smiling—she hadn't really stopped, although now her smile had a different genesis—Lucilla walked across the cottage. Although Hesta lay sprawled before the hearth, Lucilla's relatives were nowhere to be seen. Opening the front door, she found them. All four were standing in the snow a few yards before the cottage, and all were looking about with wonder in their faces.

Within two paces of walking out to join them, she, too, fell victim to the entrancement.

The sky had finally cleared completely. Stars winked and twinkled, and high above, the moon sailed free, its silvery radiance bathing a truly magical scene. She halted and, with the others, simply stared.

Drank in nature's beauty.

Cloaked in iridescent white, the wild peaks rose in splendor, line after line successively higher and, for once, readily discernible against the night sky. They were facing west; the sky was blue-black velvet sprinkled with the diamonds of a million stars.

But nearer at hand, all about them lay a winter wonderland. Snow covered everything—every fir, every rock. It coated the upper surfaces of every branch, while icicles depended below, gleaming in the moon's light.

If there hadn't been snow, the moon's glow would not have been strong, but the snow reflected and multiplied the soft radiance, transforming it into a stark and dazzling illumination that gilded every line, edged every shadow.

The final touch was the silence—the overwhelming lack of sound in the wake of the storm's cacophony.

That silence was profound. It was as if they stood in a world made new, one formed purely of elemental power... and they could feel the land, feel Nature herself, see her in all her majesty.

Lucilla felt her throat close. Her senses felt both overwhelmed and expanded.

From the corner of her eye, she saw Hesta sit down a few paces away; her shaggy gray head lifted, ears erect, as if she, too, was aware of the moment.

A presence loomed close; Lucilla looked to her right as Thomas halted beside her. One glance at his face confirmed that he was as riveted, as much in awe and wonder, as immersed in the moment and as alive to it as she.

And Marcus. Her gaze sought her twin, and despite the yards between them, she knew what he was feeling—that he was trapped, rapt, by that same awesome majesty.

She looked at the peaks again, and the moment shivered with poignancy.

This—this was theirs. Hers, Marcus's, Thomas's.

Theirs to know, to protect, to hold.

This land was both their past and their destiny; in that moment, she saw that clearly.

This land was their place. It was where they belonged. Where they would always be anchored and at home.

For a long minute, time stood still, and the power of the moment held them all.

Then Sebastian, furthest from the cottage, turned. He looked at Michael and Prudence, then commenced trudging back through the calf-high snow. "We should start back." He glanced at Marcus, met his eyes. "The cover will be lighter in the trees and on the southern slopes, but it'll still take time to pick our way through."

Marcus nodded and turned. "Let's saddle up our mounts."

The moment was past; Lucilla turned, too, and Thomas fell in beside her.

"I'll saddle your horse," Thomas murmured. "You can fetch the saddlebags."

Lucilla nodded. To the others, she said, "I'll bring the saddlebags through."

Back in the cottage, she quietly latched the front door, then tiptoed to the screen; they'd left it up to protect the baby from the worst of the drafts. Peeking around it, she saw, finally, all three of her patients sound asleep. Smiling—again—she retreated, picked up the saddlebags from the corner, cast a last glance around the cottage, then went through the door into the stable-barn.

Sebastian, Michael, Marcus, and Prudence were all cinching their girths. Prudence never allowed anyone else to saddle her mounts, not since she'd grown tall enough to do it herself. Thomas had Lucilla's black mare ready and waiting by a large log.

She handed around the saddlebags, then quickly crossed to where Thomas stood. "Thank you."

He took her saddlebag from her and settled it in place. She checked the girth strap; finding it perfectly set, she turned and he offered his hand to help her onto the makeshift mounting block.

For the barest instant, she hesitated, then she drew in a quick breath and set her gloved hand in his.

Despite the leather between their skins, the contact told her everything she'd wanted to know—confirmed all she'd started to suspect.

Stepping onto the log, she slid her fingers from his clasp and scrambled into her sidesaddle. She settled her feet in the stirrups, settled her skirts, gathered her reins, and finally met his gaze.

And saw in the deep golden amber of his eyes the same knowledge she'd just obtained.

She held his gaze for a moment more, then inclined her head. And said the words that leapt to her tongue. "Until we meet again."

He didn't answer, just slowly dipped his head.

The mounting block was close to the stable door. Now mounted, the others walked their horses to join her.

Thomas stepped back. He looked up at them all. "On behalf of the Carricks, thank you for your help." He met

Sebastian's gaze. "You were looking for the deer herds. I saw one of the bigger herds over by the crags directly to the west the day before yesterday. They might still be there."

Sebastian, Marcus, and Michael grinned. Sebastian inclined his head. "Thank you." He looked forward. "And now, we'll bid you farewell."

With a brisk salute to Thomas, Sebastian led the way out.

The others followed. Lucilla brought up the rear.

They reached the tree line and slowed as, with Marcus in the lead, they started onto the bridle path, now largely concealed by snow.

Lucilla had told herself she wasn't going to, yet just before she set her mare to follow Prudence's mount, she glanced back at the cottage.

Thomas stood exactly where she'd known he would be, watching her.

As he would until she'd passed out of his sight.

Lucilla looked back at him, looked her fill, branding him and all he was into her memory, then she turned and urged her mare into the trees.

Eight

The sun had only just risen when Devil Cynster pulled open the kitchen door of the manor and stepped out into the morning. Iced snow crunched under his boots as, his hands sunk in his greatcoat pockets, he slowly made his way past the forge and the blacksmith's house to the north-western corner of the rear yard.

About him, the land lay blanketed in white, pristine and untouched, with the sky above a cerulean blue so intense it hurt the eyes.

The wind had gone, vanished with the storm. The cold was sharp enough to cut; the air, as clear and pure as crystal.

To the east, the sun rose, painting streamers of gold and the palest blush-pink across the silent land.

Upon reaching the corner where the northern and western fences met, Devil halted. His pale green eyes narrowing, he scanned the darker snow-dappled line of the forests.

An instant later, he heard the crunch of someone else's boot.

Long lips quirking, he waited and wasn't surprised to

be joined by his cousin, Demon. He met Demon's blue eyes. "Honoria was worried—I thought I'd come and take a look."

Demon nodded. "Felicity, too. Hardly surprising." Prudence, their elder daughter, was still somewhere out there on this bright and sunny Christmas morn. Demon, too, stood and stared out.

Gradually, one after another, the others joined them. Gabriel, Vane, and Lucifer all had similar tales of worried wives who had sent them out to check...on quite what, none of them mentioned.

Finally, Richard strolled out and joined the gathering at the corner of his yard. After several moments of studying the forests, he said, "Ten minutes ago, I was reminded that our children —the five who, on Christmas Eve, stopped to help a crofter family because they were asked—are more than capable of taking care of themselves."

Vane glanced at Richard. "Did she say they would reach home safely?"

All there knew that "she" meant Catriona, and that the Lady of the Vale was not one to hand out assurances unless she *knew*. And when it came to this land, if she said she knew, she did.

Richard nodded. "She said they would be back today. I was instructed to tell you that, and to point out that us keeping a vigil out here would achieve precisely nothing. It was suggested that we should all go back inside and let their adventure run its course."

The others shifted.

"And," Richard continued, "before I came out here I went up to the highest tower and checked with a spyglass. There's nothing at all moving out there."

With various snorts and grunts by way of acknowledgment or reaction, the others scanned the landscape again, but of course, as Richard had just confirmed, there was nothing whatsoever to see.

Richard turned away first; one by one, the others followed suit, and they all trudged back to the house.

Devil was the last in the line. At the kitchen door, he paused to look back over the white paddocks to the dark skirts of the forests surmounted by the white bulk of the higher peaks. And still not a soul stirred in the crisply cold landscape.

He went into the house.

It was too early even for a pot of coffee—not on Christmas morn; they all trooped past the kitchens and went their separate ways, returning to the different towers or suites where they'd left their still-sleeping wives.

Devil entered the large suite he shared with Honoria. After silently closing the door, he shrugged off his greatcoat, tossed it on a chair, then sat to ease off his boots.

Honoria lay sleeping, curled on her side, facing the window. Devil's second boot heel clacked on the floor as he set the boot down, and she stirred.

She turned her head and squinted sleepily at him. She frowned as she watched him undress. "Has anything happened? Where have you been?"

Looking down as he unbuttoned his cuffs, Devil replied, "Nothing's happened."

When he didn't add anything more, Honoria turned fully onto her back, the better to view him. "And?"

His lips tightened, but then he inwardly sighed and admitted, "I went out to see if I could spot them riding in."

"Ah." Honoria eyed him with gentle understanding and a species of fond indulgence. "I take it they aren't yet in sight."

"Richard checked from the highest tower—there's no sign of them yet."

"I suppose that all of you were out there?"

Devil hauled off his shirt and leveled a look at her that stated very clearly that he couldn't believe she'd asked.

Honoria laughed.

But her laughter faded as he stripped off his breeches and reached the bed in one long stride.

He raised the covers and tumbled in alongside her, simultaneously juggling her into his arms.

On a laughing squeal, suddenly breathless, Honoria found herself trapped against him. She looked into his peridot eyes.

Devil looked down at her and smiled his signature smile. "Merry Christmas, Your Grace."

Then he bent his head and kissed her.

Over breakfast, the Great Hall was awash with Christmas cheer. Courtesy of the host and hostess, there were small gifts beside every plate, and the children had already found more personal presents left by their parents and siblings at the feet of their beds.

The chatter that swelled and filled the room was alive with happiness and warmed by good wishes.

Everyone had noted the section of empty table below the dais, Christopher having been admitted once again into the company of his elders. But Catriona had risen, welcomed everyone, and reassured the company that their missing members would be home for the feast that was Christmas luncheon. Everyone had cheered, and thereafter, the delight and laughter flowed without reservation.

On entering the hall, Claire had felt buoyed by the wave of festive joy; smiling unrestrainedly, she'd walked to her place beside Daniel, met his eyes, held his gaze, and said, "Merry Christmas, Daniel."

His smile had deepened; the light in his eyes had grown more personal. "And to you, Claire."

She'd given him her hand; he'd taken it and helped her over the bench.

Settled alongside him, she let the joy of the morning have her, let it sweep her up and away from her cares. It was a time for rejoicing, and she gave herself over to the warmth of the fellowship she and Daniel shared with each other, and with Melinda, Raven, and Morris. All of them delighted in the numerous small gifts and expressions of thanks they'd received from their charges, as well as from the grateful parents of those charges.

This wasn't the moment to allow her dilemma to cloud her reactions; she opened her heart and let the happiness of the day be hers. Let Daniel and the warmth in his eyes and the simple pleasure of the moment be her guide.

For his part, with Claire beside him and nothing to keep them apart through the hours, Daniel was content to let his direct pursuit of her lapse, at least for those shared hours on this most joyous of days. The son of a reverend, he'd never known a Christmas Day without a morning visit to church, but in the Vale there was no formal church, not even a chapel within the house. Instead, the household formed its own congregation, and it seemed to him that the merging of the pagan Yule, the Lady's ways, and all the elements of the Christian celebration resulted in a richer, deeper, somehow more grounded and therefore more meaningful experience.

The impromptu choir of the evening past formed again. They sang of bells ringing, of hallelujahs, of births and rejoicing. The voices rang out, the lighter tones clear and pure, the deeper voices providing a powerful rolling counterpoint.

Daniel embraced the glory of the moment, embraced the sentiment of the day, and devoted himself to enjoying every second.

At the next table, Louisa, Therese, Annabelle, and Juliet were thrilled with their gifts.

After they'd each described what they'd received, Louisa looked around the room and gave a contented sigh. "It was worth every ounce of effort we made to convince the elders to hold Christmas here."

Annabelle arched her brows. "It's not just Christmas— not just today. We've all the days to come, up to and including Hogmanay!"

Juliet bent an interested look on Annabelle. "The way you say that it's as if Hogmanay is even better than Christmas, and"—with a smile, she spread her arms, indicating the gaiety all around—"I don't see how that could be."

Annabelle's eyes twinkled. "Just wait. You'll see."

"For me," Therese said, "I'm content to take these holidays day by day—to enjoy each one. There's so much that's *almost* the same yet different up here." She glanced around. "Partly that's because here, it's not just the family, with the staff having their own celebration in their quarters. Here, everyone's together." She nodded at the choir. "It's more like a whole village celebrating all together."

"Yes," Annabelle said, "that's exactly what it's always like here. And it certainly helps with the numbers come Hogmanay." Again, she grinned as if savoring some secret.

"You're teasing, now," Louisa said, but she was smiling. "So," she continued, "what's next today?"

"Actually, girls." All four turned to find Catriona standing by the end of their table. Seeing she had their full attention, she continued, "I'm here to ask if the four of you will stand in for Lucilla and Prudence, and help me and Algaria and Mrs. Broom to box up the gifts for the Feast of St. Stephen."

The four girls exchanged a swift glance, then Louisa answered for them all. "Yes, of course." The boxing of gifts for giving to the household and estate workers on the following day, St. Stephen's Day, was a tradition on both sides of the border. Then Louisa's gaze went to the empty end of the table and her expression sobered. "But...won't Lucilla and Prudence want to help when they get back?"

Louisa looked up at Catriona; beneath her joy, Louisa was very much aware that her big brothers were still out in the snow somewhere. They were annoyances more often than not, but still, she'd been looking forward to seeing them soon. She had presents to give them and, she hoped, presents to receive from them, but more than anything else, she just wanted them there...and Lucilla and Prudence were with Sebastian and Michael. Louisa fixed her gaze on Catriona's face. "Aren't they going to be back in time to help?"

Catriona looked into Louisa's large pale green eyes and read the reality of the emotion swimming in the limpid depths. She smiled. "They'll all be back for luncheon, as I said, but I can guarantee that both girls—and the boys, too—will fall into their beds after they've eaten. I sincerely doubt any of them slept a wink last night."

"Oh." Louisa's gaze cleared. She glanced at Therese, then back at Catriona. "In that case, when do you need us, and where?"

The morning vanished in a rush of activities. Breakfast had been served early, the better to clear the kitchen for the extravaganza of a Casphairn Manor Christmas luncheon. For the staff—kitchen, household, gardeners, gamekeepers, and all—it was one of their premier events of the year.

Luckily, not only had the storm passed, but the sun, weak though it was in this season and latitude, had decided to essay forth, glinting off the hoar frost the night had laid over the snow, and transforming the icicles hanging from all the eaves into a lacework of diamonds.

The children, both Cynster and household, were happy to go outside, initially to stare in open-mouthed wonderment—then, at Raven's suggestion, to build a small army of snowmen in the drifts along the drive. The competition was collaborative, and in some instances fierce, with results ranging from the dramatic to the hilarious.

With Louisa and the other three fourteen-year-old Cynster girls busily working under Catriona's direction, Claire donned her pelisse, gloves, and a knitted hat and scarf, and went out to join Daniel in the snow. He was loosely supervising the snowmen-builders. Without allowing herself to overthink things, on reaching him, she boldly twined her arm with his; when, surprised, he glanced at her, she smiled at him. He looked into her eyes; she saw the hope that infused his gaze, but other than drawing his arm closer to his body, anchoring hers more definitely, he said nothing. Then a child called, and he looked up and answered their question.

They spent the rest of the morning promenading together. As the snow had iced over, especially along the drive, other women, too, had claimed a man's arm; that she was on Daniel's didn't draw any real attention.

But it was a different pleasure to be able to share the moments of the day—as they had over breakfast—simply being themselves without any demands or restrictions.

That, Daniel thought, as he guided Claire along the line of snowmen, was part of the magic of the Vale of Casphairn; it was so far from any metropolis, so buried in raw and untamed country, the superficialities of their more civilized lives fell away, irrelevant.

Then the great gong was struck, the deep *boong* resonating through the manor and out through the newly opened doors.

With one voice, the children cheered, a spontaneous sound that placed a smile on every adult face. Snowmen and the question of which was best were left behind as, leaping and calling, the boisterous throng, followed by their highly entertained elders, streamed back into the manor.

Among the last inside, Daniel released Claire to help one of the footmen close the big front doors. He glanced at the man. "Are the rest of the riding party back?"

The footman shook his head. "Not yet. But as the Lady said they'd be here for luncheon, they must be close."

Daniel turned back to Claire. As she retook his arm and they followed the footman into the Great Hall, she tipped her head closer and murmured, "It must be comforting to have that degree of certainty."

He glanced at her, but she was looking ahead. "Truer words," he murmured, and led her to their places at their table.

The tables were already laden with covered dishes and platters, with branchlets of evergreen set around and in between. Fir, pine, and spruce lightly scented the air, adding to the festive spirit.

Despite all beliefs and certainties, everyone's gazes drifted to the section of table below the dais, still empty—

"They're coming!" Calvin came leaping down the stairs

that debouched directly onto the dais. His face alight, he addressed the table of Cynster parents. "I've been keeping watch from Carter's studio at the top of our tower— I took the spyglass and I just spotted them walking their mounts through the snow. They're out of the forest and not far away."

By the time Calvin had finished his report, fully half the room had risen again. People made for the doors leading outside—the side door, the front door, the kitchen door. Expectant eagerness—expectant relief—had all the Cynsters bar the dowager spilling out to the rear yard, and a large number of the household followed, keen to see the absent riders home safe and to hear their story.

Everyone who crowded into the rear yard was hoping to hear a fresh, new Christmas tale with a happy ending.

The riders crested a rise, coming into view. They were walking their horses smartly.

Demon, watching with his hands on his hips, nodded approvingly. "Good to see—this snow's too deep even to trot."

From beside him, Felicity, his wife, qualified, "Not unless wolves were nipping at your heels."

Demon glanced down at her; they shared a smile, then both raised their heads and watched Prudence, their eldest daughter, guide her mount through the snow toward them.

Sebastian, as usual and as expected, was in the lead. His heavier mount had less difficulty stepping through the snow. Prudence followed, her mount treading more or less where Sebastian's had, and Lucilla followed her. Lucilla's black mare was the lightest of the horses and usually headstrong, but in these conditions, the mare clearly appreciated the track created by the two heavier horses preceding her; she followed in their wake without fuss.

Riding easily, Michael followed Lucilla, and Marcus brought up the rear, patently keeping a watchful eye on the little procession and the various tacks Sebastian chose to take over the snow-covered ground.

And then they were in hailing range.

"About time," the duke called.

Sebastian grinned, albeit wearily. "We came as fast as we could." He tipped his head in the direction from which they'd come. "The drifts along the ridge line and in the lower reaches of the forests were deeper than we'd anticipated."

"Never mind," the duchess declared. "You're here now, home and safe, and that's all that matters."

Rupert and Alasdair swung open the rear gate and, one by one, the riders passed through. Weariness, but also triumph, glowed in their eyes and lit their faces.

As they brought their horses to a stamping, drooping halt, the company closed around them with cheers and calls of "Welcome home!" and "Merry Christmas!"

Richard was the first to reach his eldest child. He lifted Lucilla from her saddle—noting as he did that she made not the slightest protest. Tiredness etched her face, but there was something else there, too—something precious and wonderful.

Lucilla shivered. "I'm cold."

Richard hugged her. Then Catriona was there. She embraced Lucilla, then held her at arm's length. The Lady of the Vale looked into her daughter's eyes, then she smiled a smile full of love and approval. Laying a hand on Lucilla's bright copper-red hair, Catriona gently stroked. "Well done. Now go inside and get warm, and we'll all feast, and then you and the others can catch up on your sleep."

Marcus came up at that moment. Catriona hugged him,

then released him and ran her gaze over him. Then, smiling in a slightly different way, she nodded. "Good. You, too—inside now. You will have to tell us all about your adventure, but get into the warmth and drink something first."

"Wassail." Marcus looked at Richard. "Is there any left?"

Richard clapped him on the shoulder. "Bound to be—ask Cook."

Many willing and able hands gathered to lead the tired horses into the stable, making light work of unsaddling and tending them. Meanwhile, with the returning riders carried along in their midst, the bulk of the crowd streamed back into the Great Hall.

Those who'd remained inside had been busy, making sure the riders' table was set, and piled platters and warmed mulled wine were waiting, along with beakers of the reheated spiced ale from the night before.

Sliding onto the bench in his usual place, Marcus lifted his beaker. "Wassail for us." He sipped and looked startled.

Polby, the butler, hovering to ensure that all was just right for the returning heroes, noticed and grinned. "It's stronger from having sat overnight. Cook said you'd want it."

"Need it, more like," Michael said, eyes closed as he savored a mouthful. Opening his eyes, he grinned tiredly at Polby. "And please tell Cook that if she ever wants to cure anybody of anything to do with being cold, reheated wassail is the trick."

"Excellent." Satisfied that the six of them—the five now having been joined by Christopher—had all they needed, with a wide smile, Polby withdrew, heading for his own place on the benches.

At the high table, Catriona rose to her feet. Gradually, the chatter subsided and an expectant hush fell over the room. Catriona smiled, ineffable grace and warmth in her gaze as she surveyed the room. "Today is a day for rejoicing, for giving thanks for the bounties of the past year and looking forward in hope to those of the year to come. Whatever your leaning, to whichever deity you cleave, please take a moment to give thanks." She paused, and not a sound could be heard. Many bowed their heads, their lips moving in prayer; others simply closed their eyes, while still others waited, wide-eyed and waiting, secure in the presence of their Lady.

Finally, Catriona smiled and continued, her voice clear and pitched to reach the furthest corners, "We are doubly grateful, today, to have our young adventurers returned to us safe and sound, and as we're all by now aware, they have a Christmas tale of their own to tell." Her gaze lowered to the section of table immediately before the dais. "But the food is hot, and I'm quite sure they're famished, too." Laughter rippled through the room, and Catriona raised her hands. "Please, everyone—join in this feast, in this celebration, and perhaps, as they can manage it, our recently returned members can entertain us with their story as they may."

Richard, seated beside Catriona, had risen during her conclusion. Now he raised his goblet high and commanded, "Come one, come all—eat, drink, and let us be merry!"

A rousing cheer went up on all sides and everyone happily complied with their host's directive.

Michael reached for a turkey leg, then looked around their table of six. "How do you want to do this?"

Christopher grinned. "As I wasn't there, I don't have to do anything—I can eat, drink, and be entertained by you lot."

Sebastian, seated alongside, accidentally-on-purpose nudged Christopher away from the dish of pullets in red wine that he was reaching for.

"Hey!" Christopher "nudged" back rather more firmly.

"Boys, boys!" Across the table, Prudence wagged a chicken bone at them both. "You're supposed to be gentlemen, now."

Unrepentant, Sebastian and Christopher shrugged and, with Marcus and Michael, settled to demolish everything edible within reach. But after piling his plate high and swallowing several mouthfuls, Sebastian said, "Why don't we just pass the baton, so to speak? I'll start, and then whoever wishes can cut in and take over." He glanced down at his plate. "That way, everyone else will be kept amused, and we'll all be able to eat while the food's still warm."

Lucilla nodded. "As I can't imagine you, Michael, or Marcus describing the birth, and as neither Prudence nor I know what actually happened when you and Thomas Carrick went out to fix that shutter, a round-robin will work better than one of us trying to cover it all."

Mouths full, the others nodded their agreement.

Sebastian wiped his lips with his napkin, then rose. Stepping over the bench, he moved to the space before the main fireplace. With his back to the flames, he looked up at the high table and saw his parents smiling down at him. He inclined his head to them. "Your Graces." Spreading his arms, he turned to include the entire company. "*Mesdames et messieurs*, our Christmas tale."

Laughter greeted his opening. Encouraged, he went on, "It started with a ride through the forests in search of game. But a storm was blowing in, and…" With deft turns of phrase, Sebastian described the sudden eruption of Jeb, the crofter, into their path, and how his plea for help had had them turning aside to ride to his cottage.

Marcus rose. Sebastian returned to the bench and his meal as Marcus described the cottage in detail, from its unprepossessing exterior and rickety shutters to the newer stable-barn built at the rear. He also filled in the immediate geography. "So the front of the cottage was fully exposed to the brunt of the onrushing storm."

Lucilla rose and replaced her twin before the fireplace. "I went in and examined Jeb's wife, Lottie. She was already in labor, and I could tell the baby would arrive before dawn and also was not in the best position. As I had been summoned there, I knew I had to stay. I needed Prudence to help, and Marcus, Sebastian, and Michael elected to remain and see to our general safety. Christopher, as you all know, led the other boys back."

Christopher stood at his place at the table to report, "And as everyone here knows, but you five don't, we arrived in good order, just in time for dinner."

Sebastian snorted. "Naturally."

Christopher shrugged eloquently, and to a round of good-natured laughter, he sat.

Lucilla resumed her telling. "So the five of us and Jeb made ready as best we could, not just for the arrival of the baby but also to weather the fury of the storm." She briefly described a few of the simple measures they'd taken—the blanket hung as a screen, the pots and pans of water.

Michael rose and took up the tale. "While neat and tidy, the cottage was not what one would describe as sound." He outlined the various repairs they'd undertaken to weatherproof the cottage.

Prudence rose briefly to mention that there had been insufficient food to adequately feed anyone, and that they'd faced the prospect of having nothing but a thin broth to help sustain the mother. "And, of course, Lucilla's tisanes—which did help."

Marcus followed with a brief description of what animals they'd found in the stable-barn.

"And then," Sebastian said, reclaiming the stage, "just as the storm was reaching its zenith and battering at the cottage as if intending to flatten it, there was a knock on the door."

"More a thump," Michael called.

Sebastian inclined his head. He went on to describe with melodramatic flair the arrival of Thomas Carrick, and all the food and drink Carrick had brought. "Like nothing so much as Good King Wenceslas, huge deerhound by his side and all. The weather meant he couldn't ride up, so he'd trudged, hauling the supplies up on a sled."

Rising to replace Sebastian, who pulled a face at her but gave way, Lucilla noted that, after an initial tensing about the high table over the news that some other male had arrived at the cottage, the older Cynster males, her father included, had relaxed somewhat; approval now tinged their features. Taking position before the fireplace, she declared, "The food Thomas Carrick brought was a godsend. As was the bottle of mead, the bottle of gin, and the bottle of whisky. The latter, sadly"—she directed a severe look at Sebastian, Michael, and Marcus—"was empty by the time we quit the cottage."

Laughter rolled around the room.

"So," she said, letting her gaze sweep the gathering, "we had Good King Wenceslas and his hound. We had a poor crofter couple, with the wife having her baby on Christmas Eve in a rude, ramshackle cottage, little better than a stable. We had animals beyond one door—sheep, a goat, an old milch cow. We had"—she waved at Marcus, Michael, and Sebastian—"the three wise men?" Everyone hooted and cheered, especially the other Cynsters. "And," Lucilla continued, as the laughter faded, "I believe that leaves Prudence and myself"—placing a hand over her heart, she half bowed—"playing the part of ministering angels."

The company laughed and clapped. Huge smiles wreathed most faces.

Michael rose and shooed Lucilla from pride of place. "Regardless of the ministering that occurred behind the blanket-screen, I feel I must tell you more about the hound—for it was not just any old hound." There were groans from various people; many there knew of Michael's obsession with the hunt. Undeterred, he assured the company, "This was a hound among hounds." He went on to describe Hesta with verve and flair, then proceeded to paint Jeb and his slowly unraveling composure, describing several of the attempts made to distract him from his wife's quite obvious agony. "Not that anything actually worked. But as the screams and groans reached their apogee, and we were all on tenterhooks, waiting for the moment…a shutter blew open and the storm stormed in."

Waved to his feet by Michael, Sebastian obliged and took up the tale. He was the only one present who knew what had happened while he and Thomas Carrick had wrestled to secure the shutter; listening as avidly as anyone, Lucilla literally shivered. She knew Sebastian well enough to read between his glibly delivered lines and to guess that both he and Thomas had come close to taking serious injury, courtesy of the iciness of the raging storm.

When Sebastian had the shutter closed and he and Thomas back inside, Lucilla reclaimed the stage. "If the shutter hadn't been closed again, I don't know what might have occurred, for the air was ice-laden and the winds were fierce, but the others built the fire up, and not long after that, the baby decided it was time."

She described the birth only as "not straightforward, but working together, Lottie, Prudence, and I brought a perfect little girl into the world." Lucilla directed a smile around the room. "At ten minutes past midnight."

There were coos and sighs of "A Christmas babe" from numerous female throats around the room.

Prudence claimed another turn. In her usual practical vein, she described how they had worked through the next hours to set the cottage to rights, and to ensure that Jeb and Lottie had sustaining meals, and that their animals were fed and watered. "Carrick said he would stay until the snows thawed enough for him to bring up a party to ferry Lottie, Jeb, and their child down to Carrick Manor."

Marcus rose to take Prudence's place. "I don't think any of us noticed when the storm ended. We suddenly realized that the winds had died, then we went outside, and silence engulfed us."

Lucilla listened as her twin described with evocative eloquence the magic of that moment; he, like she, *felt* the land.

Sebastian rose and briefly detailed the last things they'd done—the wood they'd chopped, the cow Michael had milked without getting kicked.

But then Sebastian waved the others to join him—including Christopher. "We wouldn't have been able to stay with the other lads, too, so Christopher's contribution was significant as well."

To cheers—and laughing jeers from the "other lads"—Christopher took a bow.

Then he stood with the other five as Sebastian, in the center, spread his arms and said, "Our journey home was slow, but without incident. And so that's our Christmas tale for you—how we were called upon to aid in bringing a new life into the world, with help from all the saints and deities involved, on Christmas morning."

Sebastian bowed low and the others bowed with him, and the Great Hall erupted with cheers, clapping, and the stamping of booted feet.

Many called compliments, and the Cynster elders beamed proudly on the future of their house—the leaders of the next generation—as they smiled and acknowledged the compliments, then made their way back to their seats.

At the high table, Catriona nodded to the waiting servers; they'd all gathered in the archway from the kitchen to listen to the tale. Within minutes, flaming plum puddings and jugs of rich custard were ferried out, and the hungry hordes quieted.

Seated beside Daniel and marveling at the luscious taste of the pudding—she'd never had better—Claire seized the moment when Daniel looked across the table to study his profile.

How could she tell if he loved her? There had to be a way.

She returned her gaze to her plate before he caught her staring. She accepted that she had to go forward and, one way or another, learn what she needed to know; somewhere in the dark watches of the night, she'd moved past the point where she might have backed away. Whether that had been due to Melinda's advice or some element of her own determination, she didn't know, but she no longer viewed simply turning away from Daniel as a viable path.

She had to find out what was possible between them or she would regret it for the rest of her life.

But how was she to find the answer to the question on which everything else seemed to depend?

She consumed the pudding and custard in silence, that thought revolving in her mind.

Daniel viewed Claire's silence with increasing misgiving. As matters stood between them, he had no idea if he was on the cusp of success or abject failure.

On the one hand, he was hopeful and counseled himself to patience; pressing her at this point might not be wise. Their day had been full of shared emotions——not the same emotions he hoped she felt for him and that he most definitely felt for her, but quite other emotions; trying to shift their focus to the personal in the midst of such communal engagement would, he felt, be a serious misstep.

But what if Alasdair or Rupert was summoned south tomorrow, and he or she had to leave with their respective families? What if she didn't agree while they were at the manor?

If he didn't gain her agreement to, at the very least, allow him to formally court her, then he didn't know when he might get another chance to press his suit.

And given the nebulous hurdle that, courtesy of her previous marriage, stood between them, pursuing her from a distance was not going to work.

He had to make headway in learning about the dragon he needed to slay, and as soon as possible.

But for today… As the banquet, for it had been that,

finally ended, he helped her to rise and climb over the bench seat.

And seized the few seconds when everyone around them was likewise absorbed with sorting themselves out; holding on to her hand, he gently squeezed her fingers and murmured low so that only she could hear, "I want to know everything about you—I want to know your demons as well as your desires." He caught her gaze as, eyes widening, she glanced up at him. "I will never give up pursuing my dream—pursuing you…" He searched her eyes. "Unless and until you say me nay. Until then, I'm yours, regardless of whether you move to claim me." Pressing her hand, he released it. "Remember that, my dearest Claire."

Claire held his gaze for a moment more, then had to yield to the press of bodies around them and turn toward the door.

I want to know everything about you—I want to know your demons as well as your desires.

As she strolled with the crowd, with Daniel behind her, she replayed his words. Let them sink into her heart. Into her soul.

Drawing in a breath, as she passed under the mistletoe and into the front hall, she decided she might just hold him to them.

Before Lucilla could join the others in heading for their rooms and their beds—their performance before everyone had drained the last of their energies; they'd all actually admitted to feeling wrung out—she was hailed by Algaria.

"You go on," Lucilla said to Prudence. "I doubt this will take long."

And if it did, she might fall asleep where she sat.

With an exhausted nod, Prudence went.

Lucilla stepped onto the dais; her parents and the other Cynster elders had already repaired to the drawing room or the library. Making her way past the empty benches, she reached the end of the high table and perched on the end of one bench so that her gaze was nearer to level with her grandmother's and Algaria's, both of whom regarded her with bird-bright eyes, one pair palest green, the other black.

McArdle was asleep and snoring softly in the armchair closer to and angled toward the hearth.

"So tell us." Algaria resettled her shawl about her stooped shoulders. "I want all the details you left out about the birth, and your grandmother isn't likely to have the vapors from overhearing, so talk."

Lucilla managed to keep her lips straight, but the laughing, indulgent look the dowager cast Algaria very nearly overset her. Carefully, she drew a long breath, then, her voice steady, she described the birth in the detail she knew Algaria wanted, adding what she'd observed about Lottie and the details of the tisane she'd brewed, and the mead- and gin-based potions she'd left behind for Lottie to help with the aftereffects.

Both old ladies listened without interrupting, their gazes locked—rather unnervingly—on Lucilla's face.

But when she reached the end of her recitation, Algaria nodded with patent approval. "Excellent. You did precisely as you should have throughout." Algaria bestowed on Lucilla one of her very rare smiles. "I taught you well, and you remembered when you needed the information. That's all any mentor can ask."

Somewhat taken aback by what was, from Algaria, richly fulsome praise, Lucilla hesitated, then asked a question that that been circling in her brain for the past twelve and more hours—ever since she'd come close enough to

Thomas Carrick to realize that he was Lady-touched, too. "I wanted to ask…" She looked at Algaria. "Indeed, I'm surprised I haven't thought to ask this before, but how far around the Vale does the Lady's protection extend?" *Into the lands to our north? The Carrick lands, for instance?*

Algaria's brows arched as if she, too, hadn't previously thought of that point, but then the old woman shrugged. "I know it's not limited to the Vale but spills into the surrounding areas. However, I've never known it to have precise borders." She trapped Lucilla's gaze. "Better ask instead how far Her mantle extends. Were you out from under it—did you lose your link to Her—in that cottage? You know what it feels like when you travel to London."

"Ah—I see."

"And?" Algaria prompted.

"No, I wasn't out of touch while in the cottage—or, indeed, anywhere we rode on Christmas Eve—so the mantle extends at least that far." *Into Carrick lands.*

"Well, then. You have your answer." Algaria sat back. "And now you'd better go and rest. You're at low ebb, I can tell."

Letting her weariness show, Lucilla smiled and rose.

Stowing away the knowledge that, as she and Marcus were, Thomas Carrick was also under the Lady's direct protection—and she had to wonder why that was—Lucilla bobbed a curtsy to Algaria and her grandmother. Only as she turned away did she realize that Helena had listened quietly throughout, and, unlike Algaria, Helena had *heard*.

Deciding she was too tired to even speculate as to what her unnervingly perspicacious grandmother might do with whatever knowledge she'd gained, Lucilla headed for her room and her bed.

Nine

In the quiet of the afternoon, when the manor lay somnolent in the aftermath of the huge meal, Daniel finally tracked Claire down to a window seat high in one of the manor's turrets. When he first spied her, she was looking out of the window, but hearing his boots on the stone, she turned. And smiled, although there was a hint of wry resignation in the gesture.

He smiled back—as lightly as he could, yet tension had been building inside him all day; it chose that moment to grip and tighten. His chest felt like iron bands had locked about it, restricting his breathing. He waved at the cushioned space alongside her. "May I?"

Lips curving gently, she inclined her head. "Indeed, you may."

He sat. Then he angled his head and looked at her, met her eyes. He held her gaze for several seconds, then he lowered his. To her hands, resting in her lap.

On impulse—one he didn't question—he reached over, picked up her nearer hand, and drew it across to cradle between his. She didn't resist, neither his touch nor the claiming. Driven by burgeoning need and emboldened by that acceptance, he said, his voice low, "I know I shouldn't press you, that I should give you whatever time you need to consider…whatever it is you need to consider."

She must have heard something in his voice; she swiveled on the seat to face him. She placed her other hand over his, gripping lightly.

He drew breath and turned his head. Met her eyes, briefly searched them. "But I have to ask—I have to know. Is there any hope for me? For us?"

Claire looked into his warm hazel eyes and saw—was allowed to see, openly and clearly displayed—a devotion she could count on, a depth of commitment that would always be there. Solid, dependable, unwavering.

And she sensed—felt—an answering response, the reality of a reciprocal commitment that was already there, in existence and real, a connection to another she'd spent her adult life dreaming of finding.

"I…" Searching his eyes as he had searched hers, she reached—for honesty, for the simple truth. Feeling as if she was teetering on the brink of taking some ineradicable step, she swallowed her hesitancy and said, "I need to know—"

A shrill scream cut her off.

Both she and Daniel reacted instantly. Turning to the window, rising so they could better peer down, they looked, saw—froze for just a second—then both whirled and plunged down the turret stairs.

Daniel was in the lead, and with his longer legs, he quickly outstripped her. Her heavy skirts hiked to her calves—modesty be damned, she couldn't risk falling—she ran on in his wake, praying they would get to the riverbank in time.

The scene they'd looked out on had been one of incipient disaster. A large group of children—not Cynsters but of the household families—had slipped out to play in the heavy drifts of snow. Sparkling overlays of ice had transformed the tiered terrace gardens between the manor and the burn into a winter wonderland. Inevitably, some of the children had been drawn to the banks of the burn—the treacherous banks, for despite the icy weather, the burn still flowed beneath a crust of ice and snow. Later in the season, perhaps it would freeze enough for skating, but at present, it was a trap waiting for the unwary.

One boy had fallen in, and at least two more were stranded.

Two girls, screaming and sobbing, were clinging to a crumbling snowdrift, their boots dangling in the icy waters.

Panting, Claire reached the ground floor and raced into the corridor leading to the side door. At the corridor's far end, the door stood open, no doubt thrust wide by Daniel as he'd raced through.

Ahead of Claire, heading toward the door, Polby exclaimed, "Great heavens! Leaving doors open in this weather—"

"Polby!" Claire reached him and grabbed his arm. "Leave the door." Meeting the butler's startled gaze, she gasped, "Children—several—have fallen into the burn. Mr. Crosbie rushed out to help. I'm going, too. Get others—everyone you can. We especially need more men who can fish the children out."

She could help, but in her heavy winter skirts, she couldn't risk going in deeper than her knees.

Polby's eyes flew wide, but he understood. Without waiting to see more, Claire released him and rushed to the doorway.

She went straight through, paused on the stoop to swiftly take stock, then stepped off the porch onto ice-slicked snow. She'd been to the manor often enough to know the layout of what was, in other seasons, a large productive herb garden. She could remember where the paths were, but snow covered everything and was made yet more perilous by patches of ice; she had to pick her way carefully.

Clenching her jaw against the first assault of the cold, she sternly told herself she'd be no help if she broke a leg. She was experienced enough to rein in the impulse to rush precipitously forward, yet a pounding urgency to reach a spot where she could see what was going on and then help Daniel—and ensure that he was safe, too—thundered in her blood.

Looking down from the turret, they'd been able to see the whole scene laid out below them; coming from the house, she had to clear a lip of the gardens about halfway down before she could see what was occurring along the burn.

Finally reaching the spot, she paused in what had become a mad scramble and surveyed the scene. Her heart leapt into her throat. "Oh, God."

Daniel had plunged into the burn's icy waters. He was holding a little boy up against his chest, flailing to keep both their heads above water.

The burn was a lot deeper than she'd thought; worse, she could glimpse rocks—dark gray and jagged—protruding here and there, silent threats lurking within the churning water.

Two other boys were half submerged in the rushing waters; they were desperately clinging to a large rock, fighting to hold on and keep their heads clear.

The two girls in danger of slipping in had been grabbed by other children and were being held suspended half in and half out of the icy burn; the other children weren't strong enough to pull the girls to safety.

The cold was intense, the chill sharp enough to cut.

Neither Claire nor Daniel was wearing gloves or coat, much less outdoor boots. Resuming her sliding scramble down the last section of garden, Claire shoved the discomfort already making itself known from her mind and concentrated on reaching the bank.

Glancing up, she saw Daniel slipping and stumbling on the rocky bed of the burn as he struggled to bring the boy he held to shore. She changed direction, making for the stretch of bank Daniel was angling toward.

Reaching it, she tested the bank; in several places there was nothing but snow overlaying a thin crust of ice jutting over the water, waiting to crumple beneath her weight. She stamped around, establishing where she could safely stand, then as Daniel neared, she stretched out, reaching for the boy.

Teeth gritted, Daniel found his footing in the burn. The boy's hands had frozen—he could no longer grip anything. Daniel, too, was losing body heat rapidly, but the other two boys wouldn't last long unless he reached them and got them out.

None of the three boys were large enough, heavy enough, not to be swept away in the rushing waters.

Staggering slightly, summoning his strength, Daniel lifted the boy he'd caught and held him out to Claire.

She bent forward, stretching, and tried to grip the boy's hands, then realized that wouldn't work and gripped his wrists. She nodded. "I've got him."

Daniel paused. "Make sure you're stable before I let him go." He didn't want her toppling in.

She shifted her feet, then nodded again. "Let him go."

Daniel did. Smoothly, Claire straightened, pivoted, and swung the boy safely to the bank.

Daniel immediately turned and went for the next boy. From the corner of his eye, he saw several of the other children—who had huddled in a group along the bank, unable to help their fellows and until now frozen in panic—draw closer to Claire. She beckoned them nearer. Distantly, he heard her giving the group crisp orders to help the boy she held against her; he was too weak to stand.

Closing in on the two still clinging to the rock about which the freezing waters surged and broke, Daniel swiftly assessed which one to take first; although they were only about eight years old, he couldn't ferry both of them to the bank at once.

The water below the rock was nearly as deep as he was tall; battling to maintain his position in the swirling, tugging torrent, Daniel caught the flailing legs of the boy he judged the younger, the one with the weaker grip on the jagged edges of the rock. "You next. Let go, and I'll take you to the bank." To the other boy, he said, "I'll come back for you next."

The boy whose legs he held looked at him, terror starkly etched in his small face, which was turning blue. Then the boy peeled his fingers from the rock and let go.

Daniel caught the lad against his chest, but the force set him staggering back several steps. Regaining his balance, he righted himself and the sputtering boy, checked that the boy's face was clear of the water, then he started the hard slog across to the bank.

This time he managed it more directly.

Shivers had already started to course through him, but were as nothing compared to those racking the boy's smaller frame. As he neared the bank, he heard shouts and calls from above. Other adults—Raven, Morris, and Melinda among them—had started scrambling down the last section of the gardens, but all were still too far away to help.

But Claire was there. Blinking past the hair the water had plastered over his eyes, he refocused on the section of bank toward which he was struggling, and saw that she'd already established another patch of firm ground on which to stand and take the boy from him.

As soon as he got close enough, they repeated the maneuver that had worked the time before, but this boy was somewhat heavier than the last. When Claire tried to swing him to the bank, she slipped, teetered –

In a sliding rush, Raven reached her and grabbed her about her waist, anchoring her. Lips compressing, Claire steadied and pulled the boy in.

Raven looked at Daniel, a question in his eyes.

Already turning back to the rock, Daniel waved at the two girls still suspended over the water; they were silently weeping as they hung by their arms, but were smart enough not to struggle or try to climb the slippery, barely solid mound of ice and snow. "Organize the others to pull the girls up. I'll get the last boy—no sense anyone else getting soaked."

Getting chilled to the bone, as he already was.

Setting his sights squarely on the last boy clinging to the rock, Daniel forced his freezing limbs to his bidding; pushing against the force of the burn, he angled across, then nearer.

He was almost at the rock when, with a cry, the boy lost his grip. Like a hungry beast, the waters gobbled him up and swept him away.

Daniel lunged sideways. The waters closed over him, but his fingers tangled in the boy's jacket. Fighting against pain, he forced his hand to close, his frozen fingers to grip and hold.

Getting his feet under him, he surfaced with a gasp. Steadily, he drew the boy to him and, fumbling, got the boy's head up and braced against his shoulder.

The boy's eyes popped open, panicked and wild. He gasped, wheezed, strained for air even as his body shuddered.

"Hold as still as you can," Daniel gritted out through chattering teeth. "I won't let you go." Getting the words out was an effort. He felt as if his lungs were shutting down, as if they wouldn't expand.

Doggedly, he turned—so slowly—to the bank.

It suddenly seemed a long way away.

As he forced his legs to take tortured step after tortured step, he was distantly aware of the commotion as the two girls were pulled to safety. Glancing through the fall of his hair, already crusting with flecks of ice, he saw that the first two boys he'd dragged out of the water had already been wrapped in blankets and were being carried up to the house.

He couldn't feel his feet. Or his fingers. All he could sense of the boy he held was the solid mass of his body and his weight; the boy was even more deeply chilled than he was.

Curiously, the water no longer felt that cold. Daniel didn't think that was a good sign.

He felt so deathly tired...

The toe of his boot stubbed against a rock, and he nearly pitched headlong.

"Daniel!"

Claire's voice reached through the cold. Opening his eyes—he hadn't realized he'd closed them—he looked and saw her leaning forward, not that far away, reaching for him.

He pressed forward another step. Two.

Raven and Morris were waiting with Claire to help him up the bank. So was Richard Cynster and an agonizingly worried-looking man— the carpenter, Daniel realized. It must be his lad that Daniel was holding.

The riverbed started to slope upward. Ignoring the screaming of his thighs, Daniel pressed on Another step, and another, and the water had fallen to mid-chest. He paused and gathered his strength; he was still too far away from the bank for the others to help, but the boy now hung limp, an awkward, destabilizing weight.

Weaving, with a final spurt of effort, Daniel managed to keep his balance as he swung the boy up out of the water and across his upper chest. Anchoring the lad there, Daniel lowered his head and forged on.

Another step. Another.

Then hands seized him and dragged him forward; he stumbled and they held him upright.

The boy was lifted from him. Eyes closed, Daniel relaxed and started to tip back.

Hands seized him again, even more ungently. Even more urgently. Then he was half lifted, half dragged out of the burn.

The chill of the air had him blinking his eyes open, then a blanket—oh, blessed warmth!—was flung over his shoulders.

A towel fell over his head and someone—Claire—briskly rubbed his hair dry. Or at least drier.

"Right. Let's get you into the house." The voice belonged to Richard Cynster, as did the shoulder that slid under Daniel's raised arm.

Then another Cynster—the duke?—matched Richard on Daniel's other side, and in concert the brothers started him walking toward the house.

Up the sloping path over which some quick-thinking soul had thought to fling salt and gravel.

Daniel walked—weaved—slowly up through the garden, but he had no real sense of intentional physical action; it was as if his body floated alongside his corporeal self, which, puppetlike, moved under someone else's guidance. But he was aware of Claire; he could feel her gaze constantly on him, anxious, concerned, watchful.

He wanted to smile at her and tell her he was all right, but at that moment, he wasn't in command of his tongue or even his face.

The upper reaches of the path had been hastily shoveled, and then they were at the side door.

The two Cynsters helped him up over the step and into the house, and carefully released him into the multitude of hands waiting to help him.

Raven and Morris stayed with him. Claire and Melinda hovered as close as they could.

Uncounted minutes later, relaxing in a tub filled to the brim with warm water, Daniel finally came fully back to himself.

He groaned, then tipped his head back and slid beneath the water. He stayed under for as long as he could, letting the warmth penetrate his scalp and bring his ears back to life in a rush of prickling, rather painful sensation.

After resurfacing, he wiped water from his face and took stock. His shivers had subsided to tremors, yet although his skin was warmer, he still felt chilled to the marrow.

Beside the tub, Raven popped into view. The other tutor studied Daniel's eyes, then grinned. "Good. You're back with us." Raven reached to the side and produced a glass holding a good few inches of amber liquid. "We're supposed to give you these to drink in order. This is from our host—the very best whisky in the world, I'm told." Concern returned to Raven's face. "Can you hold it?"

Daniel raised his right hand from the water. His fingers still didn't feel quite right, but they closed well enough around the cut-crystal tumbler. He nodded and took the glass; using both hands, he carefully brought it to his lips and sipped.

Liquid fire streaked down his throat and exploded in his stomach. As the warmth spread, he closed his eyes and sighed. "That's…indeed very good." The words emerged as little more than a croak, but at least his vocal cords worked.

Morris appeared on the tub's other side. "We're under strict instructions." Morris bent to dabble his fingers in the water, then straightened. "We're only allowed to let you lie there until the water starts to cool, then we have to get you up, dry, dressed, and down to sit before the fire in the Great Hall."

Taking a larger sip of the whisky, Daniel frowned. "Can't I just sit by the fire in our room?" Perhaps with Claire to keep him company. There was some notion niggling in the back of his brain—something about him and her—that he wanted to pursue.

Morris snorted. "Not a chance. You're the hero of the

hour, and everyone wants to get a look at you, if only to make sure you really are all right."

Daniel sighed and rather plaintively said, "I didn't *mean* to be a hero."

Raven studied him for a moment, then smiled. "I rather think that's what makes you one. Now"—he reached for the tumbler which, miraculously, was empty—"this is the next thing you have to drink. It's from our hostess, and she says it will ensure you take no lasting harm from spending too long in her icy burn."

Daniel accepted another glass, this one a simple beaker. He examined the very green concoction it contained, then sniffed it. A plethora of herbal aromas flooded his senses, with the underlying hint of strong spirits. Cautiously, he sipped—and instantly knew the potion was incredibly strong. It was, he suspected, a distillation, but even that first sip gave him strength.

"What does it taste like?" Morris asked.

Daniel sipped again, savored the elixir, then licked his lips. "Think of the tastes of every green and growing thing you've ever come across—blend them all together, and you have"—he raised the glass—"this." He sipped again, then tipped his head. "Actually, it's not bad."

Half an hour later, with Morris and Raven hovering on either side, Daniel managed to walk under his own power into the Great Hall. It was too early for dinner, yet with the day already fading to night, the majority of the household, summoned by the excitement, had already gathered, sitting about the long tables in chattering groups, retelling the story of the rescue of their children.

The instant those assembled laid eyes on Daniel—the rescuer—they sent up a cheer, one that rolled around the room as others turned to look and joined in.

Clapping started from the high table, then spread throughout the room. Daniel couldn't recall blushing so fierily before in his life as, following Morris's directions, he found himself escorted to the end of a table that was now angled close to the main hearth.

Beaming, Claire rose and waved to the end of the bench alongside her. "That's reserved for you."

Seeing nothing in the arrangement with which he wished to argue, Daniel moved forward to claim the spot.

Everyone—children as well as adults, his charges and all those he'd overseen over the last days, over the last years—had risen to their feet, clapping and cheering. Halting beside the bench, realizing he stood in much the same position the six older Cynster children had earlier occupied when telling their tale, Daniel borrowed from Sebastian Cynster's repertoire of charm. First inclining his head to those at the high table, then looking out over the room, he said, "I would bow if I could, but I fear that if I try I'll land on my nose." Laughter rippled around the room. Smiling, Daniel placed his hand over his heart and inclined his head to them all. "I do thank you for your concern and good wishes, but I am, indeed, well, and the best reward I could have is to know that the three boys who tumbled into the river are also recovering."

Calls of reassurance came from several points around the room. Daniel nodded. He glanced at the others at the table—Raven, Morris, Melinda, and Claire. "In that case, all is well." He stepped around the end of the bench as everyone else in the room sat.

Everyone except their hostess. Still standing at her place at the high table, Catriona caught Daniel's eye. About to sit, he halted and straightened.

Catriona smiled. "On behalf of us all, Mr. Crosbie, I

wanted to thank you for your signal service today. Through your prompt and selfless actions, you prevented the joy of this day—of this week of festivities—from being marred by the deepest tragedy. We cannot thank you enough. However"—Catriona's voice took on a slightly different note, a different timbre—"you must now allow us to do what we can to repay our debt. As you can see, we have rearranged the tables so that you may sit in your usual place beside Mrs. Meadows and yet remain close by the fire. Throughout the rest of the evening, you will oblige us all by remaining no further from the fireplace than that."

Finding all eyes on him, Daniel inclined his head. "As you wish, ma'am." There was really no other answer possible.

Catriona smiled. With a graceful wave, she sent him to his seat and resumed her own.

Daniel subsided onto the bench with an inward sigh. He smiled at the others; each of them had come to help by the burn. "Are the children really all right?"

They nodded, and Melinda reported, "Mrs. Broom came past earlier. She said all three boys and the two girls, plus many of their young friends who were out with them by the burn, are all tucked up in their beds and will, in all likelihood, find themselves all but tied either to said beds or their parents' sides for the next few days at least. But our hostess has seen them all, and she dosed the five who got wet and has declared she expects no lasting ill-effects."

Morris snorted. "One lasting effect I believe I can predict is that none of that crew—or any of ours, come to that, all of the younger ones who saw the end of the drama— will ever again venture onto snow banks bordering rivers."

"Well, life's all about learning, isn't it?" Melinda flicked out her napkin as the footmen and maids appeared with platters piled with food and jugs brimming with spiced ale.

After the extravagance of the manor's Christmas lunch, dinner was a much lighter meal, still festive, but less frenetic and definitely more relaxed. Despite the dramas—of the storm and the worrying absence of the older Cynster children, capped by the near-loss of five of the household's youngsters—the day had ended well; if anything, said dramas and the dealing with them had fostered a greater camaraderie between those present, no matter from where they hailed.

Daniel sat on the bench before the fire, felt the warmth of the flames bathing his back, and as the meal wound down and the lingering excitement faded into remembrance and people started drifting from the room, he quietly gave thanks for his blessings.

Claire held to her position beside Daniel, keeping up her part in the conversations as, along with Melinda, Raven, and Morris, she set herself to entertain Daniel and otherwise let him rest.

When most of the company had departed and the Great Hall had grown quiet, the other three rose.

Raven smiled at Daniel. "According to our gracious hostess, you should remain by the fire here until at least ten o'clock. Thereafter you may retire to your couch, but you've been given a new room, a warmer one at the top of a tower." Raven glanced at Claire, then looked back at Daniel. "Do you want me to return and show you or—"

"I know where it is," Claire said. "I'll show him."

Daniel smiled at her, then at the other three. "Thank you for your help."

"Nonsense, my boy." Morris lightly clapped Daniel on the shoulder. "You did us proud."

"Indeed, you did." Melinda tightened her shawl about her plump shoulders. To Claire, she said, "I'll check on our charges—don't concern yourself with them tonight."

"Thank you." Claire waited until the others had made their way to the archway before turning back to Daniel. Meeting his eyes, she held his gaze for several seconds, then glanced into the shadows behind them. She looked back at him. "Why don't we move into the inglenook again?" It would give them more privacy, and after the revelations of the day and their discussion that had been interrupted by having to rescue children from the burn, a discussion they needed to resume, a touch more privacy wouldn't be remiss.

Turning his head, he considered the spot. "If anything, it's closer to the fireplace than here and is nicely warm, so I doubt our omniscient hostess will consider it an infringement of her dictates."

Smiling, Claire rose and stepped over the bench. "She is rather... I was going to say overpowering, but she's more correctly 'powerful.'"

Daniel nodded. "Indeed." He moved slowly, carefully, out from the bench, then straightened fully, stretched—and winced.

Claire's concern flared again. "Are you all right?"

He smiled. "Yes—just a twinge. The sort that will be history by morning."

She didn't wait for him to take her hand; she took his, and together they walked the few paces to the inglenook and sat side by side.

When she glanced at him, he arched a brow, then glanced down at their linked hands. "Should I read anything into this?"

Despite the superficial flippancy, the question was genuine. Given where they had left their earlier discussion, that was hardly surprising.

She was waiting when he returned his gaze to her eyes. She looked steadily back at him and discovered it was actually quite easy to say "Yes."

His brows rose again, but gently, inviting more even as his gaze grew more intent.

She drew in a deeper breath—deeper than any she'd drawn that day—and stated, "Earlier, when we spoke, I said I needed to know…something." She searched his eyes, and he nodded.

"I remember." He paused, then asked, "What was it—that something you needed to know?"

"What it was," she replied, "was irrelevant." She cast a swift glance about, then returned her gaze to his face. "I don't know what it is—whether it's something to do with this place—but just as I started to ask my question, the children screamed, and you raced down to rescue the boys and I followed, and everything that subsequently happened—all I saw and felt, that I not just understood but experienced and so cannot deny—made it abundantly clear that what I had been about to ask"—*why you wanted to marry me, whether you loved me*—"wasn't the critical point."

He was watching her intently, his gaze locked on her face, on her eyes. "So…what was your revelation? What was your true critical point?"

Looking deep into his eyes, Claire saw all she needed to know of him revealed in the steadfast depths of his gaze. "The critical point—the one that matters most to me—is that I love you." Her heart had literally choked her when she'd reached the lip above the burn and seen him half drowned in the icy water, with the boy clutched against him. Her heart had hammered and leapt, again and again, throughout his valiant battle to rescue the three boys; not even she could possibly doubt the meaning of her reaction.

It had been too strong, too visceral, too powerful, and like nothing she'd ever felt before.

Those moments had affected her too profoundly for her to possibly doubt. Only a real and true love could have moved her so.

A true love that she already felt, that already lived within her.

She no longer needed to know whether he would say he loved her in order to trust him with her hand. Her heart had already made that decision.

Her soul was already linked with his, no matter the debates of her rational mind.

Daniel searched her eyes and found nothing but calm certainty where previously the very opposite had reigned. She was assured, confident—even determined; she had made up her mind. In his favor. He tried to control his own reaction and failed. His heart soared. Shifting to face her, he took her hands in his. "Marry me, Claire. Marry me and make me the happiest man upon this earth."

Her lips curved; she returned the pressure of his fingers, but she wasn't a green girl to be swept off her feet. "I'm not sure the shoe isn't on the other foot, in that marrying you will make *me* the happiest woman on the planet. And yes, I will most assuredly marry you"—the curve of her lips deepened—"now that you have, finally, actually proposed. But, my darling Daniel, I have to admit I haven't yet thought through the how of it all—I don't have much by way of savings put by."

He shook his head. "The how isn't insurmountable— we'll find our way. Now we've found each other, the rest will come." He glanced at the walls around them. "And yes, I agree that this place seems to have fostered our union, so perhaps it will help us solve that issue, too."

Gripping his fingers more tightly, she raised her brows. "Perhaps we're fated by the Lady to share our lives?"

He smiled and leaned closer. "The Lady appears to be a distinctly benign deity—I'm happy to have our union blessed by Her."

Bending his head, he pressed his lips to Claire's. Slipping free of his clasp, one of her hands rose to his cheek, then her lips firmed beneath his.

The kiss...this kiss was a plighting of their troth.

A statement by both of them—a commitment freely given and declared.

A promise, one fully reciprocated, one Claire had been waiting all her life to give.

To truly give.

To truly love.

Daniel raised his head.

Claire looked into his eyes, sensed, as she always did, the steadiness, the steadfastness of his focus, and heard her heart sing.

The large clock in the corner whirred, then started to bong.

Ten times.

When the last resonant *boong* had faded, she smiled; she no longer cared if her emotions—if her very heart—showed in the gesture. Retaining one of Daniel's hands, she rose. "Come along. If you recall, I'm under strict instructions to see you up the stairs to your new room after ten o'clock."

Daniel made a huffing sound but slowly got to his feet. Somewhat to his surprise, the twinges and aches he'd been conscious of earlier had faded. "I'd much rather sit here and talk to you all night, planning our future."

"Perhaps, but planning our future might be better done after a good night's sleep." Claire turned toward the main archway.

He let her tow him along. "I have to admit to some curiosity over my new room. I thought the manor was full to the rafters."

Her answering smile was mischievous. "It was—almost. As their contribution to your recovery, McArdle, Polby, and Mrs. Broom declared that you needed to be housed in a room high in one of the towers, because those rooms are the warmest. And as it happens, there's a box room in the attic of one of the towers." She paused and turned to him, her eyes dancing. "The staff threw themselves into clearing it, cleaning it, and setting it up for you. It's warm and has its own little fireplace. Raven and Morris moved your things in, and Melinda and I were allowed to assist in making up the bed and hanging the curtains."

They walked on. This time, as they passed under the archway, it was Claire who halted. She looked up at the mistletoe, then turned to him, stretched up on her toes, and kissed him.

Slipping his fingers from hers, he closed his arms about her, and this kiss was more—distinctly warmer—than either of their previous exchanges.

She finally broke from the caress, but she didn't pull away. Leaning back in his arms, she smiled—radiantly— up at him. "I love you." There was wonderment in her voice—such joy.

It moved him to reply, "And I love you." His own truth, an emotion that had lived and grown within him for so many months it was now as familiar to him as breathing.

She blinked, then searched his eyes.

He realized... "Ah—I hadn't told you that before." He grimaced. "Forgive me—I had thought it obvious."

She paused, then said, "Melinda said earlier that life is all about learning. One thing life has taught me is to treasure words given sincerely, and to otherwise rely on the evidence of my eyes." She held his gaze. "I did see your regard for what it was, but I didn't have the confidence to trust that I was seeing correctly—to trust in my instincts. Now, I know better, and indeed, all along my heart believed, even if my mind refused to. Somewhere underneath all my fears, I did know you loved me, but it took the events of this afternoon to show me that I loved you."

He hesitated, but he had to know, no matter what the question revealed of his vulnerabilities. "More than or at least as well as—you loved your late husband?"

She held his gaze for a long moment, then she smiled lightly—mysteriously—and retook his hand. "Let me show you to your room, and then I'll tell you a story."

Ten

Daniel climbed the winding tower stairs two steps behind Claire, and tried to keep his eyes from focusing on her shapely derriere and her perfectly rounded hips as they swung gently from side to side, all the way up the very high tower.

They'd passed a yawning footman banking the fire in the front hall, making sure the latest Cailleach set alight continued to smolder. Small lamps set high in the walls lit their way, casting a golden glow over the gray stone. The day had been long and full of excitement; the very crowded manor had already quieted for the night.

When they reached the landing on the tower's topmost level, Daniel felt a touch lightheaded, an effect that had nothing to do with his exertions of the afternoon, much less the altitude. The dual tonics his host and hostess had provided, followed by the meal and the constant warmth, had in large part ameliorated, if not eradicated, the lingering effects of his dousing in the burn.

And Claire had said that she loved him.

He'd finally been able to say the words he'd come to the manor desperate to utter; he'd asked her to marry him, and she had agreed. And now she was leading him to his room—

He cut off his thoughts. Wiser to simply follow her lead than make any assumptions.

Claire opened the nearest of several narrow doors, and he followed her into a small attic room, tucked under part of the tower's conical roof.

The room was a quadrant with a curved outer wall and two straight inner walls. One of the buttresses that supported the roof intruded and filled one corner. Two small windows were set in the curved wall, both screened by curtains. Daniel had expected a mere cot—a truckle bed at best—but a proper bed with a headboard and footboard had been carried in, even though it filled most of the space. With its plump pillows, fresh linens, and thick feather-filled comforter, the bed was a very welcome sight.

Other than that, the room contained a small nightstand beside the bed, a washstand with basin and pitcher, and a chest on which Raven or Morris had left Daniel's brushes; his traveling bag sat alongside.

Every surface was spotless, and beeswax scented the air, noticeable even over the tang of the logs burning cheerily in the small grate.

A lamp had been left on the nightstand, its flame turned low. Claire adjusted the wick and warm light filled the room, combining with the flickering flames of the fire to create a golden glow. Straightening, she glanced around, then, with no other option offering itself, sat on the bed and looked up at him.

He held her gaze for a second, then he closed the door and crossed to sit beside her.

Claire clasped her hands loosely in her lap; she glanced once at Daniel—took in his encouraging expression—then fixed her gaze on her fingers. "I know that you, Melinda, and the others—everyone, in fact—thinks that the reason I've so trenchantly turned my back on a second marriage is because I loved my husband so deeply that I did not wish to replace him. That because I had loved him to that degree, and because our marriage was such a loving one, I had vowed to cleave to his memory and not remarry."

She drew breath, then said, "That's true in one way and entirely false in another." She glanced at Daniel. "When I tried to explain and dissuade you from pursuing me, I told you that I did not know whether I could ever commit properly to another marriage. That was the truth at that point, and the reason for it lies in the real story of my marriage."

Shifting her gaze to the flames in the hearth, she went on, "I was the second of two children, but my much older brother was killed in the wars. Then when I was sixteen, my parents died in a carriage accident. They were reasonably well connected and had been comfortably well-to-do, so they left me decently provided for, at least financially. But they had no close relatives able to care for a sixteen-year-old young lady-to-be. They left me to the guardianship of older friends—a family who lived happily in the Dales, largely out of society. When I turned nineteen, the family arranged for me to go to London and be presented under the aegis of a Lady Mott, a kindhearted soul who made her way by using her position in society to launch… well, young ladies like me. She took me in and duly presented me, and I caught the eye of a dashing gentleman by the name of Randall Meadows. He was the grandson of a viscount on his mother's side, and as handsome, charming, and debonair a gentleman as any young lady could possibly wish for.

"I… I fell in love, or thought I did. But to my surprise,

Lady Mott tried to steer me away from Randall. When I challenged her, she could say nothing definite against him. However, she wrote to my guardians, as she was bound to do, and they wrote firmly advising me against accepting a proposal from Randall." She paused, then said, "Over all the hours we had together, Randall was never once anything other than handsome, debonair, and charming to me. He proposed and I accepted. I knew that although my guardians might disapprove, they would never cause a scandal by trying to overturn a marriage."

She looked down at her now tightly laced fingers. "Randall and I married via a special license—I wrote a letter, supposedly from my guardians, giving their permission. Looking back, I realize that even his friend who stood up with him had concerns, but Randall carried all—me included—before him. In hindsight, I was impossibly naive, but…" She paused, then went on, "Throughout the months of our marriage, I was deliriously happy. Our marriage seemed perfect—Randall was attentive, or at least as attentive as I expected, and although we only lived in lodgings, I accepted that we needed to take the time to find the right place to live, the right house."

Daniel said nothing; he could tell from Claire's expression that some painful revelation lay ahead. He wanted to reach across and take her hands in his, to give her comfort, but he reined in the impulse. She was having a difficult enough time facing her demons; she didn't need distraction.

As if to confirm his guess, she drew in a slightly shaky breath. Her gaze still locked on her hands, she said, "I've never told anyone this—the only other who knows it all is my family solicitor. He handled the marriage settlements and helped me later." She drew breath again, steadier this time. Raising her head, she stated, "Five months after we wed, Randall overturned his curricle in a ditch—he was participating in some race. He was killed instantly, leaving me a widow. What transpired... For that, I have only myself, and my naivety, to blame. Like me, Randall had been born to some wealth. He was an only child and had inherited some years before we met. Unbeknown to me, he was also a spendthrift, a profligate one. By the time he met me, he'd already run through his fortune and was deeply in debt. On marrying me and gaining access to my funds, he paid off his debts, then proceeded to run through what was left. When he died...his creditors immediately came calling. I was grieving, in shock, and to then discover that he'd left me with barely two pennies to my name—"

Abruptly, she looked up, blinking rapidly.

Daniel softly swore. Reaching across, he closed one of his hands over hers and gently squeezed. "You don't have to tell me anything more."

"No." She met his gaze. "I want to. You deserve to hear it all so you'll understand." She paused, then went on, "My old solicitor helped me settle with all the creditors. After that...as I said, I had barely enough left to bless myself with. Lady Mott very kindly took me back into her home—I had nowhere to stay. She offered to sponsor me again, but even she could see I...simply couldn't. Quite aside from being in mourning, I'd lost all taste for marriage—for trusting men. And I no longer had any dowry. My guardians wrote and offered to take me in, but I wouldn't have been able to even pay them board. I would have been a penniless pensioner in their house, and they didn't need or deserve that, and neither did I."

Claire looked down at Daniel's hand, warm and strong

over hers. Shifting her hand, she stroked his with her fingertips. "The only skill or qualification I possessed was that I had been well educated—my parents had seen to that. The only path forward was to become a governess. Lady Mott steered me to the Athena Agency, which proved a godsend. They took me in, checked my background and abilities, then sent me to the Rupert Cynsters. Two days later, I was on my way to Somerset."

For a moment, she held still, then, lips curving, met Daniel's eyes. "I've been with the family ever since, and countless times have blessed my luck. I left my past behind long ago—I let it all go. All except..."

He tipped his head. "All except your entirely understandable distrust of marriage and of men who offer it?"

Her smile deepening, she nodded. "Indeed. And it's you I have to thank for freeing me of that last shackle by asking me whether it was right that Randall's memory should hold me back from knowing happiness for the rest of my life." She held his gaze. "Until you said that, I had simply never seen it in that light. I'd only known that the distrust, not just of men who offered marriage but of my own feelings, ran deep, deep enough to stop me from moving down the path of matrimony again."

"And now?" Daniel quietly asked.

Her smile broadened, her expression softened, and the glow he needed to see filled her eyes.

"Now," she said, "I know beyond a shadow of a doubt that I never loved Randall. I thought I did, but I was merely infatuated—and even that was with the façade he projected rather than the man he actually was. I never really knew him. There never was any true connection—if there had been, he wouldn't have done as he did, nor would I have been so unaware of his failings." Focusing on Daniel's eyes, she continued, "Now, I know what love is. It's what I feel for you. It's…very different from infatuation. It's much deeper, more powerful, infinitely more riveting."

He smiled. Tugging one of her hands free, he raised it; cradling her curled fingers between both of his hands, he pressed a kiss to her knuckles. "I'm no callow youth. Although I've never felt this emotion before, I know what it is—I know that it's love. I love you, Claire, and I will until I die."

Her face glowed, radiant with that same emotion. Leaning closer, she raised her other hand to his shoulder. She slid it further to cup his nape as she shifted on the bed to face him.

He shifted, too, so that he could fully meet her eyes, could bask in the acceptance, the joy, the steady flame of her love that shone there.

Leaning closer yet, stretching up, she lifted her face, her lips, to his. On a breath, she softly said, "I love you. I trust you. And yes, Daniel Crosbie, I will most definitely marry you."

With that, she closed the distance and pressed her lips to his.

She kissed him—and with a soaring heart, he recognized and accepted, drank in and savored, all the pent-up longing she allowed to pour out.

Into the kiss. Into the steadily heating exchange that fanned the flames of wanting, of need and desire that had smoldered, latent, between them.

He released her hand and reached for her, closed his arms about her and drew her closer, and she came. Eagerly, enthusiastically.

Exactly as he wished.

The kiss deepened, driven not by him or by her but by

them both, into a heady, glorious melding of mouths, lips, and tongues that excited all their senses. That sent heat spreading beneath his skin, then sinking deeper.

Her hands, gentle but deliberate, framed his jaw, and she met and matched him in what had transformed into a battle of delight. One palm rising to cup her head, he held her steady as he parted her lips further and, slanting his lips over hers, with his tongue claimed every inch of her sweetness; she tasted of warmed honey laced with promise and spiced with joy. He couldn't get enough, was already past addicted.

She sighed into the kiss and leaned into him.

For an instant, they swayed, then, locked together, he tumbled them down onto the bed.

She allowed it, falling with him and laughing softly as they landed with their heads on the pillows.

He would have come up on his elbow to hover over her, but she moved first. Rising to lean over him, her soft weight on his chest, she looked into his face; with one hand, she brushed aside the lock of hair that had tumbled across his forehead.

Smiling, her heart lighter than she'd ever known it to be, Claire looked down into Daniel's eyes—eyes that promised her all and everything she'd ever wanted in life. A husband, a happy marriage, and if they were so blessed, a family of their own—but most important of all, she saw love.

Solid, unwavering, immutable, his love was so strong it caught her breath and left her wanting to plunge giddily in and bathe...the curve of her lips deepening, she said, "I suspect that by now Melinda will be sound asleep. I really shouldn't wake her."

His brows arched. "She was kind enough to absolve

you of the need to check on your charges. In the circumstances, it seems appropriate to avoid disturbing her well-
earned rest."

"So"—she arched her brows—"where should I rest my
not-so-weary head?"

His smile lit the room. "I have a suggestion, Mrs.
Crosbie-to-be, if you'll entertain it—why not spend your
night here with me?"

She laughed, and even to her ears, the sound was joyous. "I believe, sir, that I should, indeed, do just that."
Propped above him, she looked into his eyes, and all that
was in her heart welled. She felt the power of what lived
there, now a palpable thing, and let it show. Her tone serious, her diction clear, her eyes confirming the depth of
her conviction, she said, "I came here determined never to
marry again—never to take the risk of loving again. Yet
here I am, so deeply in love that I feel giddy and breathless, and I can't wait to be yours and have you be mine.
You've been my salvation—you've saved me from my
past. You are and will always be my love. You will always hold my heart."

She didn't give him a chance to reply but swooped
and covered his lips with hers. She kissed him and let all
the sheer need—the need to love and be loved that she'd
been holding within her through all the years—pour out.
Let it free.

Let it consume her. Let it drive him.

Let it guide them both on.

He met her, held her, as she knew he always would.

He drew her down, rolled them over, and then he was
kissing her and her head spun.

Her senses waltzed as, with slow, reverent care, he
learned her curves. They were both experienced enough,

it seemed, to hold back the urgency, to better and more fully savor every little step along their passionate journey. While the end of that journey was not in any doubt, she was grateful that he'd chosen a longer route. She wanted their first time to be a glorious memory, an interlude steeped in the passion they would each bring to their marriage bed for the rest of their days.

His passion. Her passion.

The former surged hot and strong in the languid stroking of his tongue against hers, in the heavy heat of his hand as he cupped her breast through the fine wool of her gown.

He found her nipple and gently squeezed. She arched beneath him.

Deep within her, her own passion stirred, long forgotten but lured to life by him, by the supping of his lips, the claiming of his tongue, the artful caresses of his hands on her body. He drew back a little from the kiss, not releasing her lips but releasing her senses enough that she was exquisitely aware as he splayed his hand across the width of her waist, lightly gripping, then releasing and skating lower to span her taut belly.

Then his hand drifted lower, tracing her limbs, the hollows and curves, making them his.

She shivered and rejoiced. They were both still fully clothed, yet he commanded her awareness utterly, to the point where every last iota of her conscious mind was filled with the moment, focused on the drift of his fingers over her body and on the sensations that provoked to the exclusion of all else.

His fingers skated on a long light caress from her knee upward, lazily tracing the long length of her leg before lightly delving into the hollow at the apex of her thighs.

Heat bloomed in her belly, pooling low.

Lovemaking had never been this all-consuming.

The thought pressed her to send her own hands searching to see what more delights—what more depths—she could uncover and explore. She unbuttoned his coat and waistcoat, then spread her hands greedily over the expanse of linen-draped chest within. Although his lips didn't leave hers, her touch caused him to pause in his own explorations; she seized the opening, the moment, to extend her discoveries. To exult in the width and breadth of his chest, to test the resiliency of the heavy muscles that banded it.

Then to sweep her hands lower, learning the rigid corrugations of his abdomen before, with one hand, reaching farther...

He sucked in a breath when she found him, hard and rigid and, even through the fabric of his trousers, scalding hot. She palmed his length, and he made a guttural sound.

She traced his erection, with her fingers circled the broad head.

He groaned and caught her hands, leaned into her and kissed her hungrily as he raised her arms and anchored her hands, one trapped in each of his, on the pillow to either side of her head.

His hunger evoked and incited hers; abruptly, the kiss turned ravenous, both of them wanting more.

More.

Daniel mentally swore and hauled back his desire, reined his passions—too close to slipping their leash—back, in. Not yet. He wanted this night to be everything it could be, not just for him but for her. They had the night for themselves; why not make it perfect?

Even without words, with just the communion of their mouths and bodies, she seemed to understand; her hands shifted beneath his, and her fingers lightly gripped his—in reassurance. In agreement.

Accepting her encouragement, he eased his lips from hers and sent them trailing over the delicate curve of her jaw, then down, tracing the long column of her throat as she arched her head back, giving him better access. Inviting his next touch, his next direction.

Her shawl had fallen open; it lay beneath her, spread across the bed. He left it where it was and instead set his fingers to slipping free the tiny jet buttons closing the front of her gown. He opened the gown to below the line of her hips, then drew his lips from the soft silk of her throat and eased back.

Looking into her face, into her eyes, luminescent with burgeoning desire and just visible beneath the fringe of her lowered lashes, he eased his hand past her gaping bodice and cupped her breast.

The fine cotton of her chemise was no real barrier to the heat of his touch, to the inherently masculine strength of his hand as he closed it about the peaked mound; Claire caught her lower lip between her teeth, let her lids fall as she arched into that oh-so-welcome caress. Her breasts were swollen and heavy, aching for more caresses; her nipples had ruched so tightly, every time he brushed them, sensation flashed through her. For the first time in her life, she fully comprehended the concept of being driven wild.

Then he pressed aside her bodice, cupped her breast, dipped his head, and through the thin cotton, laved her nipple.

She cried out. She was shocked by her own sensitivity—if he could set her nerves afire with lightning even before they were skin to skin, what would it be like when...

Suddenly, she had to know.

She reached up, caught his head and, rearing up, planted her lips on his. Kissed him with her own brand of demand, made her own claiming. Palms cradling his lean cheeks, holding him captive she delved deep into his mouth, and with every feminine wile she possessed, she called to him, her counterpart, her mate.

And on a surge of molten passion, he responded, meeting her fire with his. Their desires waged a sensual war, first his, then hers in the ascendancy, control of the kiss passing from her to him and back again, yet neither held any supremacy in this sphere.

Neither could hold on to their reins, either.

They snapped and cindered in the erupting heat.

Released, passion welled and swelled.

Between them, the heated tide swirled dizzyingly higher, hotter, sizzling and scalding as they both poured every ounce of their need onto their fire.

Every last iota of their urgency—of their urgent, escalating need to be one, to join, and share, and ride the wave of their runaway desires to the passion-filled end.

Their fire roared and flames licked their flesh, tempting, cajoling. Ravenously riveting.

They broke from the kiss, gasping, panting, chests heaving like bellows as their eyes briefly met and they sensed the onrushing tide.

On a hitched breath, on a wordless cry, they dove back into the kiss and the wave of their need crashed over them both.

Heat escalated, flames seared, and the conflagration expanded. Senses heightened, muscles tightened and locked, they clung together in the maelstrom, lips fused, desires matched, and in desperate accord let the swelling power sweep them up and on, until one and only one consuming need filled them.

More.

They were greedy, ravenous, desperately wanting.

All control went tumbling. Hands shaking, fumbling, heated and panting, she pushed his coat wide and back off his shoulders. Fired with need, he slid her gown over her shoulders and down her arms.

They had barely enough sense left not to rip their clothes; it was a wonder no buttons went flying.

This garment, then that, fell to the floor. He had to sit up to remove his boots. He hissed with pleasure when, clad only in her fine chemise, she pressed herself to his back, reaching around him to run her hands over his naked chest.

His boots hit the floor, dropped any old how. He stood and, his back to her, stripped off his breeches and under-garments; her busy hands were already caressing his hips and buttocks as he tossed the clothing aside.

Then he turned—and saw her look directly at his jutting member, saw delight spread wide across her face as she reached—

He caught her hand, tumbled her back onto the bed. Leaning over her, he wrestled and worked and finally drew her chemise away. He held it out from the bed, suspended from the fingers of one hand as he looked down on her, looked his fill at all he'd revealed.

Wonder dried his mouth.

Desire seized him by the throat.

Need—pure and unadulterated—sank its spurs deep.

"You are…glory personified." The words were gravelly, harsh and low.

The siren he'd had no notion lived inside prim Mrs. Claire Meadows looked up at him from her honey-gold eyes.

Then her lips curved in the most wanton smile he'd ever seen, and she reached up and drew him down to her.

He went. He had no will left beyond the compelling need to have her. To love her. To make her his.

She welcomed him with her arms, with her eyes, with her lips, with her body.

They fell into each other, back into the kiss.

Back into the still-swirling maelstrom of their passions.

Urgency pounded in their heads, in their hearts, in their blood, yet...

Despite being in a room at the top of a tower, despite the fire in the hearth, despite the flames that even now heated their skins from the inside out, the air was too chilly to lie naked and exposed.

Both realized and accepted that at the same time. Between them, with swift, urgent, jerky movements, they stripped back the covers, then tumbled beneath.

Straight into each other's arms.

He settled upon her, and she held him close. He parted her thighs with his, and she shifted and made space for him there, cradling his hips between her silken limbs. Even as he reached down to fit himself to her, the scalding wetness of her welcome bathed the head of his erection.

She shifted, tilted her hips in the same instant he pressed in.

Lids falling, he pushed deeper.

He heard her breath catch as, on a slow glide, he forged on; heard that breath release on a soft sigh as he came to rest embedded deep within her.

Eyes closed, Claire let sensation swamp her. She had never felt so full, so stretched. So complete. Had never felt the same intimacy—the same passionate closeness— she was experiencing now. Lovemaking had never been this intense.

Then he started to move, and she realized on a mental gasp that she had never truly made love before.

Not like this. Not with desire searing her nerves, with passion thudding in her veins, with love overflowing her heart.

Surrendering to the force that drove her, that had compelled her to accept him no matter the risk, that had shown her the way to love and be loved, she wrapped her arms about him as far as she could reach and went with him, into the dance that was like no other, onward on their journey to the end of the known world.

As if to make amends for their earlier impetuosity, they started slowly and only gradually increased the tempo, taking the time, stealing the moments, to meet each other's gaze, to wordlessly share...everything.

Intimacy.

Daniel had always imagined it would be like this, that when he found the right lady the act with her would be infused with this incredible, indescribable togetherness. But that had been pure speculation and he'd never known if he was simply being fanciful...

She'd taken his heart and made it come alive.

Now she took his dreams and made them real.

And as they traveled on, skins slick with desire, their bodies ceaselessly merging, their senses wrapped around each other, their conscious awarenesses entwined and submerged, each in the other, as he hung his head and, gasping, breaths mingling, they pushed on and the pace escalated and they climbed the final peak, she stayed with him. Her body eased as he withdrew, clung when he pressed in, accepting and embracing.

Urging him on.

Then they were there and the pinnacle beckoned, and

in joyous accord they raced the last way and flung themselves from the peak—

And shattered.

Glory shot down every vein, frazzled every nerve, and filled their minds with blinding wonder.

Their senses fragmented.

The supernova of sensation expanded, swallowing them and their world.

And in that moment of utter openness, blindly reaching, she touched her lips to his.

Drank in his soul, gave him hers in return, and finally made him whole.

She gave him all she was; she gave him her everything.

Slumping upon her, wracked beyond belief, Daniel held her close, held her deep in his soul, and knew beyond question that she was and always would be his all.

Later, when they'd finally disengaged and settled in the bed, lying with legs entwined, him on his back and her wrapped around him, courtesy of the narrowness of the mattress—an amenity about which he felt no reason to complain—she sighed and sank deeper into his arms. "I'll have to give notice and move down to Devon."

He angled his head, trying to see her face; she didn't sound too perturbed… "How do you think they—the family—will take it?"

"Actually, I hadn't really allowed myself to dwell on it before." She glanced up at his face. "It was a trifle disconcerting. But Juliet is already fourteen, and like all the females of the family, she is, if anything, precocious. I've already taught her most, if not all, I can. She really needs a finishing governess, one who can prepare her to take her place in the haut ton, which is not something I can do."

"So you don't think they'll create a fuss?"

"I'll be surprised if they do." She paused, then said, "But how will we manage? Are there any families near Colyton with whom I might be able to get a day position?"

"You won't need to work, not unless you wish to. As I mentioned, I have a new position with an increased stipend, enough to support a wife and family—especially in Colyton, which is not London, after all." He caught her gaze as she glanced up again. "My only concern was that the Rupert Cynsters might have felt hard done by if I lured you away, and Alasdair and Phyllida would therefore not approve…although, truth to tell, that's not generally their way."

"No, I agree. The families are usually quite supportive of their staff… Well, just as they have been with you."

"Indeed." He lifted her hand from where she'd spread it on his chest, raised it to his lips and placed a kiss in her palm. "So tomorrow we'll take our respective bulls by their horns and explain our wishes, and see what comes."

She didn't like taking—facing the prospect of—any sort of risk; he could see that in the anxiety that seeped into her expression, but she drew in a breath and, lips firming, nodded. "Yes. Let's do it tomorrow. Delaying won't solve it, and one never does know when one or the other gentleman might be summoned south again."

"Precisely my thoughts." He set her hand back on his chest.

She seemed to settle, sinking more deeply into his arms as he closed them about her.

With the bliss of aftermath thrumming like a golden chord throughout his being, he was content to let the matter rest; they would deal with it tomorrow, and he felt sure all would be well.

His lids grew heavy, and he let them close.

He was on the cusp of sleep when she murmured, "I don't know why, for I can't possibly know it for fact, yet somehow I feel certain that our path forward will be clear. That there will be no impediment and all will work out perfectly." She paused, then even more quietly said, "I think it's this place. It's not exactly alive, yet it feels as if it's sentient—as if it has power and can make things happen."

Hovering close to the land of dreams, he saw no reason to argue. He flattened his hand over hers where it lay over his heart and murmured back, "I think it's the Lady and her magic."

Eleven

At the manor, the principal celebration of the Feast of St. Stephen was literally a feast that started at noon and rolled on through the afternoon. The revelries were well under way, the food served and consumed and the platters cleared, and Richard and Catriona, standing at one end of the high table, had commenced the presentations of the traditional boxes, one to every family who lived and worked on the manor lands, when from the corner of her eye, Lucilla saw a footman enter from the front hall.

The footman made his way to Polby and spoke quietly. Polby looked surprised. He glanced toward Lucilla and Marcus, then Polby rose and followed the footman back into the front hall.

Lucilla had noticed the footman because she was keyed up. On some edge, although which edge and why she had no idea.

Which only made her even more fidgety.

Something was about to occur, but she had no idea what.

A minute passed before Polby returned and, as she'd expected, made for her table.

Reaching Lucilla's side, Polby leaned down so he could speak beneath the ongoing cheers and laughter occasioned by the short speeches Richard and Catriona made as they called each family to the dais. "My lady," Polby said. Most of the staff had taken to addressing her thus, even though she wasn't her mother, the formal Lady of the Vale.

Lucilla plastered on a calm smile even though her heart had sped up. "Yes, Polby?"

"There's a gentleman at the front door asking to speak with you, my lady."

And just like that, she knew who it was.

Knew why her lungs had constricted and her heart was thudding.

She inclined her head. "Thank you, Polby. I'll come and see him now."

Without glancing at her twin, seated alongside her, she slid out from the bench seat.

As she wound her way between the other tables, making for the archway into the front hall, she didn't need to look over her shoulder to know that Marcus, eyes narrowed, had risen and was following at her heels.

Her brother took his duties as future Guardian of the Lady quite seriously.

Unfortunately, having Marcus at her heels meant she couldn't stop before the hall mirror to check her appearance before continuing to the door; that would have been far too revealing, certainly to her twin.

Polby had gone ahead and now stood by the open door; although his butler's mien remained impassive, Lucilla could tell he was intrigued.

The day had been brilliantly fine, weak sunshine glinting off the snow and turning the landscape an eye-searing white; as she approached the door, the brightness outside made it impossible to see clearly… She walked onto the front porch more or less blind.

Behind her, Marcus swore softly; from the corner of her eye, she saw him duck his head, trying to shield his eyes.

She knew there was no danger lurking. She paused at the edge of the porch to let her eyes adjust. They did, and she saw who she'd expected to see—Thomas Carrick. He was standing before his horse, a fine roan stallion, with Hesta, as huge as ever, sitting by his side.

What Lucilla hadn't foreseen were the two wriggling, squirming bundles of gray fur Thomas was struggling to hold, one under each arm.

Seeing her, he sent her an imploring look.

A spontaneous smile flooding her face, she picked up her skirts and swept down the shallow steps.

The instant she reached him, Thomas raised one excited, quivering bundle and deposited the beast into her arms. "That's Artemis—a female."

The pup was young, yet already the size of a lot of other dogs; Lucilla registered strong bones, firm muscle, and significant weight. The pup's head was large and impossibly shaggy; it squirmed and wriggled to look up into her face. Bright amber eyes studied her, then the pup grinned, gave a little yip, and bobbed up to lick her chin.

Lucilla laughed and turned her head away. Tightening her grip on the pup's body, she found its muzzle and stroked. "Calm down."

Amazingly enough, the pup gave an ecstatic shiver and relaxed in her hold; she kept stroking the huge head, the fine ears.

Thomas had been watching; he nodded approvingly.

"And this one"—gathering the other pup, he finally shifted his gaze beyond Lucilla and held the wriggling bundle out to Marcus, who had halted at Lucilla's shoulder—"is Apollo."

Marcus accepted the pup almost reverently. The hound immediately turned and tried to climb Marcus's chest to get to his face. Despite his clear intention to remain grim and forbidding, Marcus grinned—he couldn't help it. He had to give his attention to avoiding the pup's determined attempts at affection, but eventually, he and the pup came to an understanding, and Apollo settled in Marcus's arms.

Both pups, each comfortable in their new owner's arms, looked at Hesta and woofed.

"Is she their mother?" Lucilla asked.

Thomas nodded, his gaze going to the huge hound. "They were weaned a few weeks ago."

Lucilla exchanged a swift glance with Marcus. Deerhounds of Hesta's type and lineage were rare. The pups would be worth a small fortune on the open market, and to a clan like the Carricks, whose wealth was uncertain, they would be worth even more.

But what should she say? They couldn't refuse a gift like this, offered clan to clan. When Thomas turned back to them, Lucilla caught his eye. "We helped as we should have—we didn't expect such a valuable gift in return."

Thomas looked at her for a moment—long enough for her to wonder what he was thinking—then he lightly shrugged. "What value a baby's life? Without your help, we wouldn't have her." He shifted his gaze to Marcus, almost as if challenging him to argue. When Marcus said nothing, Thomas's lips eased. "No—I believe the exchange still leaves me and the Carricks in your debt."

Lucilla resettled Artemis and, looking down at her, continued to pet the pup. She could feel Thomas's gaze on her face. "Have Jeb and Lottie chosen a name for the baby yet?"

"Yes," Thomas said. "They're calling her Lucy."

Lucilla glanced up. Meeting amber eyes more complex and intriguing than the pup's, she smiled. "Please tell them I'm honored."

He inclined his head. "I'll send word once we know when the naming ceremony will be held."

She nodded and looked back at the pup. She got the distinct impression that, given the choice, Thomas would have happily stood and watched her—watched her stroke the puppy he'd given her—for the next hour, but instead he forced himself to look at Marcus, who was silently communing with Apollo.

Sliding his hands into his breeches pockets, Thomas nodded at Apollo. "They'll need plenty of exercise until they're grown."

He took a step back, and Lucilla abruptly recalled the tenets of hospitality. "Won't you come inside and join us—take a drink, at least?"

Thomas met her gaze. "Thank you, but no. I must get back."

With a fluid bow that included them both, he turned and strode to his waiting horse.

Gathering the reins, he swung up to the saddle. He looked at them—Lucilla, Marcus, and the puppies—for a moment, then his gaze focused on Lucilla. With a last slow inclination of his head, he wheeled the horse, called to Hesta, and set off down the drive.

Hesta rose, stretched, then without a glance at her puppies, fell in behind and a little to the side of the big horse.

With Marcus beside her, Lucilla watched Thomas Carrick ride away. The puppies, too, lay silent in her and Marcus's arms and watched their mother lope off.

Thomas rounded the curve in the drive and passed out of their sight.

Hesta stopped before the curve and looked back.

The monstrous hound stared—and Lucilla would have sworn the dog was not looking at either her or Marcus, but at her pups.

And the pups stared solemnly back.

They didn't whine; they didn't squirm. It was as if mother and offspring communed across the distance via that long, meaning-laden look.

Then, still without a sound, Hesta turned and loped after Thomas.

Marcus quietly exhaled. "Do you have any idea what that was all about?"

Peering down at Artemis's face, Lucilla shook her head. "No more than you."

They walked toward the open front door. As they neared the steps, Marcus asked, "Would the babe have been lost if you hadn't been there? If we hadn't heeded Jeb's call and turned aside to give aid?"

Starting up the steps, Lucilla nodded. "Very likely."

Marcus halted on the top step and frowned at her. "How did he know?"

Thomas had known before she'd told him. Pausing before the door, Lucilla glanced at her twin. "The Lady only knows." With that, she turned and stepped over the threshold. "Now stop questioning fate and bring Apollo, and help me make Sebastian and Michael turn green."

That drew a laugh from Marcus. "Oh, I'll very happily be a part of that." Accepting her tack, he hoisted Apollo up and followed her into the house.

* * *

Daniel and Claire could think of no better day than the Feast of St. Stephen on which to approach their respective employers with a view to discussing their futures. Both had received boxed gifts from the families they served, and both sets of employers had readily agreed to a meeting immediately after dinner—once again a lighter and therefore shorter meal.

Following Rupert and Alathea Cynster, as well as Alasdair and Phyllida Cynster, into the drawing room, Claire was grateful that the other Cynster couples—and, indeed, virtually everyone else—had remained to sing songs and be entertained by charades in the Great Hall.

The drawing room was a large, well-appointed chamber. Like all the rooms in the manor, it did not boast wide or long windows; while there were windows, the climate demanded they be smaller and, in this season, well curtained. The result was a room that was cozy and comfortable, with few if any drafts to disturb those who sat there.

The Cynster couples arrayed themselves on a pair of opposing sofas, the gentlemen relaxing alongside their wives, their arms stretched along the sofa's backs; the brothers, almost certainly unknowingly, had struck nearly identical poses. Meanwhile, Alathea and Phyllida had settled their skirts and now turned serenely inquiring gazes on Daniel and Claire and, with similar graceful waves, invited them to avail themselves of the numerous straight-backed chairs that, with so many to accommodate every evening, were left scattered about the room.

Daniel steered Claire to a pair of chairs helpfully set facing the hearth, making the fourth side of the rectangle created by the twin sofas and the fireplace. He waited until she sat, then sat beside her.

Together they faced their employers—who were smiling upon them, the ladies with blatant encouragement.

"We understand you have some news for us," Alathea said.

Daniel nodded. "Indeed." He paused, then surrendered to impulse, reached across and took one of Claire's hands in his. It wasn't something he would normally have done in public, but in the circumstances it seemed appropriate. The feel of her fingers lightly gripping his imparted both strength and affirmation. "Mrs. Meadows and I have decided that we wish to marry."

"Excellent!" Alathea beamed.

"Wonderful!" Phyllida lightly clapped. "That couldn't be more perfect."

"Congratulations." Alasdair smiled.

Smiling, too, Rupert inclined his head.

Daniel felt a moment of irrational panic; he hadn't anticipated such instant and open support. He glanced at Claire and saw the same dawning consternation in her eyes. Gripping her hand more tightly, he cut straight to the heart of their concern. "Naturally, Mrs. Meadows—Claire"—again he glanced at her, and he read encouragement in her eyes—"would need to move to Devon." He took his heart in his hands and looked at Alasdair. "We had hoped, with my new position as your secretary, that perhaps we might take a small cottage nearby—"

"I would not expect to be paid, of course," Claire rushed to assure Alasdair and Phyllida. "As you know, it's not customary for a governess to be married, but I thought that perhaps I might find some pupils in the vicinity..." She trailed off, then looked at Alathea. "Regardless, I'm afraid—ma'am, Mr. Cynster—that I will be leaving your employ. That said, although I know we've touched only briefly on the issue, Juliet is, in truth, past the stage of needing an academic governess—she really needs a finishing governess to prepare her for her entry into the haut ton."

Somewhat to Daniel's relief, Alathea was nodding as well as smiling. "I agree. But I believe you sell yourself short, my dear. You are an exceptional academic governess, because not only do you know your studies, but your pupils like and enjoy working with you." Alathea glanced at Phyllida.

Following her gaze, Daniel saw Phyllida nod with open encouragement at Alathea, patently urging Alathea to go on.

Returning her gaze to Claire, who was looking faintly nonplussed, Alathea paused. Then, her smile taking on a self-deprecatory edge, she admitted, "We haven't been entirely oblivious to your evolving connection. Consequently, as is our wont, we have already discussed the eventuality of you, Claire, marrying Daniel and therefore removing to Devon. As I said, you are too good a governess for us to allow to slip through our collective fingers, at least not without making an effort to retain your services, but as you say, your work in our household, with Juliet, is done. So we wondered if, in moving to Devon, you would consider accepting a position in Alasdair and Phyllida's household as governess to Lydia and Amarantha."

Claire blinked. She looked at Phyllida.

Phyllida leaned forward, her expression eager. "Please say yes. Although I have to warn you, Mrs. Meadows—Claire, if I may?" After Claire, faintly stunned, nodded, Phyllida went on, "As I was about to confess, my girls, Lydia in particular, will not be such easy pupils as Juliet.

Lydia believes that there must always be an easier way—in anything. She's not precisely lazy. She's…"

"Too clever for her boots," Alasdair, Lydia's father, supplied. He cut a glance at his wife. "I have no idea where she gets it from."

Phyllida humphed and bumped his arm, but she immediately returned her dark gaze to Claire. "So, you see, we would be thoroughly pleased if, in moving to Devon as Daniel's wife, you would consent simultaneously to take up the currently vacant position of Lydia and Amarantha's governess."

"No need to find any cottage, either," Alasdair said. "We've plenty of rooms in the house—you can have your own suite. I appreciate having you"—he nodded at Daniel—"under our roof and close at hand to help deal with anything that arrives at our door, and I also know Phyllida and the girls"—he glanced at his wife—"will prefer to have Claire close, too."

Alasdair looked at Daniel and Claire. "Later, perhaps, when our girls are grown, we can look into other arrangements, but for now"—Alasdair smiled winningly at Claire—"just say the word, and we'll be delighted to welcome you into our household."

Daniel's head was spinning. Beneath his breath, he murmured, "Which word?"

Claire heard him. Absorbing Alasdair's encouraging smile, she looked at Phyllida and saw hope, real and sincere, shining in her eyes. Claire glanced at Alathea, read her calm certainty, then looked at Rupert, relaxed, assured, and entirely supportive.

Her survey had taken no more than two seconds; looking back at Alasdair, Claire beamed. "Yes. And I—we—thank you from the bottom of our hearts."

"No, no!" With a look of patent horror, Alasdair waved her thanks away. "Just wait until you're mired in our unruly household—you won't thank us then."

Everyone laughed.

Rupert uncrossed his long legs, rose, and walked to the fireplace. He tugged the bell pull, then turned. He looked at Daniel and Claire with very obvious approval, then he raised his gaze and looked past them as the door behind them opened. He smiled and waved whoever was there inside. "Excellent—just what we need."

Swiveling in her chair, Claire saw all the other Cynster couples streaming into the room. She and Daniel came to their feet. The duke and duchess helped the dowager in, and Algaria followed slowly on McArdle's arm. Melinda, Raven, and Morris were there, too, while Polby and two footmen bearing large bottles and balancing serving trays filled with glasses brought up the rear.

Straightening from seating his mother in the corner of one sofa close by the fire, the duke turned to smile at Daniel and Claire. "This is exactly what this holiday season required to be complete."

"At least for this family." The duchess handed the duke a glass, and raised the one she already carried to Daniel and Claire.

Glasses filled with fizzy champagne were rapidly handed around. Most of the Cynsters stood in a wide horseshoe with its center about the fireplace, the ends of the horseshoe's arms enclosing Daniel and Claire as they stood facing the duke and duchess, with Melinda, Raven, and Morris ranged behind them.

The duchess glanced around, confirmed that everyone, Daniel and Claire included, had been given glasses, then she smiled and again raised her glass. "To Daniel and

Claire—felicitations on your engagement, and may your future life together be as happy as those of all the couples here. You have given us the perfect highlight for this season's holidays—may your life together be long and filled with contentment and joy."

"Hear, hear!" came from all around, and everyone drank.

"To Daniel and Claire." Richard, their host, raised his glass high. "Congratulations—not just on your impending trip to the altar, but also on your sterling contributions, both past and those to come, to not just this family but the wider communities you both so devotedly serve. Your efforts yesterday will never be forgotten. So here's to you both." Richard glanced at Catriona and smiled. "And may the Lady, God, and all the saints, too, smile upon you."

Everyone laughed, cheered, and drank to Daniel and Claire's health.

People gathered around, shaking hands with Daniel, pressing Claire's fingers.

At one point, Daniel and Claire were summoned to speak with the dowager. They duly presented themselves before her, wondering what she might want, but she only regarded them smilingly, then—in her customary, somewhat unsettling way—informed them that all would be well.

Shortly after, they were allowed to escape. Raven, Morris, and Melinda had gone before; Morris had paused to tell Daniel and Claire that the trio would be waiting to celebrate further with them in the schoolroom upstairs.

Closing the drawing room door on the celebratory party, Daniel met Claire's eyes and saw the same stunned happiness he felt reflected there. The relative dimness of the corridor and the sudden quietness enfolded them.

As his wits started to settle, and the realization that, yes, they really had done it and all had gone so well sank in, the release of tension was so great he laughed—and heard his own joy in the sound. "I was so sure that would prove much more awkward. Much more difficult."

Grinning back, Claire nodded. "I did, too." She waved at the drawing room. "I thought we would be walking on eggshells, and instead…" She blew out a breath. "Well, they are a family who enjoys weddings, after all."

"Apparently even when it's not one of them being wed." Daniel grinned back; he couldn't seem to stop smiling. He took Claire's hand and tugged her toward the front hall. "It's a little hard to take in. I came here determined to speak to you—to woo and win you—but I wasn't sure that I would succeed…and now here we are, mere days later, with our engagement an acknowledged fact, our wedding pending, and our future life together all arranged."

A smile wreathing her face, glowing in her eyes, Claire readily kept pace. "Nothing ventured, nothing gained. I would say that's your lesson."

"Hmm." Daniel cast her an assessing look. "I must remember that."

Claire laughed and, beside him, started up the stair that would lead them eventually to the schoolroom. "I'm finding the changes a little discombobulating, too." She glanced at him, met his eyes. "Mere days ago, I was all alone, and possibly facing the end of my days as a governess to the Cynsters. Now…" She gestured.

"Now you have me, and I have you, and"—Daniel waved behind and around—"we have people who value us and our skills, we have roles to fulfill, ones that suit and will satisfy us, and we have friends with whom to share it all, friends we are not going to lose with the years."

They reached the landing, and in the patch of moonlight before the landing window, Claire paused. Facing Daniel, taking his hands, she looked into his eyes. "And most important of all, we have what's grown between us. We have love to warm us, to carry us through."

"To carry us on." Daniel raised first one of her hands, then the other, to his lips, brushing kisses across her knuckles. "Because we have love, we have all we'll ever need."

Her fingers holding fast to his, Claire stretched up and touched her lips to his.

And for one bright moment, time stood still.

Then a flash of light beyond the window startled them. They looked, and in the blue-black velvet of the night sky, they saw a shooting star.

"Oh." Claire turned and leaned back against Daniel. He closed his arms about her, and they watched the star streak across the firmament.

When it passed behind the mountains, they sighed. Stepping apart, gazes touching, they linked hands and continued up the stairs—to the schoolroom, to their friends, to the many blessings of love.

The following morning dawned clear, and after a conference over breakfast, the hunting party convened in the rear yard.

All those who had ridden out on Christmas Eve had turned out again. Mounted on her black mare, Lucilla watched as several of her male relatives checked shotguns and ammunition.

Prudence wheeled her bay and came up alongside. "I was wondering if you would come. You seemed in two minds, earlier."

"I was." Lucilla studied Sebastian with a critical eye. He handled the shotgun her father had allowed him to take with nonchalant ease, sliding it into the saddle holder before catching the reins and fluidly mounting.

Only Sebastian, Michael, Marcus, and Christopher had been allowed weapons, even though most of those present would regularly hunt with guns on their home estates. The reason for the restriction was simple. The Lady and all those Lady-touched—such as Catriona, Lucilla, Algaria, and even Marcus—did not approve of unnecessary killing, not on Vale lands. Not on lands under the Lady's mantle, which, as Lucilla had now learned, also meant at least some of the Carricks' lands, too.

That said, some culling of deer and other game was necessary, and as they used every bit of any slain animal, hunting in general was not forbidden; however, it was normally engaged in only by those who had been born in the Vale, who understood the local ways.

Whenever those not born to these lands were allowed to hunt, Lucilla generally felt a vague yet insistent need to be present. Whether it was the guns themselves and the consequent risk of accident or perhaps a need to ensure the hunt remained acceptably controlled that compelled her, she couldn't say. Yet it was true that, of all those present, she was the only one who could be certain of influencing the Marquess of Earith. Sebastian was only one step down from his father, and was therefore very close to being a law unto himself, and he was the eldest of the cousins. Against that, Lucilla was the eldest female of the cousinly tribe, and although she didn't quite understand it, that had always given her near-equal footing with Sebastian. On top of that, there, in the Vale, she had the added imprimatur of being the Lady-in-waiting.

Marcus could and would argue with Sebastian, but only Lucilla could be certain of turning her powerful cousin from a path he'd decided on.

As the others all mounted and settled into their saddles, Lucilla inwardly sighed. "I would much rather have spent the day playing with Artemis, but"—she gestured about—"duty calls."

Prudence studied her. Lucilla's cousins rarely questioned statements like that—she suspected they really didn't want to know—but in this instance, Prudence cocked her head. "Duty over what?"

That was part of Lucilla's problem. "I'm really not sure." She grimaced and rubbed a gloved finger between her brows. "It's just a nagging prod that I should ride with the hunt today." She shrugged and turned her mare as the party formed up. "It doesn't mean anything's going to happen."

She didn't really believe that, but she had no idea what adverse possibility was behind the unusually strong compulsion.

That morning, as Prudence had noted, she had been vacillating, questioning the need for her to ride with the hunt given that Marcus assuredly would, and after all, Sebastian and the others knew the local rules. But then Catriona had looked in to confirm that Lucilla would be riding with the others, which, of course, had set the seal on it. She'd penned Artemis in a corner of her room with an old pair of slippers to chew, donned her riding habit, pulled on her riding boots, picked up gloves, hat, and quirt, and headed for the stable.

Leaning down from his saddle, Marcus swung the gate at the rear of the yard wide and Sebastian led the hunt out.

They spread across the barren winter fields, riding in

staggered formation. Sebastian and Marcus rode side by side in the lead, with Michael and Christopher exchanging remarks behind them. Settling with Prudence behind the latter pair, Lucilla rode out into the morning and wondered what awaited her and where.

She knew, beyond doubt, beyond question, that Christmas Eve and her hours in the cottage had fundamentally changed her. It was as if those hours had been some sort of test, and she'd passed from being an apprentice to a journeyman.

That analogy seemed apt; even those at the manor who had known her from birth now treated her with a new respect, an acknowledgment of her altered status.

But that change wasn't all that had occurred over those icy hours in the cottage.

She'd been afforded a glimpse into her own future—a gift very rarely bestowed. While she often saw things, they were usually about other people or, as with the hunt, she felt pushed to do certain things regarding others. Very rarely did she receive any revelations solely about herself. Yet although such an occurrence was rare, her mother had also had a similar revelation, although in Catriona's case, she had actively scried for the insight.

And as had happened with Catriona, Lucilla didn't know what she was supposed to do with the knowledge. Or even if she was supposed to do anything at all.

One thing she did know—her time, and his, was not yet. They had years before some unknown occurrence would force them to act and seal their fate, so she didn't need to do anything about him *yet*.

Which in no way explained why, today, he was taking up such a large part of her brain. Perhaps it was Artemis, acting as an avatar, but Lucilla didn't think so.

Determined to force her mind from fruitless speculation—time enough to deal with whatever might happen once it did—she focused on the line of trees rapidly
drawing nearer.

They retraced their route up onto the bridle path that
ran along the northern ridge.

Prudence called across, "Are they going to head to
where that Carrick fellow said the deer had taken cover?"

"I assume so," Lucilla called back. She hadn't really
paid much attention to the planning.

But their supposition proved correct. Sebastian and
Marcus led the hunt to the point where the bridle path ran
into the skirts of the forest on the slopes of the western
hills. There, they dismounted and tethered the horses. Taking the guns and ammunition, and the various bags and
implements, the group followed Marcus and Michael—
the best hunter of the lot of them—as the pair led the way
forward on foot.

"This is the part of the hunt that I hate," Lucilla grumbled as she and Prudence, hampered by their full skirts
despite the fact both wore riding trousers underneath,
slogged along in the rear. The boys strode blithely ahead,
while they had to wrestle with their skirts every few steps
of the way.

They crept into the valley below the craggy outcrop
that Thomas had mentioned. While it was obvious that
deer had, indeed, been there, in number and not that long
ago, there were no deer anywhere in the narrow defile.

Lucilla paused to listen, head tilted to catch any rustle
carried on the light wind, then she sighed and let the skirts
she'd been carrying bundled in her arms fall. "There are
no deer here." Or even close.

Glancing at Marcus, she found him looking at her. The

shared glance was enough; both of them knew there were no deer in the area, not anymore.

But what puzzled her was the sense she had that the animals had been spooked.

She debated whether to mention it, but predictably, the others, led by Michael and Christopher and supported by Sebastian, were not of a mind to simply accept that there were no deer to be hunted today and return meekly home.

As neither she nor Marcus could explain how they knew that there were no deer to be found, neither said anything and, instead, resigned themselves to following the others in their unknowingly fruitless quest.

Called on to confirm direction, Marcus again took the lead with Michael, and they led the pack of would-be hunters on through the forests.

Keeping together, they explored various rocky valleys, gradually descending through the swath of forest. On the lower slopes, the trees were a mixture of the very old—towering giants that stretched toward the sky—interspersed with lots of younger trees replacing those that had been logged. The dense growth made for poor visibility. It was sometimes difficult to see the sky, or even the mountains, despite them being so close. And as the foothills were undulating, it wasn't always easy to tell direction; just because they were pacing uphill didn't mean they were heading west toward the mountains—they might just as easily be heading east and away.

Trudging along at the rear of the pack, Lucilla decided she might as well get something from the day; opening her mind, she *reached* for the Lady and felt Her. She'd never thought to do that simple test before, but it confirmed that, as Algaria had said, they were still beneath the Lady's mantle, still on land She considered her own.

That was comforting.

It was also a little confusing. Lucilla had always been able to sense the manor like a beacon, likewise the sacred grove where she and her mother prayed. But now…glancing around, she confirmed that she was also sensing a tug from a different direction. "Must be Carrick Manor," she muttered to herself.

That realization washed through her and brought her mind alive to the possibility that they might be approaching Carrick lands. She assumed that the Carricks' western boundary lay along the edges of the forest, but exactly where the edge lay wasn't clear, not in the foothills they were presently traversing.

The boys ahead of her stopped abruptly. Lucilla nearly plowed into them. She grabbed hold of Nicholas's arm—with his help, she kept her feet.

"Sssh!" Nicholas held a finger to his lips. His admonition had been barely more than a breath.

Lucilla followed his and everyone else's gazes to the sight of a buck—or at least the beast's antlers—slowly moving down the slope opposite the one they were presently descending.

They'd just come over a heavily wooded crest; between them and the opposite slope the land fell sharply into a narrow valley along which one of the thousands of burns in the area ran. The tinkling of the water sounded like distant bells, distracting the senses and masking other sounds.

No one moved; slowly, in response to Sebastian's signal, all the boys sank to their haunches.

Lucilla remained standing, her eyes trained on the buck. Nicholas reached up and tugged her sleeve, but she gently, absentmindedly disengaged. They were standing deep in forest shadow. The wind was blowing off the peaks. Unless they made some abrupt movement, the chances of the buck seeing them and taking flight were negligible.

The bushes between them and the buck concealed its body completely; only the antlers showed, moving with the telltale gait as the animal paced, presumably along a path just below the opposite crest.

Lucilla stared, and something very strange started rising inside her.

Something akin to the most god-awful fear.

Silently, soundlessly, her gaze locked on the buck, she started moving forward, stepping around her younger cousins, ignoring their frowns.

Drawing closer to the group in the lead—Sebastian, Marcus, Michael, and Christopher—she heard Sebastian whisper to Marcus, "Is it a legal kill?"

Narrow-eyed, Marcus was studying the enormous antlers.

Lucilla knew her brother's eyes were as sharp as hers. As she halted a few steps behind him, she wasn't surprised to hear her twin answer, "He has to be ancient. It's doe season at present, but in this area, bucks that old are always legal kills."

"Excellent," Sebastian breathed.

He already had his shotgun in his hands. He brought the barrel up, sighting along it—aiming, no doubt, for where the buck's head would be; the position of the body was too hard to guess. Lucilla knew her cousin was an excellent shot, and at this distance, he could hardly miss.

The buck would be dead—his life cut off cleanly—in seconds.

She told herself it was a better end for the animal that way. Tried desperately to calm her sudden panic—this was *normal*. They culled bucks this old all the time.

Clenching her fists, she tried to suppress the sudden, swirling, intensely black fear that rose up—choking her.

What is wrong?

Her senses were sharp, her perception acute.

At the edge of her vision, she saw Sebastian's shoulders fall almost imperceptibly as he exhaled to take the shot—

"No!" Lucilla dived forward, over Sebastian's shoulder.

The shotgun thundered, but she'd pushed the muzzle down and the shot furrowed into the ground.

Sebastian had let go of the gun and shifted to catch and support her. "What the devil?" He wasn't angry so much as shocked. Rattled.

But Lucilla had no attention to spare for him. Her gaze, her every sense, was locked on the body below the antlers…which slowly rose.

Finally fully upright, eyes narrowing to pierce the shadows, Thomas Carrick stared across the intervening ravine. The antlers were strapped to his head.

All of them stared back. Sebastian swallowed. Somewhat shakily, he said, "I repeat—what the *hell*?"

Lucilla finally managed to drag in a breath; the blackness that had threatened had vanished. Struggling upright—and through that attracting and fixing Thomas's gaze—she explained, "He's playing the part of the Horned God in the Chase—Herne, Herian, Herla, call him what you will. It's a very old tradition in these parts. I didn't know anyone still followed it."

"God!" White-faced, Marcus rose. "I had no idea." Holding his hands out to his sides, he mouthed across the ravine, "Sorry."

Sebastian dragged in a breath and opened his mouth to call an apology—

Lucilla elbowed him. "No. We have to be quiet—the hunt will be near."

On the words, they heard calls and thrashing and the sound of running feet rolling up and over the opposite crest, drawing nearer. They all looked to a spot above and behind Thomas.

So did Thomas, then he turned back and looked directly at the group—at Lucilla. Everyone else was nothing to him, but as the sounds of pursuit drew nearer, Thomas slowly inclined his head—dipping that wonderful rack of antlers—to her, then he turned and ran.

In seconds, he'd disappeared into the trees and bushes; less than a minute later, they glimpsed him leaping over the crest—running as Herne through the forests.

As his pursuers—mostly excited children with a smattering of youths—boiled in a rushing, tumbling wave over the crest, the Cynsters faded soundlessly back into the trees.

Once the hunt had passed in joyous obliviousness, the Cynsters turned and, in a loose group, trudged back through the foothills toward the bridle path.

No one said anything; they were all still deeply shocked over what had so nearly occurred.

Eventually, Sebastian, the shotgun broken and resting over his arm, fell in beside Lucilla. They walked side by side for a little way, then Sebastian exhaled. "Thank you. From the bottom of my heart. That was so nearly...horrific."

Lucilla met his gaze. After a moment, she nodded and looked forward. "Yes. Horrific."

Her voice sounded hollow, even to her.

Mistakenly killing Thomas Carrick might have been horrific for Sebastian.

It would have been as good as death for her.

Epilogue

January 1, 1838

Her arms wrapped around her knees, Louisa sat in the window seat of Annabelle's room and looked out over the snow-smothered gardens to the snow-draped forest beyond.

Hoar frost had claimed the land. Icicles glinted and twinkled, and smaller ice crystals formed a diamond-studded lacework over every surface, winking in the winter sunshine.

Hogmanay was past; a new year had begun.

The festivities that had filled the previous day, that had rolled on through the night and into the morning—at least those she and her three peers had participated in before they'd stumbled up the stairs and fallen into their beds—had been filled with an almost frenetic sort of joy. A farewell to the delights and sorrows of the year past, and a heightened anticipation for what the new year would bring.

And now that new year was here.

Resting her chin on her knees, Louisa stared, unseeing, at the winter landscape. She'd been the one who had worked the hardest to persuade their parents that the Vale was where this season's celebrations had needed to be held; looking back on the happenings of the past week, she considered the implied promise to have been more than met.

The room had been quiet, the other three girls still slumbering, but Therese had woken; wrapping her robe about her, she came to join Louisa in the window seat. Therese looked out, then, with one finger, traced the pattern of ice crystals frosting a portion of one windowpane. "So this will be our last day here—I wonder if it's snowed at home."

Annabelle and Juliet had been sharing Annabelle's bed, while Louisa and Therese had slept on truckle beds by the fire; at the sound of Therese's voice, Annabelle opened her eyes, saw the pair by the window, and sat up.

Juliet grumbled, but when Annabelle slipped from beneath the covers, Juliet, too—still grumbling—followed.

There was only space for two on the window seat. Annabelle pulled up a narrow-backed chair, and Juliet dragged over the dressing stool.

Plopping down upon it, dragging the shawl she'd picked up over her shoulders, Juliet looked at Therese, then Louisa. "So it's our last day here, but if the party downstairs continued long after we left—as it most likely did—then I can't see anyone doing anything more than recovering today."

Annabelle nodded. "Perhaps a walk at the most, just to clear heads, and then later there'll be the cleansing of the fireplaces—the removal of the ashes of the year past and the ashes of the Cailleach logs."

"Like a banishing of the spirit of winter?" Therese asked.

Annabelle nodded. "Exactly."

"I have to admit," Therese said, "that after the last day, I'm ready for a little quiet. I had no idea Hogmanay had so many elements to it—much more than our simple New Year celebrations."

"It's different up here," Louisa said, "but, after all, that's why we came." Tipping her head, she regarded the other three. "And you have to admit, we've had more to enjoy than even we could have planned, what with our very own romance and the Christmas baby, even if we weren't directly involved in the latter. Incidentally, Grandmama told me that our mistletoe worked for Mr. Crosbie and Mrs. Meadows—that it was very definitely helpful in bringing them together."

Juliet wriggled deeper into her shawl. "Good. And it is good because Medy so deserves a happy life and a family of her own, and Mr. Crosbie is nice, too. Mama told me that Medy will be leaving us to go to Uncle Alasdair and Aunt Phyllida—lucky Lydia and Amarantha—but that means I'll still see her when they come to visit or we visit them, which is often enough."

"And," Annabelle said, "Mama spoke to me last night. Apparently, all four of us are to have finishing governesses—it was one of the things our mamas discussed and decided while they were here."

All four girls considered that prospect, then Louisa arched her brows. "That will be interesting."

They all laughed, the camaraderie, the closeness, the four had always shared bubbling up. All Cynsters, all born within a single year to different branches of the ducal family tree, they'd been fated from the first to share life's experiences; for each, it was hard to imagine any other who might share more completely the gamut of decisions that living their lives would entail.

"So," Therese said, "we are, it seems, heading into the final stretch of preparing for our come-outs. Four more years, and then we'll be launched—on the unsuspecting ton, as old Lady Osbaldestone would say." The other three grinned, and Therese went on, "But what are our aims— for this year, for the next? What are we aiming for? What are our goals?"

She looked at Annabelle and Juliet, then all three looked at Louisa.

Louisa noted the implied invitation; she smiled one of her more enigmatic smiles. But it had faded and her tone was serious when she said, "Our goals... To define those, we need to know what we want. What we most want to see in our lives, what elements are most important to us." She glanced at the others, meeting their gazes. "Do we know that yet?"

A second passed, then Therese caught Louisa's eyes. "I don't, but I will own to surprise if you don't."

Louisa shook her dark head, the rippling mass of her black hair shifting over her shoulders. "I know some, but not all." She looked out, and her gaze settled once more on the landscape, although her focus had turned inward. After a moment, knowing the others were waiting and that they always shared such things, she said, "I know I want to be in control of my life—that I will never be happy being someone else's pawn, a husband's ornament, my importance dependent on his. I know that I want to make my own decisions in all those issues important to me. I want...to find a place in society, within society, in which I am of society but it does not rule me. I want a family, a home, children, a love of my own—all the things we, as Cynsters, all but take for granted and assume we will somehow find." A small smile played over her lips in acknowledgment of their familial expectations. "And while there's nothing wrong with that—and, indeed, I see those as goals very much to be desired—while I want all those things, above and beyond everything else, I want the freedom to be me."

She paused, and the other three were silent, all following her thoughts, drawn by the power already resonant in her words, in the ideals they described. Then Louisa continued, "I know I will need to be determined, that I will need to remain focused and vigilant to achieve the outcome I want." She glanced at the others. "That much I do know."

She looked back at the landscape and the others followed her gaze, yet none of the four were seeing the present, but rather were looking ahead.

After a moment, Louisa hugged her knees more tightly and softly said, "I might face a battle, but I can't see any other way it can be." Her quiet words fell into the crystalline silence. "In order to live fully, I have to be me."

Later that morning, Lucilla brought Artemis down for a run in the rear yard. Rugged up in her pelisse, her hands warm inside her fur-lined gloves, a thick shawl for extra warmth wrapped about her head and shoulders, and her thick riding boots on her feet, she followed the pup outside. Ambling in the questing pup's wake, she walked out from the house into the silence of the Vale.

Despite the hour, few had yet stirred; most were still sunk in slumber, sleeping off the effects of the various beverages that had been in goodly supply the previous evening. Drinking was a serious part of the seeing out of the old year, an essential ritual of Hogmanay. Lips curving at the memory of some of the drink-fueled revelry she'd witnessed, Lucilla continued in Artemis's wake.

Eventually, the staff would rise; later, a light luncheon would be served in the Great Hall. But until then, with even the younger members of the various families inclined to rest, the house would remain peaceful and quiet.

Letting the new year steal up on the occupants on silent feet.

Reaching the barred gate at the end of the yard, Artemis dove between the two lowest bars and loped on; opening the gate, leaving it wide, Lucilla followed.

There was, quite literally it seemed, no other person in the white world but her, no animal beyond the gamboling pup.

The silence was pervasive, but beneath it she could sense…something akin to a beating heart. A presence that, to her senses, was very real, tangible, although not in a way others could feel.

Closing her eyes, Lucilla opened her mind, her senses, her soul.

And communed with the world around her.

Uncounted minutes later, a sharp yip interrupted her meditation. Opening her eyes, she saw a second shaggy gray bundle tumble and stumble past, big paws slipping and sliding as Apollo rushed out in his sister's wake.

Smiling, Lucilla glanced over her shoulder. She met her twin's dark blue eyes as Marcus came to stand beside and a little behind her.

Marcus looked back at her, reading her eyes, then in their usual wordless accord, he and she looked out—at the pups now playing, mock-growling and leaping, then further, to the white fields that ultimately would be their domain, theirs to nurture and care for.

Then both lifted their gazes and looked further yet, to the hills beyond.

They rarely needed words, yet it wasn't even thoughts that passed between them so much as *knowing*.

Lucilla couldn't imagine not having Marcus there, knew without hearing it that he felt the same. But she didn't know whether the link they shared was simply and solely because they were twins or whether it was more because they were both Lady-touched.

Regardless, he and she looked to the north, and knew. Knew that for each of them, their future was inextricably connected, not just with the manor, not just with the Vale, but also with what lay beyond.

Neither questioned that insight; neither denied it.

Even though neither fully understood exactly what was meant. What would come to be.

There was a sharing in that, too.

Lucilla found it hard to draw herself back in, to pull her wider awareness back from the distant hills; there was a part of her that was drawn to seek and find, to discover, learn, and truly know, even though their time, hers and Marcus's, was not yet.

Eventually, Marcus stirred. Quietly, he called Apollo, and the pup came loping back, ears flapping, jaws parted, tongue madly lolling.

Marcus grinned. Raising his head, he looked out at the hills for one last, long moment…then he turned and headed back to the house.

Lucilla heard him go, yet she remained looking out, her gaze on the hills, wanting to know more, reluctant to leave without—

A whine jerked her back and had her glancing down. Artemis sat at her feet, looking up at her through strangely wise, pale amber eyes. The puppy raised a paw and lightly scratched the skirt of Lucilla's pelisse.

She couldn't help but smile. "Yes, you're right. There's no point, is there?"

Artemis cocked her head and looked earnestly back at her.

Lucilla chuckled softly. "All right. Let's go back inside."

She looked up at the hills—one last lingering look—then she turned and, with Artemis in the lead, followed Marcus back to the house.

High in the tower overlooking the rear yard, Helena, Dowager Duchess of St. Ives, sat in the window seat and looked down on her grandchildren—on Marcus's black head, on Lucilla's flame-colored mane—as they passed back into the house.

Many throughout the ton believed Helena to be uncannily perspicacious, yet her ability owed more to her habit of observing people carefully, and noting the little things others missed, than to any peculiar talent.

And when it came to her grandchildren, she was especially observant; there was little she allowed herself to miss.

As the pair below disappeared from her sight, she softly smiled.

"What is it?" Noticing Helena's smile, Algaria came to the window to peer out.

Still smiling, Helena shrugged. "It was just Marcus and Lucilla—they've come inside now."

Algaria regarded Helena, then arched a brow. "And?"

"And," Helena responded, "it pleases me to see the young ones finding their way."

Tightening her shawl about her shoulders, Algaria snorted. "If only they would simply follow their noses, their lives would be so much simpler—that ought to come naturally, after all."

Helena's smile deepened, serenely confident, unshakably assured. "I wouldn't be too sure of that. For some, the worth of the prize is reflected in its price, in the battle to win it. And just think of what we have seen over this last week." She spread her hands, inviting Algaria to consider the facts, then Helena's gaze shifted to the window, to the landscape beyond, to the hills in the distance. "As we have seen," she softly said, "for some it requires a sprig of mistletoe. For others...it's a touch of magic."

* * * * *

For alerts as new books are released,
plus information on upcoming books,
sign up for Stephanie's Private Email Newsletter,
either on her website, or at:
http://eepurl.com/gLgPj

Or if you're a member of Goodreads,
join the discussion of Stephanie's books at the
Fans of Stephanie Laurens group.

You can email Stephanie at:
stephanie@stephanielaurens.com

Or find her on Facebook at:
http://www.facebook.com/AuthorStephanieLaurens

You can find detailed information on all
Stephanie's published books, including covers,
descriptions and excerpts, on her website at:
http://www.stephanielaurens.com